DUPLICITY

ALSO BY SHAWN WILSON

Relentless

DUPLICITY

A BRICK KAVANAGH MYSTERY

SHAWN WILSON

OCEANVIEW PUBLISHING

SARASOTA, FLORIDA

ISBN 978-1-60809-510-0

Published in the United States of America by Oceanview Publishing

Sarasota, Florida

www.oceanviewpub.com

10 9 8 7 6 5 4 3 2 1

PRINTED IN THE UNITED STATES OF AMERICA

For Lady

"The plans of the righteous are just,
but the advice of the wicked is deceitful."

PROVERBS 12:5

ACKNOWLEDGMENTS

My sincere thanks to:

Bob and Pat Gussin and the Oceanview Team for welcoming me and turning my dream/goal into reality.

Helaine Mario who I will always think of as my North Star for pointing me in the right direction at Bouchercon, 2018.

Anne Dubuisson for our brainstorming sessions that made all the difference.

Ruth Ann. Great having you as my West Coast cheerleader, even better having you as my sister.

Bob, retired ATF agent. Great having you as a consultant, even better having you as my cousin.

All my family and friends, near and far, who enrich my life. May real hugs be our future and virtual hugs our past.

CHAPTER ONE

September 2013
Inishmore, Ireland

BRICK KAVANAGH STEPPED to the edge of the cliff and watched the waves crash against the rocks. He closed his eyes, hoping this sight would be seared in his brain the same way his mind tended to store images from twenty years of being a cop.

During all those years with the Metropolitan Police Department in Washington, D.C., he didn't recognize the emotional toll the job was taking. But there was no denying the price he paid after the devastating conclusion of his last homicide case. How to deal with the aftermath of a case that became so personal? The sage advice of bar owner Eamonn Boland provided the answer—a one-way ticket to Ireland. He figured he'd probably be there for a week, maybe two. Now, with his stay closing in on ninety days, he needed to leave or be in violation of the country's visa-free travel regulations.

Brick fumbled in his pocket for the slip of paper Eamonn had given to him before he left D.C. It was wrinkled and the ink was smudged but it didn't matter; he almost knew the quote by heart.

"We are tied to the ocean. And when we go back to the sea, whether to sail or to watch it—we are going back from whence we came."

When Brick first arrived, the words John F. Kennedy delivered to the America's Cup crew didn't have much significance for him. But the longer he stayed, the more they resonated. Spending time in a place surrounded by the ocean had a cleansing and calming effect he hadn't expected. He was grateful he would be leaving in a much healthier state of mind than when he had arrived.

Brick checked his watch. He still had time to take in one last view from Dun Aengus. He made his way to the prehistoric fort, being careful not to photobomb any of the selfie-taking tourists along the way. He didn't feel like a tourist himself anymore as he stood on the highest point of the cliffs. He looked in every direction absorbing the breathtaking panorama before he fell in step with the others making their way in the direction back to the boat dock.

Dark clouds were now blocking the sun and the wind had picked up. In the three months Brick had been here, he had gotten used to the weather changing quickly. Part of the charm, although it would probably mean a choppy ferry ride back to Rossaveal. For the sense of tranquility he had experienced, forty minutes of rocking and rolling was a small price to pay. Standing on the upper deck of the boat, Brick watched as Inishmore became shrouded in fog.

*   *   *

It was after six o'clock when Brick arrived back in Galway. He was starving and knew where he wanted to have his farewell dinner. He headed to Gaffney's, a small pub that served the best lamb stew he had ever eaten. Tonight, he would be dining alone, but when he was here previously, he had had dinner with a woman he met earlier in the week at Charlie Byrne's Bookshop on Middle Street. Nora Breslin introduced herself after a brief conversation in which they discussed a book of poetry by Seamus Heaney. Upon hearing her name, Brick jokingly asked if she was related to Jimmy Breslin. Surprisingly, he was a distant cousin and the well-timed question led to more conversation about the legendary American journalist and his connection to Son of Sam. With the bookstore about to close, the nearby pub provided the perfect place to continue talking over a pint of Guinness and a view of the swans on the River Corrib.

Two nights later, they met again for dinner at Gaffney's. Unfortunately, plans for a trip together to Dublin got derailed when Nora, a flight attendant with Aer Lingus, had to unexpectedly fill in for a colleague. Before leaving, she suggested getting together on the other side of the Atlantic since her regular assignment was the Shannon-to-O'Hare route. Would it happen? Brick wasn't sure, but he had enjoyed the brief time they had spent together. One thing he had learned recently was that it's far better to appreciate what was, than anticipate what might be.

Brick seated himself at a small table with his back to the wall so that he could have an unobstructed view of the restaurant. Some habits die hard; some never do. When the waitress approached with silverware and a menu, he placed his order. She returned shortly with a pint of Guinness. Brick would never mention this to Eamonn or his nephew Rory when he got back home, but the Guinness seemed to taste better here than what they served at Boland's Mill. Then again, maybe it was his imagination. He'd chalk it up to that.

Boland's Mill. As long as tomorrow's flight wasn't delayed, Brick figured he'd probably be having dinner there and thanking Eamonn for suggesting—well, insisting—that time away from D.C. wasn't an option, it was a necessity. The old man knew what he was talking about, but now it was up to Brick to figure out what to do next. He was young, forty-two, owned his condo, and his pension from the police department would be enough to pay the bills and keep food on his table, but Brick was a live-to-work, not a work-to-live kind of guy. Aside from an email he had received from the Assistant Director of the School of Public Affairs at Abraham Lincoln University, regarding a project involving graduate students attempting to solve a cold case, he didn't have any other employment prospects. He would check it out, but it didn't sound like his forte. Working a cold case was right in his wheelhouse but teaching a group of college kids would be a whole lot different than mentoring a detective newly assigned to the Homicide Squad.

One thing was for sure—he wasn't going to figure it out tonight so he might as well just savor the stew the waitress placed in front of him. Maybe he would suggest to Eamonn that the chef at Boland's should consider adding barley to their lamb stew recipe. Maybe he should consider an entirely new career and enroll in culinary school. On second thought, for the sake of the dining public, probably not a good idea. Best to leave cooking to the pros. That's why he frequented Boland's Mill far more often than the Giant or Safeway.

Brick wasn't about to waste a slice of brown bread. He used it to soak up the last of the herb gravy on his plate.

"Another Guinness?" the waitress asked as she cleared the table.

"No thanks, just the check when you get a chance."

Brick took the long way back to his airbnb. Most of the shops were closed, but the bookstore was open for another half hour and he needed something to read for tomorrow's flight back to Washington. After browsing for a few minutes at a shelf displaying a number of books by contemporary Irish authors, he chose an autographed copy of *The Guards* by Galway-born Ken Bruen. Even though he had to leave the west coast of Ireland, at least he could be there vicariously by reading about it.

CHAPTER TWO

Washington, D.C.

CASA KAVANAGH. FOR the first time in three months, Brick woke up in his own bed. He had slept well, but figured that was as much a result of a long, tiring day of travel as it was being home. While he was away, Rory Boland had kept an eye on the place. In exchange, Brick gave him the club-level Nats tickets he wouldn't be using. Upon walking in the door, Brick knew Rory had done an outstanding job. The place looked neater than when he had left. His prized Madagascar Dragon Tree was thriving, and a philodendron appeared to have doubled in size. Still, this morning as Brick rubbed his eyes and looked around his bedroom, it felt oddly unfamiliar. He yawned and stretched before throwing back the covers and heading to the kitchen.

Stocking the fridge with breakfast food was a "welcome home" gesture Brick really appreciated. He poured a glass of orange juice and while he waited for two frozen waffles to finish toasting, he listened to the *Local on the 8's* weather report.

According to the calendar, there were still two weeks of summer, but with any luck, he had missed the hot, humid days that make most Washingtonians miserable. A forecast of eighty-three degrees with low humidity sounded good. Business casual would be appropriate for his afternoon appointment. When he finished breakfast, there was a stack of mail he needed to sort through and two suitcases to unpack.

On a scale of one to ten, Brick's enthusiasm for meeting with Professor Grace Alexander hovered around four. But since she had gone to the trouble of tracking him down, he was willing to hear what she had to say. The Uber dropped him at the front gate of Abraham Lincoln University. Set on a large tract of land in Northwest D.C., the campus of Lincoln U., as it was more commonly known, seemed to have a split personality. The modern glass and steel buildings on the eastern end of the campus contrasted sharply with the ivy-covered brick buildings on the western end. But that also spoke volumes about the success the university had achieved. Nobel Prize–winning chemistry professors and a men's basketball team that had made it to the Final Four several times went a long way toward raising money. It was a school that Brick's younger self wanted to attend instead of a community college and state university, but the tuition was prohibitive. All these years later, he would probably still be paying off student loans. He checked the directory and located the School of Public Affairs Building. On his way there he didn't pass many students, but the ones he did seemed totally preoccupied with whatever device they held in their hands.

After checking in with the security guard at the entrance to a modern building resembling those found on K Street filled with deep-pocketed lobbyists, he was directed to a bank of elevators. He got off on the third floor where a receptionist announced his arrival. Immediately, Grace Alexander emerged from her office. Brick guessed her to be in her early fifties, but when she stepped closer and greeted him with a warm smile and a firm handshake, he realized he was mistaken. Despite her silver, chin-length hair, she could easily be ten years younger.

"Let's talk in the conference room. Would you like coffee, tea, water?"

"Water, please."

Brick followed the professor into a room with a view of the soccer field. As he settled into a leather chair that probably cost more than all the furniture in his apartment combined, the receptionist arrived with a bottle of Fiji water and a glass filled with ice.

"Thank you for agreeing to meet with me and hear what I'm proposing. I touched on it in the email I sent you but I'm sure you have some questions."

"I do. And frankly since I don't have teaching experience, I'm wondering why you think I'm the best person to work with a group of students."

Alexander leaned forward, resting her manicured hands on the table. "May I call you Brian?"

"Brick is better." Despite a few strands of gray, the nickname from his youth based on his red hair would, undoubtedly, always be his preference.

"Oh, yes, I remember that from the article in the *Washington Post Magazine*."

Without realizing it, Brick rolled his eyes. He felt heat rising around his collar and shifted in his chair.

"I take it the article makes you uncomfortable," she said.

Brick nodded. "For most of my career, I flew under the radar. The Delgado case changed everything. Now total strangers know where I live, where and what I drink, and things about me that I never planned to share, but others who were interviewed did. Case in point, it's how you were able to find me."

"That's correct. Although Eamonn Boland protected your privacy by just passing along my contact information to you. I had no idea where you were until you responded."

"I'm not surprised. Eamonn always has my back. Anyway, I am curious why you think I'm the best person for the job."

"Aside from the fact that you were a homicide detective for . . . was it eight years?"

"Ten."

"I think the complexity of the Delgado case showed the determination a detective needs in order to succeed. Who better to mentor graduate students pursuing careers with the FBI or ATF than someone who has, as the saying goes, walked the walk."

Brick uncapped the bottle of Fiji water and poured some into the glass. He appreciated her logic but "walking the walk" often comes with a price. Rather than students being motivated, they may end up reevaluating their career choice when the reality of the job sets in. He took a sip of water then set the glass aside. "What exactly do you have in mind for this project?"

"As I mentioned in my email, this would be for a select number of graduate students. In the past, there have been programs where students worked on innocence-type projects. To their credit, two inmates serving long prison sentences have been freed after DNA showed they didn't match the evidence from the crime scene. I would like to see a group of students have the experience of investigating a cold case with a goal of finding the perpetrator."

"Given that many cases will never be solved, that could be more challenging and disappointing," Brick pointed out.

"I understand, but isn't that a reality of being in law enforcement?"

"Definitely. Arrests always bring satisfaction, but an unsolved case is the one that wakes you sweating in the middle of the night." Brick thought for a moment. Being involved in solving a cold case did appeal to him. It's not that he believed in being able to provide closure for victims' survivors; knowing what happened is always preferable to living in limbo. "Do you have a specific case in mind?"

"I have and it hits very close to home. About three years ago, a Lincoln U. student named Henry Yang was the victim of a hit-and-run in Rock Creek Park. His death was, of course, a shock to everyone here, but what was even more shocking was how quickly the case went cold. You must have been working homicide at the time, right?"

"Yes."

"Do you remember anything about it?"

"Henry Yang?" Brick shook his head. "No, the name isn't familiar."

"What do you think? Does this project sound like something you would be interested in doing?"

"Maybe. But it would require the approval of Lieutenant Sonia Hughes. She's the current head of the Homicide Squad."

"I understand." Professor Alexander hesitated for a moment. "If you're willing to get involved, I'm thinking a request from you would carry more weight than if I contact the lieutenant first."

Brick was silent for a minute. "Thanks for offering me this opportunity, but I need to think about it for a day or so."

"Fair enough." Professor Alexander smiled warmly as she handed Brick her business card. "I look forward to hearing what you decide."

As Brick headed to the elevator, it occurred to him that had he taken a day or two to think back in April instead of acting impulsively, in all probability, he'd still be a homicide detective.

CHAPTER THREE

WALKING USUALLY HELPED Brick clear his head when he needed to make decisions. As he turned south on the section of Massachusetts Avenue known as Embassy Row, he weighed the pros and cons of the proposal. The more he thought about it, the more interested he was in getting involved even though working with graduate students from an elite university was a bit intimidating. Not in the same way as facing down an armed career criminal, but more like being cross-examined by an aggressive defense attorney with Ivy League credentials and attitude to match. Still, it might be worth the trade-off and experience he could add to his resume. Plus, it wasn't like there were other offers on the table. He crossed the street. Rowhouse mansions that had been single family homes were now embassies and flying flags of countries as diverse as the Philippines, Sudan, and Paraguay. At least on this street, there was a sense of peaceful coexistence.

In the next block, Brick recognized the red flag with the emerald green pentagram in front of the Embassy of Morocco. He immediately thought about Adil, the owner of a Georgetown salon where he had gotten his hair cut for several years. As picky as Brick tended to be about his clothes, he was even more particular about his hair. Adil never failed to please, and earlier in the year, Brick had attended his naturalization ceremony. Afterward, he was invited to Adil's home where his wife prepared a traditional meal of lamb, dates, and almonds cooked in a tagine. Over dinner, their stories of growing up in Casablanca fascinated Brick. He wouldn't need a haircut for a couple of weeks, but he made a mental note to give Adil a call.

This area was like a walk down Memory Lane. Even though Brick wasn't a world traveler, he thought about the immigrants he had met over the years. A few weren't on the right side of the law, but several had become his friends and he had learned a lot about their cultures and traditions. Once every four years when the World Cup was being played, except for being at the games in person, D.C. was the next best place to be.

A few blocks from Dupont Circle, Brick passed a site where a dry cleaner and a mom-and-pop convenience store had been a few months before. Now, it was a deep hole with a construction crane towering above the other buildings nearby. A sign advertised luxury one-bedroom condos starting at 1.5 million. At that price, he assumed a high-end feature would be well-insulated windows to block the constant cacophony of car horns and sirens on Connecticut Avenue. While crossing the Calvert Street Bridge, Brick felt his phone vibrate. He figured it was a breaking news alert but instead was pleasantly surprised to see a text from Nora. *"Guessing you're back home. So am I. Do you think we crossed paths somewhere over the Atlantic?"* An airplane emoji followed. Two-thumb texting was a skill Brick hadn't mastered—and probably never would. With his right index finger, he tapped out a response. *"Didn't you see me waving?"* He smiled as he slipped the phone back into his pocket.

* * *

"Well, look who's here!" Rory Boland made the announcement as Brick walked into Boland's Mill for the first time in three months.

Over the years, the pub had been his go-to place in good times and bad. If he missed three days in a row, it would have been noticed. A call from Eamonn or Rory was sure to follow. Brick noticed that the two guys seated at the far end of the antique oak bar turned their heads in his direction. If they were thinking a Washington VIP had just walked in the door, they were probably disappointed. Brick claimed the barstool he usually occupied next to the wall.

"Guinness?" Rory asked.

Brick nodded. "Thanks again for taking care of my place. I really appreciate it, especially the breakfast stuff you left in the fridge."

"No problem. Figured it was the least I could do given the tickets you gave me. A couple of times I came so close to catching a foul ball. I swear one whizzed right by my ear, but I had a beer in one hand and a hot dog in the other."

Brick laughed. "And that probably set you back twenty bucks."

"Right. For a split second, I thought about dropping them but after standing in line for the beer, I would have been pissed if I missed the ball. Anyway, I saw some exciting games." Rory set a pint of Guinness in front of Brick.

"Where's Eamonn?" Brick asked.

"He's upstairs, taking a nap. Got a flu shot yesterday and now he's convinced he's got the flu." Rory laughed. "I mixed up some cure. He'll be fine. Plus, Elvis is looking after him."

Brick knew the "cure" was a reliable mixture of honey, lemon, and Jameson, heavy on the whiskey. And Elvis, the female cat rescued as a tiny kitten and named before her gender was determined. Eamonn and Rory adopted the cat after her original owner was tragically killed. Thoughts of the beloved employee were never far from Brick's mind, especially in this place. Jose always had a smile on his face as he bussed tables as if it were the best job ever. Compared to his life in Guatemala, maybe it was. Brick took a sip of Guinness. It was good, just not quite . . . but that didn't matter, it was definitely good enough.

Rory checked with the other customers to see if they needed anything before making his way back to Brick. He leaned his elbows on the bar and lowered his voice. "I could use a little advice."

"Okay." Considering the request was from Rory, any subject from blackjack to financial planning to sex was possible. Brick took another drink and braced himself.

"Next week is Kelly's birthday and I'm planning to surprise her with a party. Here, of course." Rory hesitated and seemed to swallow hard. "I . . . ah, I'm going to propose to her."

"At this surprise party?"

"Yeah."

"Have you two talked about getting married?"

"Sort of. I mean we've talked about living together but if we're going to do that, I want it to be permanent." Rory shrugged his shoulders. "I figure if I screw up, it will be harder for her to kick me out."

"Always good to plan ahead." Brick laughed and took another drink. "Is that really the reason?"

"No, although I have been known . . . anyway, I want us to have a life together, to be a family. Have kids someday."

"Is that what she wants?"

"I think so."

"But you're not sure?"

"Not a hundred percent." Rory shook his head. "You're a good judge of people. What do you think I should do?"

There was a time when Brick felt he deserved Rory's confidence, but not anymore. Trusting the wrong person was a regret he would live with for the rest of his life. Still, he saw no harm in answering Rory's question. "I don't know Kelly that well, but she strikes me as someone who isn't comfortable being the center of attention. Am I right about that?" Rory nodded as Brick continued. "I think the surprise birthday party, as long as it's not too big, is okay. But save the proposal for a private time, just the two of you."

"Like a romantic dinner?"

"Better yet, go to a country inn or a B&B. You know, one of those places in Charlottesville or Williamsburg."

Rory winced. "I hate those feckin' places. It's like trying to have sex at your grandmother's house."

"I know but it's one night out of your life. Suck it up."

"Yeah, you're right. Kelly has mentioned a place in Charlottesville."

"Well, there you go. That should seal the deal."

Rory seemed to consider what Brick had said, but he didn't look convinced. "I guess that makes sense and if she says no, I won't feel like a feckin' eejit." Rory picked up Brick's empty glass. "I mean I will, but at least no one else will know."

Brick couldn't help laughing. "There is that to consider."

"Thanks, I'll let you know how it goes. Another Guinness?"

"No, but I'll have a corned beef sandwich and an order of fries. You can make it to go." Brick tried unsuccessfully to stifle a yawn. "I know this place will get crazy soon and I'm just not up for it tonight."

"That makes two of us." Rory sighed and walked away.

*   *   *

Maybe jet lag was catching up with him after all, but Brick was determined to get back on East Coast time and not give in to it. He watched the local news while he ate his sandwich then cleared the table. He logged on to his computer and checked email. Nothing that needed his immediate attention except an Evite from Ron and Jasmine for the baptism of their twins. Brick confirmed he would attend. Seeing his former partner was something to look forward to. Then he hit *new message* and started composing a memo to Lieutenant Hughes. He described the program Professor Alexander had proposed, mentioning the case of Henry Yang as a possibility.

He concluded with a request that if the lieutenant was interested, a meeting with him and the professor should be arranged to discuss the specifics. Brick reread what he had written, making sure auto-correct hadn't screwed up something. Satisfied, he hit *send*.

Before turning off his computer, Brick checked the Nationals' website. Although he tried to keep up with their season while he was in Ireland, it was difficult because he spent very little time online and it had been months since he had actually watched a game. Tonight's was in New York against the Mets so he might be able to stay awake for most of it.

CHAPTER FOUR

"MAYBE MY MOTHER was right. My sister, too." Jasmine Hayes reached for a Kleenex from a box on the end table next to her chair. In doing so, she knocked over her cup of coffee and cried harder. "Oh my God, I'm so sorry. I can't do anything right."

Dr. Lynn Reznick grabbed a couple of paper towels, soaked up the spilled coffee, and wiped the top of the table. "What is it that your mother and sister were right about, Jasmine?" Dr. Reznick asked as she took off her glasses and set them aside.

Jasmine didn't answer immediately, and when she did, the words seemed to catch in her throat. "That marrying Ron was a mistake."

"They're entitled to their opinion, but what's important is whether you think it was a mistake. Do you?"

Jasmine dabbed at her eyes. "Certainly not at the time. I couldn't wait until we got married. Aside from just being happy to be together no matter what we were doing, I felt safe with him in a way that I never did before. Now, I don't know how I feel. Everything is so different than I thought it would be." She twisted the tissue in her hand. "I guess that's the trouble with having expectations. It's just a setup for disappointments."

"And what is it that's disappointing to you?"

"Everything is out of control. The laundry is piling up, the house is a pigsty, and just look at me—I'm a mess. It's been six months and I'm *still wearing maternity clothes because I can't even squeeze into my regular clothes. I haven't washed my hair in a week and this morning . . . I couldn't produce any breast milk. It's bad enough failing as a wife, but now I'm failing as a mother. The babies didn't ask to be born. They deserve better."*

"Jasmine, every new mother has moments of doubt, plus hormones are doing all sorts of crazy things that affect your emotions. I sense that you're feeling overwhelmed today. Am I right?"

Jasmine nodded as she reached for another tissue.

"Babies are a blessing but they are demanding and unpredictable and no matter how prepared you think you are, any day can present a challenge you're not prepared for." Dr. Reznick paused and wrote something on her notepad. "Taking care of one baby is exhausting, and you're taking care of two infants. Let's talk about a support system. Is Ron doing his share?"

"The way he sees it, his job is going to work and bringing home a paycheck. And lately, he's been working a lot of overtime because we can use the extra money."

"Are you saying he doesn't help out at home?"

"He does, but I think he could do a lot more. Only helping on his days off isn't enough."

"Especially since babies need care 24/7."

"Exactly, I don't get a day off. It's really hard. I'm trying to get the babies on a schedule and then his work schedule changes every couple of weeks. It's insane. He needs to sleep, sometimes during the day if he's working the midnight shift, and if the babies are crying, he gets angry, and then I start crying. Yesterday, I just locked myself in the bathroom and hoped it will all go away." Jasmine shrugged her shoulders. "I never thought it would be like this."

"When things are somewhat calm, have you talked to Ron about this?" Dr. Reznick asked.

Jasmine twisted her mouth into a scowl as she shook her head. "I've tried, but he doesn't understand. Like right now, the twins are down for their morning nap. I know what he'll say when I get home. 'What's the big deal? They slept for a couple of hours—that's plenty of time for you to get stuff done.' He just doesn't get it and trying to talk to him causes an argument." Again, she started to cry. "I don't have the energy for that."

"I understand. Motherhood—or I should say parenting— is a huge adjustment and in the short term, it might be wise to have some help."

"I'd like to hire someone, but we can't afford it."

"Maybe your mother or sister would be willing to help."

"And when they say, 'I told you so,' I guess I just have to swallow my pride."

"Sometimes, that's what we have to do." Dr. Reznick glanced up at the clock on the wall near the door. "We'll have to stop for now, but would you like to meet again next week at this time?"

"I need to check Ron's schedule first." Jasmine reached in her purse and retrieved her phone. "He's still working the 4-12 shift so he can watch the twins in the morning."

"Good, then I'll see you next week."

CHAPTER FIVE

TWO DAYS AFTER sending Lieutenant Hughes the email outlining the cold case project, Brick found himself at his former haunt where caffeine ruled. Different barristas at the Judiciary Square Starbucks, but otherwise everything looked the same. Knowing what to expect had advantages and might explain the loyal following. He ordered a tall English Breakfast tea and a cranberry scone and waited for Grace Alexander at a table near the door. He glanced at his phone. Before he left for Ireland, he had cancelled his home-delivery sub-scription to the *Washington Post* and started reading it online in-stead. Even though he didn't plan to restart his subscription, he missed the print edition. His crossword puzzle–solving skills had suffered and he tended to just scroll through headlines rather than reading articles. Nothing piqued his interest except the baseball standings even though he knew the Nationals' ninth season had them in second place in the NL East Division.

Brick glanced out the window. A group of Metro commuters was exiting the station and he saw that Professor Alexander was among them. As she entered the Starbucks, she looked around and smiled when she spotted Brick. She joined him at his table as he stood and extended his hand.

"Professor."

"Please, call me Grace. I would have been here sooner, but there was a door problem on the train. Had to offload at Farragut North and then the next train was too crowded. So frustrating." She set her briefcase on the chair across from Brick. "Even without coffee, I'm feeling wired. Guess I'd better go for the decaf."

"Ever notice how they raise the fares and service declines? I've learned to always allow plenty of time. We're good."

She returned to the table and sat down. "I don't know that there's anything we need to go over prior to the meeting. I'm just encouraged that she's willing to consider the proposal. Since you've worked with Lieutenant Hughes—"

Brick interrupted. "That was just a onetime emergency situation, but I can tell you she has a stellar reputation. Now that she's in charge, she may be open to innovative ways of getting things done."

"Good to know. That may work to my advantage." Grace took a sip from her cup. "I just think it's important for students to have real-world experiences. Basing a career on what they've watched on TV is probably not the best indication of what it's really like."

"You mean like on *CSI*—or as most cops I know refer to the show—*CSI Don't Think So.*"

Grace laughed as she set down her cup. "I had never heard that expression, but yes, that's what I'm talking about."

* * *

Brick and Grace Alexander left Starbucks, crossed Indiana Avenue, and headed toward the Henry J. Daly Building. Commonly referred to as Police Headquarters, the building was named in honor of a veteran police sergeant who was killed along with two FBI agents when an armed intruder opened fire inside the building. For the last ten years of his career, this was the place where Brick reported. The place where he had his own cubicle, which was as close to an office as most cops can ever hope for. Then one day, five months ago, it abruptly ended.

Walking up the steps to the revolving-door entrance felt routine and strange at the same time. And he wasn't sure which emotion was stronger. He motioned for Grace to go ahead as she placed her briefcase on the conveyer belt to be x-rayed before she walked through the metal detector. Brick placed his keys and cell phone in a basket and waited for the rent-a-security-guard to motion for him to walk through. On the other side, they gathered their belongings and headed toward the elevator bank.

"Is that who I think it is, or do my eyes deceive me?"

Brick immediately recognized the raspy voice and turned in the direction from which it came. He fist-bumped with Otis Johnson, the night janitor, who had worked at headquarters for well over twenty years. "How are you, Otis?"

"I've been better, but I've been worse. And since my shift is over, it's all good now." He paused for a moment. "Does this mean you're back on the job?"

Brick shook his head. "No, just here for a meeting."

"Damn, I'm sorry to hear that, my man, but it's good seeing you just the same."

"Thanks, Otis. Take care of yourself."

It was inevitable Brick would run into people he knew. He had already checked with his former partner to see if he was working days, but Ron was on the four-to-twelve shift. He was hoping that was also the case for a few former colleagues he'd rather not see. Brick hit the up arrow on the elevator panel and waited for the door to open. When it did, he motioned for Grace to step in first. He followed along with a couple of uniformed officers. Everyone got off on the third floor where the Homicide, Robbery, and Sex Squads were located.

At this hour, more desks were empty than occupied. Most detectives were probably in court, meeting with assistant U.S. attorneys, or on the street interviewing witnesses. Brick directed Grace through the maze of cubicles to the private office now belonging to Lieutenant Sonia Hughes. The receptionist who had previously taken the role of gatekeeper as seriously as a Rottweiler was gone. In her place, the much friendlier face of a woman who appeared close to retirement age. Brick introduced himself and the professor.

"Lieutenant Hughes is expecting you, please go on in."

The lieutenant was seated behind her desk but immediately got up when Brick opened the door. She smiled as she introduced herself to Professor Alexander before shaking hands with her and Brick.

"It's good to see you, Brick. It appears your time in Ireland served you well."

"It did. Maybe sabbaticals should be required for all first responders."

"Sounds good to me but convincing the taxpayers might be problematic." Hughes gestured toward a round conference table with four chairs. "Please make yourselves comfortable and we'll get started." Before joining them, she went back to her desk and picked up a file and a yellow legal pad.

Grace took the lead and described what she had in mind just as she had when she met with Brick. She concluded by explaining why she thought the case involving a Lincoln U. student would be especially meaningful for the graduate students.

Lieutenant Hughes nodded. "I understand your thinking, but my concern is that there is very little to know about the Yang case." She held up a thin official police department file. "This is it. There are other cases that are stored in boxes, some in multiple boxes. I'm not suggesting that one of them would be a better experiment, but before we proceed, I think it would be appropriate for Brick to see what we have and look into the case a bit. That way we can determine if the project has the potential to provide the students with a worthwhile experience and hopefully close the case."

"Think that's what we call a win-win," Brick said. "I'm certainly willing to check it out."

Hughes looked first at Grace and then at Brick. "Good. I like the idea, and if this case doesn't meet the criteria we're looking for, we have plenty of others. Not something we're proud of, it's just the way it is." If she intended to continue, she didn't get a chance.

"Sorry to interrupt, Lieutenant," her receptionist said as she stood in the doorway. "The chief needs to see you ASAP."

"All right then. Brick, I'll draft a Memorandum of Understanding, which will grant you the authority to investigate this specific case and email it to you. If you have any questions, call me. Otherwise, sign it and fax it back to my assistant. Once that's taken care of, you can have access to the file and start investigating."

CHAPTER SIX

JASMINE TOOK OFF *her sweater and grabbed a couple of tissues before she sat down across from Dr. Reznick. She glanced over at the double stroller where Jayla and Jamal slept peacefully. "At least they don't know what's going on," she said as she dabbed at the tears flooding her eyes. "Thanks for seeing me. I know my appointment isn't until next week." She blew her nose, threw away the Kleenex, and reached for another. "I didn't know where else to go."*

"It's good you're here," Dr. Reznick said. "From the message you left on my voicemail, I'm worried about you. We should talk about your options."

"What?" Jasmine asked. "I'm sorry, my mind is wandering in a million directions."

"It's okay. I said, we need to talk about your options."

"Options? I'm not sure I have any."

"It can feel that way, but I can assure you that you do. But first, tell me why you are so upset."

"I'm not sure where to start."

"Take a deep breath and try to relax." Dr. Reznick removed her glasses and set them aside. She crossed her right leg over her left and balanced a notepad on her knee.

"Okay." Jasmine took another deep breath and exhaled slowly. "The baptism is set for tomorrow. I want it to be special." She looked up and glanced directly at Dr. Reznick as if seeking her approval.

"Of course. It's a very important occasion that only happens once."

Jasmine nodded. "Although I guess Ron doesn't see it that way. When he found out what I spent on the outfits for the twins, he threw a fit. He said it was stupid to waste money on clothes they'll outgrow in a month." She glanced over at the twins. "I tried to explain that it was important to me because it would be the first time most of my family would meet Jayla and Jamal, but I didn't get very far."

"Why was that?"

"He stormed out of the room and went to bed, leaving me with lots of stuff to do, like laundry and cleaning the bathrooms. Things he said he would help me with."

"It sounds like his behavior was immature and disrespectful. I can understand why you were upset."

"Oh no, this was just the beginning. It was close to midnight when I finally went to bed. I was exhausted, but I was too keyed up to sleep. I was still awake when Ron's cell phone pinged and a picture popped up on the screen. He woke up and tried to grab it, but I was closer to the nightstand and got to it before he had a chance." Jasmine swallowed hard and appeared to be fighting back tears. She leaned back against the sofa pillow and stared up at the ceiling. "It's like I'm still seeing that image of her in that slutty outfit."

"Who . . . who are you talking about?"

Jasmine looked directly at Dr. Reznick. "Holly Beltran."

Dr. Reznick checked through her notes. "I don't recall you ever mentioning her."

"I didn't think there was any reason why I should, but it just shows how stupid I've been."

"Jasmine, why do you feel that way?"

"Because I thought she was my friend . . . our friend." Jasmine brushed a strand of hair out of her eyes. "She works with Ron."

"Is she a police officer?'

"Yes, a detective, new to the Homicide Squad. She gave Ron gifts for the twins, which I thought was really nice, so I invited her to the house to see the babies. She told me about her nieces and nephews and how she hoped to have kids of her own some day." Jasmine shifted her position and glanced over at the twins. "I trusted her and when she offered to babysit so Ron and I could have a date night, I accepted. Now it makes me sick to know she was in my house, probably snooping through my stuff . . . some friend, right?"

"I sense you're feeling betrayed."

"Of course I am." Where there had been tears, Jasmine's eyes flashed anger. "When I saw that picture, I knew."

"Knew what, Jasmine?"

"He's cheating on me. The babies are six months old, and he's cheating on me with Holly. It was written all over his face."

"Did you confront him?"

"I sure did! He denied it, of course, with some lame excuse that it was a mistake. She meant to send the picture to her boyfriend. Well, it seems to be that's exactly what she did. When I said as much, Ron got angry because I didn't believe him."

"Jasmine, did it escalate to anything physical?"

"No, but for the first time since I've known Ron, I was afraid it might. He's a cop. There's guns in our house."

"That's definitely a concern," Dr. Reznick said. "How many guns does he have?"

"Two. His service revolver and a gun he uses for target shooting."

"Where are they kept?"

"On a shelf in our hall coat closet. It's okay for now, but they'll have to be locked up when the twins get older. We've already agreed on that."

"That's good for the future, but we need to talk about now." Dr. Reznick glanced down at her notes before continuing. *"Jasmine, I'm not saying this to scare you, but there was a study recently conducted in New York City. Homicide is the leading cause of death during pregnancy and the first postpartum year. African American women are at highest risk. It is critical that we discuss options for your safety and the safety of the babies."*

Jasmine nodded. "I know."

CHAPTER SEVEN

BRICK WALKED INTO Boland's Mill just after it opened and was glad to see Eamonn Boland behind the bar. No surprise that the old man whose face, for better or worse, always revealed what he was thinking broke into a broad smile.

"Welcome home, lad! Rory told me you were here the other day, but I was a little under the weather."

"Feeling better now?"

Eamonn nodded. "Cure works every time. And looks like your time away worked as well. I didn't say it then, but I'll say it now, I was worried about you. Glad to see you've gained a couple of pounds and you look relaxed."

Brick was getting used to hearing that. He took off his jacket and draped it over the back of his barstool.

"You're a bit dressed up for a Sunday morning," Eamonn commented as he wiped down a section of the bar.

"Maybe this is what I was wearing last night, and I haven't been home to change."

"Well, if that's the case, good on ya. But what are you doing in here? You should be serving her breakfast in bed."

Brick laughed. "Remember Ron, my former partner? His twins are being baptized at noon."

"Ah, that's grand. A boy and a girl, right?"

Brick nodded. "Figured I'd better have some breakfast first." He looked over the menu and considered the traditional Irish breakfast but decided on a less hearty entrée. "I'll have two eggs over easy, bacon, and O'Brien potatoes. And a glass of tomato juice."

Eamonn keyed in the order and returned to the end of the bar with the tomato juice. He placed it on a coaster in front of Brick.

"Thanks." Brick squeezed a lemon wedge over the top of the glass before taking a drink. "I met with the professor from Lincoln U., the woman you talked to. She's interested in having me work with a group of graduate students on a cold case project."

"But are you interested?" Eamonn asked.

"Maybe. A lot depends on the case. I need to check it out to see if it might be the kind of experience she'd like the students to have."

"The professor seemed like a nice woman when she came here asking how to contact you. Plus, I'm sure you noticed, she's easy on the eyes. Who knows, might lead to a job, or—"

"Don't even go there."

"Hey, if I were twenty years younger . . ."

"Eamonn, this is about a business relationship, not a social one."

"You never know. An opportunity could land in your lap when you least expect it."

"Has that been your experience?"

"Feck, no." Eamonn shook his head. "But I have a little advice on the job front—don't open a bar." He laughed when he said it, but Brick knew that running a business which operates sixteen hours a day, seven days a week isn't easy. And Eamonn had been doing it for many years. Although now that Rory had taken over a lot of the responsibility, he was putting in fewer hours on a daily basis.

While Brick ate breakfast, he thought about what Eamonn had said regarding the professor. It wasn't like him to play matchmaker although he was right about Grace Alexander being "easy on the eyes." But Brick had a strict rule about mixing business and pleasure. And for now, finding meaningful work was a higher priority than his social life. Still, he couldn't help but wonder if there would come a time when he would find himself thinking in terms of "if I were twenty years younger" or regretting letting opportunities pass him by.

*　*　*

After breakfast, Brick hailed a cab outside Boland's Mill. He wasn't opposed to using Uber but knew that cab drivers, especially older ones, were struggling. As he adjusted the seat belt, he gave the driver the address for the Southeast AME Zion Church.

It wasn't the first time Brick had entered the historic church that, along with its school, parsonage, and parking lot, occupied a city block. At least this time it was for a happy occasion; the last time was anything but. The funeral for the only MPDC female officer killed in the line of duty filled every pew in the sanctuary and overflow crowds lined the streets outside. Brick thought about the other funerals for cops he had attended over the years. How many? The answer was easy . . . too many.

The baptism was being held in the chapel, a much smaller and intimate setting. The afternoon sun provided natural light as it shone through the colorful stained-glass windows. Brick entered and saw Ron and Jasmine surrounded by a small group. Two of the women bore a striking resemblance to Jasmine, her mother and sister no doubt. As Brick made his way down the aisle, Ron turned away from the group. Upon seeing Brick, he immediately came over and greeted his former partner with a handshake that quickly turned into a bro hug.

"Hey, great to see you. You're looking good, man. Thanks for coming."

"Glad to be here." Brick noticed that Ron seemed nervous, which was to be expected given the significance of the occasion. He also had the new-parent sleep deprivation look times two. And if twins weren't enough, having to adjust to changing shifts every two weeks wreaks havoc on the body, even an athletic one like Ron's.

"We'll be getting started soon and afterward there'll be a reception downstairs. We'll get a chance to talk then but, hey, it's so good to see you. Appreciate you being here."

Brick was sure he did. One of the things the two men had in common was a lack of family members. Both grew up without siblings or father figures. Brick's mother died when he was a teenager and Ron's mother died when he was in college. Even though Brick didn't dwell on it, occasions such as this tended to be happy and sad if he allowed himself to give it too much thought.

Brick took a seat near the front and remembered to silence his cell phone. An older couple sitting in an adjacent pew leaned over and introduced themselves as Jasmine's aunt and uncle. Other family members arrived and from some of the comments Brick overheard, this was their first time meeting the twins. Their excitement was contagious.

Just after noon, Rev. Marcus Walker, the senior pastor, entered and addressed the group with the words, "Let us pray." Following the prayer and a collective "Amen," he spoke briefly about the responsibility of being a parent before baptizing each baby. Ron held Jayla who entertained everyone with cooing sounds while Jamal slept in his mother's arms until drops of holy water woke him and his earsplitting shrieks filled the chapel. The sacrament ended as it had begun, with a prayer.

It was over quickly, and the family members and friends filed out after stopping to congratulate Ron and Jasmine. The pastor led the way to the room where the reception was being held. Various relatives took turns holding the twins who seemed to enjoy the attention at first but were starting to fuss. After having a piece of cake, Brick didn't intend to stay much longer and looked around so he could say goodbye to Ron and Jasmine. He heard their voices out in the hallway and was about to approach them but immediately realized it wasn't the best time to interrupt. He stayed out of sight.

"I told you to bring their pacifiers. One task, Ron, was that asking too much?"

Brick saw Jasmine glare at Ron before continuing to rifle through the twins' diaper bag.

"Jasmine, I'm sure they're in there."

"Really? Well then you find them!" She shoved the diaper bag into Ron's chest, walked down the hall to the ladies' room, and slammed the door.

Brick was sure Ron hadn't seen him in the doorway and could probably use a minute to himself. He went back to where the refreshments were being served and helped himself to a glass of fruit punch. Shortly thereafter, Ron joined him. In his hand were two pacifiers—one pink, one blue.

"I hoped we'd have a chance to catch up," Ron said. "But now just isn't a good time."

"I understand. Let me know when it is, and we'll grab a beer."

"Will do. I'd better get these to the twins, before everyone suffers hearing loss."

Brick knew the polite thing to do was to speak to Jasmine before leaving, but all things considered, he figured speaking with Ron was sufficient. As he left the building, he saw Jasmine and Pastor Walker talking in the parking lot. He watched the pastor hand her a handkerchief and she dabbed her eyes. Brick couldn't hear anything being said, but he could read their body language. He saw Jasmine nod and smile as the pastor, an older and handsome man, bearing a slight resemblance to Attorney General Eric Holder, placed his arm around her shoulder and led her back inside the building.

CHAPTER EIGHT

BRICK WASN'T SURPRISED the weather forecast was wrong, but this time it worked in his favor. The afternoon showers predicted earlier hadn't materialized. Rather than flag down a cab, he decided to walk from the church to Police Headquarters to pick up the copy of the Yang file Lieutenant Hughes had left for him. On the way, he passed Nationals Park and stopped outside the gate. The team was on the road, but just walking by the ballpark put a smile on his face. He was visualizing some of the times spent here as vividly as if flipping through a stack of photos. A game or two still might be in his future before their season ended.

After arriving home, Brick was anxious to review the file, but first he changed into jeans and the green-, white-, and orange-striped shirt he bought at O'Neills' Irish Rugby Shop in Dublin. Before grabbing a Heineken from the fridge, he cleared the sorted piles of mail taking up too much space on his dining table.

Lieutenant Hughes had been right about the file being thin. But just as detectives are stuck with whoever witnessed a crime, Brick knew this was what he had to work with. He started by reading the report prepared by the medical examiner. Yang had died from internal injuries as a result of being hit by a car. He was eighteen days shy of his twenty-second birthday and prior to being injured appeared to be healthy. No indication of comorbidities. Brick flipped through the autopsy photos but stopped and studied the one showing the head injuries Yang sustained. As he had done many times, he tried to look past the bruised skin and abrasions and for a moment imagine the victim before he was injured. A conservative haircut and no facial hair or piercings gave the impression of a serious young man. After reading that a fractured skull and multiple internal injuries were the cause of death, he set the autopsy report aside. He didn't need to know how much various organs weighed. How Henry Yang lived may yield clues as to why he died, and Brick intended to learn everything he could.

If he accepted the job of mentoring students, Brick knew he would stress the importance of exploring everything they could about the victim's life without passing judgment or jumping to conclusions. Objectivity and persistence were critical traits for success, but could they be taught or were they characteristics determined by genetics? He wasn't sure but he might be in a position to find out.

Brick turned to the report written by the investigating homicide detective. One look at the signature and name typed below it was like being dealt a lousy poker hand. Of all the possible names of investigators, this was one he didn't want to see. Fred Stewart was never outstanding, but at one time he was regarded as a detective who did a satisfactory job. That changed about a year before he retired. He made it abundantly clear he was counting the days. This case was assigned to him just three months before he pulled the plug on his career.

The brief report Stewart had prepared indicated that the victim was observed jogging in Rock Creek Park and using the exercise equipment along the path. As Yang was leaving the trail, sometime between 6:43 and 7:00 p.m., he was struck by a car. The witness did not see him get hit but heard the impact, saw the car speed away, and called 911. He stayed with the victim until EMTs and police arrived.

Brick felt encouraged. Since only three years had elapsed, there was a reasonable expectation the witness could be located and interviewed. He turned the page expecting to see the witness statement. It was there, but the name of the witness had been redacted.

"What the fuck!" Brick threw down his pen and leaned back in his chair. Why was the name redacted? That made absolutely no sense. If, by chance, the witness was a confidential informant, the name wouldn't have appeared in the first place. Brick was baffled but it was exactly the type of inconsistency that fueled his curiosity. He set the file aside. It was after six and other than the piece of cake at the reception for the twins, he hadn't eaten since breakfast. There were plenty of options in the neighborhood. Although keeping up with openings and closings tended to be a challenge. He grabbed his jacket and headed out hoping the Chinese carry-out next to the hardware store in the strip mall was still there.

Lotus Inn was open and busy. Thirty minutes later, Brick returned to his apartment with enough food for a couple of days. After filling a plate with kung pao chicken, twice-cooked pork, and shrimp fried rice, he turned on ESPN. On this Sunday night, the Nats were playing the Cubs. Seeing scenes of the Chicago skyline made him think of Nora. Interesting that she seemed to embrace the Windy City as much as she did Galway. Even though he had never been to Chicago, he figured the two places had little, if anything, in common.

* * *

The next morning, Brick awoke to an apartment that still smelled like Chinese food. He opened the window in the kitchen, regretting he hadn't done that last night. Looking around his kitchen, which was probably last updated in the '70s, he knew his home needed some extensive renovations, but do-it-yourself projects weren't his strong suit and just the thought of dealing with contractors was a giant pain in the ass. Although at a minimum, he figured he should replace the microwave.

Brick was feeling unsettled, and he wasn't sure why. He was glad to be home and grateful for an assignment that could potentially lead to a job, but unlike the years he spent investigating homicides, the motivation just wasn't there. Maybe the time in Ireland had spoiled him. It was easy to let the day lead where it may and he had felt justified doing so. Could three months with no specific agenda or responsibilities undo years of a structured lifestyle? Intellectually, Brick knew his brain hadn't been rewired. No doubt, this was just a readjustment phase, not unlike what plenty of new retirees experienced. Eventually, he'd figure it out. For now, breakfast was the priority.

While Brick waited for the bowl of instant oatmeal to finish cooking in the microwave, he channel surfed between the local news, CNN, and MSNBC. Who won or who was snubbed at the annual Emmy Awards didn't interest him. He hit the power button on the remote to turn off the TV. The first spoonful of oatmeal was cold and the next burned his mouth. No more excuses, it was time for a trip to the Best Buy in Pentagon City. And while he was at the mall, he'd reward himself with a stop at Nordstrom's. On any given day, he would much rather shop for clothes than electronics and his walk-in closet, seriously in need of purging, was proof. As Brick dumped the oatmeal into the garbage disposal, he heard his cell phone ping. He glanced at a text from Ron.

Change in plans—the microwave replacement project had waited this long; it could wait another day.

CHAPTER NINE

RON WAS ALREADY seated at a table at the Hawk and Dove. In a city as transient as Washington, this Capitol Hill establishment had been around since Lyndon Johnson was president and before Brick was born. He took a seat across from Ron.

"I thought I'd be in court all day, but the bottom-feeder had a come-to-Jesus moment and did us all a huge favor. He pled to second degree."

"Nice when that happens."

"Yeah, as the prosecutor said, we dodged a bullet. She was worried there'd be a hung jury because two of the witnesses were shaky, kept changing their story."

"That's never a good sign." Brick picked up a menu. "Are you still working four-to-twelve?" he asked.

"Yeah. So, it didn't make sense to go back home for an hour or two." Ron leaned forward, his elbows on the table. "Been a while, partner, how are you doing?"

Brick smiled at Ron's use of "partner." Even though they had only worked together for just over a year, their partnership had been one of mutual respect and trust. Brick took a deep breath before he answered Ron's question. "I don't know if a trained therapist would agree, but I think I'm doing okay."

"Regardless of what they may say, something must have worked because you look a whole lot better than when you left. Got to say, I was worried about you." Ron glanced at his phone then slipped it back into his pocket. "Anyway, tell me about your meeting with the lieutenant. Are you thinking about reinstatement?"

The server returned with two Cokes and took their order before Brick continued. The enthusiasm in Ron's voice made Brick smile as he shook his head. He went on to describe the cold case project under consideration. "I have a small favor. Can you ask around and see where Fred Stewart is now?"

"Sure, no problem."

"Hopefully, if he's still in the area, I can talk to him in person."

"Because you can't read body language over the phone." Ron picked up his soda. "One of the first lessons I learned . . . the hard way."

Brick nodded as he thought about that particular situation shortly after Ron arrived in Homicide. "C'mon, you make it sound like I was a tough taskmaster."

"In case you've forgotten, you kind of ripped me a new one." Ron smiled at his recollection and Brick laughed.

"I don't remember it that way, but to your credit, you didn't make the same mistake twice."

Ron picked up his Coke and took a drink. "Hey, a lot has happened while you were away. Lieutenant Hughes broke up the A Team. And we have our first female detective, at least the first since I've been there. Holly Beltran. She transferred over from Robbery."

"What's the latest on Blancato?" While he was away, Brick had tried not to think about the former lieutenant in charge of the Homicide Squad and the very person responsible for his impulsive decision to retire back in April, but now he couldn't resist.

"He's got a fancy title, acting something or other at Homeland Security. Not that it matters, but my money says he'll screw up another organization." Ron shook his head. "With all his political connections, I guess we should have known he'd land on his feet."

"He always does because it's how this town works," Brick said.

"Yeah, and I'm trying not to let it get to me anymore. I've got enough to deal with on the home front."

Brick thought he heard a hint of frustration in Ron's voice. "Glad I got to see the twins on Sunday. I can tell Jayla has you wrapped around her little finger."

Ron smiled broadly. "You're right, she does."

"And I'm guessing they keep you and Jasmine busy."

"That's an understatement. I mean I knew babies change your life, I just wasn't prepared for . . . well, it's tougher on Jasmine than it is on me."

Knowing Ron's positive attitude about most things, it wasn't the kind of answer Brick expected and it confirmed what he had previously picked up on. "Because you leave and go to work and she's with the twins 24/7?"

"That's part of it, but she's been having issues with postpartum depression. I'm trying to cut her all the slack she needs, but it's not easy. Sometimes I feel like I can't do anything right."

Brick thought about what he had observed the day of the baptism. "Is there medication for postpartum depression?"

"I've heard birth control pills can prevent the cause. But it's a little too late for that now." Ron laughed, so did Brick. "Seriously, she's breastfeeding so she doesn't want to take anything. She's been seeing a therapist so I'm hoping that will help." Ron glanced away, then back in Brick's direction. "Sorry, man, I didn't mean to get into all that. I'm sure you'd rather talk shop."

"Not really. I can't live in the past, Ron, but if you need an opinion, it's just that I feel qualified to give you work-related advice. Considering my track record with women and my total lack of experience with kids, I have nothing to offer other than an ear. You know you can call me anytime."

"Thanks, man. I appreciate it. I think that was three nights of sleep deprivation talking. Don't get me wrong, fatherhood is awesome, and I highly recommend it. It's just a big adjustment. The whole family dynamic thing has changed." Ron finished his Coke and asked the server for another as he left the cheeseburgers they had ordered. "It'll all work out."

"I'm sure it will," Brick said. "Just remember, being their father is the most important job you'll ever have."

CHAPTER TEN

"So have you completely recovered from jet lag?" Rory asked as Brick took his usual seat at the bar.

"I think so. Seemed to affect me more flying west than when I traveled east."

"It's weird, that doesn't bother me." Rory reached for a bottle of Gatorade he kept in the small refrigerator under the bar. "But north to south, I'm knackered for days." He took a swig of the orange liquid.

Brick was used to hearing Rory make nonsensical comments although late-night drunks were his usual audience. To keep from encouraging him, Brick assumed Rory knew that wasn't a possibility and let it go without responding.

Rory took another drink before throwing the empty bottle into the recycling bin. "Glad to be home?"

"Yes and no." Brick thought for a minute as he waited for his pint of Guinness to settle. "It's good to be back around friends, but I could have easily stayed another month or two."

"Except for the visa requirement?"

"Right. Had I known I might want to stay longer, I would have applied for one." Brick picked up his glass and took a drink.

"Driving on the left was a little dicey, but once I got used to it, I didn't feel like a tourist anymore. It was kind of weird, I've lived here most of my life and there were times I felt more at home there, especially in Galway. If I could sing or juggle, I might have stayed permanently and become a busker."

Rory nodded. "Yeah, I can really see you doing that on a cold, rainy day. Earning a couple of euros, if you're lucky."

"I know. That pipe dream could easily be a nightmare. It's just that now it's back to reality. Time for me to figure out what to do with my life."

"Aw, you don't need to do that today. At least, not right now." Rory wiped his hands on a towel. "Want to order any food?"

"In a while. I'm meeting someone and will wait until she gets here." Brick noticed Rory's raised-eyebrow look. "No, it's not like that. Might lead to a job."

"Well, there you go. Maybe you've already figured out your future."

Brick shook his head. "I'm not counting on it." He was about to explain why, but spotted Grace Alexander walk past the window. "Hey, there she is now." Brick slipped off his barstool and waved as the door closed behind her.

"Sorry I'm running late . . . again. Seems there's always one more thing to do before leaving the office."

"Ten minutes doesn't require an apology."

Grace smiled. "Guess I'll file that under 'Habits to Break.' Women tend to apologize too much. At least, women of my generation. Not sure if the Millennials suffer from the same tendency."

"If I'm going to be working with Millennials, I guess I should look into the traits that define them. But now that I think of it, my former partner is a Millennial. I just never thought of him that way. Maybe it's because a squad room is a whole lot different than a classroom."

"I'm sure you're right. And I don't think you need to be overly concerned. From what I read in the *Post Magazine* article it seems your communication skills have served you well throughout your career."

"Don't believe everything you read." Brick smiled. "Can I get you something to drink?"

"I didn't have time for lunch today, so I'll pass. Otherwise, this meeting may not be productive."

There were times when a flirty cheap-date comment would have been okay, but this wasn't one of them even though Brick agreed with Eamonn's observation. Grace was definitely easy on the eyes, especially when she smiled. "Let's take the table over there." Brick pointed to one in the corner in front of the fireplace.

After looking over the menu, Grace chose the fish and chips. Brick returned the menus to the bar and placed the dinner order with Rory. Back at the table, he saw Grace slip her cell phone into her purse.

"I'm convinced technology is going to turn us into a nation of obsessive-compulsives."

"I think it already has," Brick said. "While I was in Ireland, I unplugged. Sometimes I went days without checking my phone or email."

"Sounds tempting, but was it hard to do?"

"Not when you don't have kids, pets, or a job to check on." Brick took a drink. "But now that I'm back, I'm slipping into the old habits of checking email a hundred times a day and grabbing my phone every time it pings. Maybe I should start my own file of habits to break."

"Or move to Ireland?"

"Thanks to my mother, I can qualify for dual citizenship. The thought has crossed my mind, but no baseball. Not happening."

"We all have our priorities." Grace smiled as she looked around the pub. "It's crazy, even though I live in the neighborhood, I hadn't been in here until I wanted to get in touch with you."

"Is that because you prefer wine to whiskey or beer?"

Grace nodded. "And somehow drinking wine in an Irish pub seems..."

"Sacrilegious?"

"Something like that." Grace took a sip of water. "Obviously, it's been my loss. It's a very comfortable place, and just as the *Post* article described, Eamonn is charming."

"Charming?" Rory set a plate with a generous portion of fish and chips in front of Grace. "You were referring to me, right?"

Grace smiled. "Of course."

Rory left and returned to the table with a bottle of malt vinegar for Grace and a steaming bowl of potato soup for Brick. "Let me know if you need anything else." Behind Grace's back, he gave Brick a double thumbs-up.

For the next few minutes as Grace ate her food, conversation ceased except for a few comments as to how much she was enjoying it. "I can't believe how hungry I was." She wiped her hands on a napkin before reaching into her tote bag and removing a large, sealed envelope. "I didn't have time to go through all of Henry's academic records but made copies of what I thought might be helpful. My sense is that he kept to himself, didn't participate in sports or campus activities. At least the transcripts will give you the names of his professors, and the emergency contact sheet lists his last roommate. Sorry there's not more for you to work with, but I'll keep looking."

Brick noticed Grace seemed less formal than she had when they met at her Lincoln U. office. "You just did it again," Brick said.

"Excuse me?"

"You apologized for something that isn't your fault."

"You're right." Grace laughed. "Thanks for pointing it out. I'm worried it's gone from a habit to a reflex."

"Need to guard against that," Brick said.

"I'll try. Have you had a chance to review the police file?"

Brick nodded. "I have and unfortunately it raises more questions than it answers. I'm hoping the detective assigned to the case can shed some light on what happened."

"Is the detective still with the Homicide Squad?"

"No, he's retired and based on what my former partner was able to find, he's living in Purcellville."

"That's in Virginia, right?"

"Yes, Loudoun County, which is about forty miles west of the District. Close enough that I can meet him in person, if he agrees to talk to me."

"Would he have reason not to?"

Brick sidestepped the question. "Only one way to find out."

missing . . . life can be so feckin' unfair. Weren't you just at the
baptism?"

"Yes." Brick wondered if Eamonn's comment about life being unfair was referring to more than Ron's situation. Eamonn cared about
his employees and . . . . gado had affected
everyone who had known him but especially Eamonn. And it occurred to Brick that for all the years he had known Eamonn, he really knew little about him before he came to the States and settled
in D.C. Had something unfair in his life been the motivation for
him to start over in a new place?

CHAPTER ELEVEN

BEFORE BRICK CALLED Fred Stewart, he needed to do a little re-
search. As much as he would have liked to save time and cut to the
chase by just asking why the name of the witness was redacted, he
figured that could be counterproductive. He Googled Purcellville
real estate. Several websites popped up showing single family homes
for sale but none in a price range a retired cop would be likely to
afford. He continued scrolling until he found a new townhouse development that met his requirements. Brick copied down the name
and address of the subdivision and a few pertinent details.

Now, he was ready. Brick put his cell phone on speaker and entered the number Ron was able to get. After four rings, he was expecting a recorded voicemail message, but a man sounding out of
breath answered.

"Fred Stewart? It's Brick Kavanagh."

"Hey, a blast from the past. Hang on a minute."

Brick heard water running.

"Okay, I'm back. Had to fill the dog's water bowl. Just took him
for a walk or more like he took me."

Brick figured you can never go wrong asking someone about their
dog. "What kind is he?"

"Good question. Not even the vet can figure it out." Stewart laughed. "Hold on again." It sounded like he had set the phone down, but Brick could still hear his voice in the background. "That's a good boy, now go lay down." A few seconds passed. "Hey, I'm back again. Anyway, I started volunteering at the local shelter and when they brought in this little guy, I knew he was going home with me. So how the hell are you?"

"Good. I joined the club a few months ago. I'm retired now."

"You . . . no way."

"It's true and there's nothing keeping me in D.C., so I've been checking out some places in Loudoun County. You're in Purcell-ville, right?"

"Yeah, and one of the best decisions I've ever made. I'll tell you, it's a whole different world out here. The only way I'd leave is in a box."

"That's quite an endorsement. I've been looking at a townhouse development online and plan to check it out soon. Any chance you're available for lunch this week?"

"Sure. How about tomorrow?"

"That works for me."

*   *   *

As he had on a few other occasions when he needed a car, Brick borrowed Rory's. After adjusting the seat to accommodate his one-inch-shy-of-six-foot height, he turned down the volume on the radio and searched for NPR. Following the directions he had printed from Google Maps, Brick traveled outside the Beltway for the first time in over a year. Cookie-cutter condos, strip malls, and chain restaurants had sprung up on both sides of the highway like toadstools after a rainstorm. To Brick's way of thinking, he had of-ficially entered suburbia hell.

After about an hour, he passed a sign indicating the Purcellville exit was a mile ahead. Brick changed lanes, and as he left Route 7, he saw the Gateway Commercial Center that Stewart had mentioned. Next to the drive-through Starbucks, he spotted Jim's Barbeque. Finding a parking space was no problem in the sprawling lot. Even Brick had to admit that was one advantage the 'burbs had over the city. Before getting out of the car, he checked his phone and saw a text from Stewart. He was waiting at the bar.

At first, Brick didn't recognize the former detective. Fortunately, there were only three other guys sitting at the bar and by process of elimination, he figured out which one to approach. He took the empty barstool next to him and ordered a Coke Zero.

"Looks like retirement agrees with you," Brick said.

Stewart nodded. "Between playing golf twice a week, walking Shiloh a couple of times a day, and paying attention to what I'm eating, I've lost over thirty pounds." He patted his stomach. "As much as I like this place, I don't come here very often. Want to eat at the bar or get a table?"

"A table."

They picked up their drinks and followed the bartender's direction to sit wherever they like. Brick pointed to a table in the corner by the window. He looked over the menu but followed Stewart's recommendation for the pulled pork sandwich with coleslaw and fries.

"Got to say, I'm surprised you're looking for a place out here. You always struck me as a city guy."

Using a ruse was something Brick had done routinely throughout his career but misleading a former colleague didn't feel right. "Well, I have to level with you. This isn't about real estate, it's about a case." Brick went on to explain about the cold case project without mentioning which case was under consideration.

Stewart leaned back against his chair and glared at Brick. "So why the bullshit about looking for real estate?"

"Because it's too easy to hang up on a phone call. The case we're considering—"

"You don't need to tell me. I know which one you're talking about—Henry Yang."

Brick nodded as an awkward silence prevailed.

Stewart finished his beer but held onto his glass. "Fuck it . . . guess I've been wearing this albatross around my neck long enough." Before continuing, he looked in all directions as if to make sure no one else could hear what he was about to say. He took a deep breath and exhaled slowly. "It was more than a hit-and-run, it was a deliberate hit."

What Brick heard sounded far-fetched. Twenty years on the job and he had never worked a case that had been a "hit." A college kid, unless he was heavy into drug dealing or some other criminal enterprise, seemed like an unlikely target, but true to form, Brick kept an open mind while Stewart continued. "Someone knew when Yang would be jogging in Rock Creek Park."

"How can you be so sure?" Brick asked.

"From what the witness said, there was no reason for the car to veer off the road. And right after it struck Yang, it sped away."

"And you think what the witness said was accurate?"

"After it was confirmed by the accident reconstruction team, yeah, sure. I believed it."

"But, Fred, I've seen the file. There wasn't a reconstruction report. And in the witness statement, the name was redacted."

"You're not telling me anything I don't know." Stewart took a swig of beer. "I wanted to go balls to the wall on the investigation, but it wasn't my decision to make. Word came down from on high— Blancato said to deep-six it."

Brick had picked up his Coke and was about to take a drink. "Why?"

"Two words—diplomatic immunity."

For a second, Brick felt dumbfounded, but at the same time it was beginning to make sense. Diplomatic immunity was often looked upon as a necessary evil to protect diplomats serving in foreign countries. Abusing the privilege had resulted in perpetrators getting away with some horrific crimes, a few of which were in D.C. Still, something wasn't adding up. A thorough investigation should have been conducted even though prosecuting anyone was unlikely unless others without immunity were involved.

"Why would Blancato call off the investigation?" This time, just saying the name of his former boss sent Brick's blood pressure into the stratosphere.

Stewart shrugged. "That was back when he was making a name for himself and had his sights on moving up the ladder. Maybe he didn't want to rock the boat, but I think there was more to it than that."

"What do you mean?" Brick asked.

"I can't prove anything. It's just a gut feeling, and I'd appreciate you keeping it between you and me."

"Of course."

"For a cop, even a White Shirt, Blancato was living pretty high on the hog." Stewart looked around the restaurant and started to laugh, as did Brick. "Guess that was a bad phrase to use given what we're having for lunch."

Brick agreed with both comments. "Did it ever occur to you to go over Blancato's head?"

"Of course it did." Stewart avoided eye contact with Brick. "But I was three months short of retiring and my wife was dying from

COPD. I couldn't risk crossing the lieutenant. Without my pension and insurance, we would have been fucked."

It was obvious that Stewart was embarrassed, but as far as Brick was concerned, the decision he made was understandable. "Sounds to me, you were between the proverbial rock and hard place."

"Yeah, but that's not a whole lot of consolation." Stewart shook his head. "I took a second statement from the witness where he stated the car was a late model Mercedes, but that never made it into the file. A few days later, I called him and told him for his own good to forget everything he saw. He was reluctant to do that until I told him a foreign government official was involved. That convinced him and it's the only part of the whole mess I don't regret because it kept him safe."

"Better than spending the rest of his life in witness protection."

"You're right about that. This probably wasn't what you were expecting to hear but that's how it went down." Stewart picked up a napkin and wiped barbeque sauce off his hands. "Definitely not how I wanted to end my career, just laying low and calling it in for the last few months. I was better than that. I know the guys I worked with lost respect for me, but it was a tough time. My wife's condition was deteriorating. Six months later, she went into the hospital for the last time."

"I'm sorry, Fred. And I'm sorry if this stirred up some bad memories for you, but I appreciate you being straight with me."

"Thanks. I'm probably not telling you anything you don't already know, but just because you retire doesn't mean you leave all those cases behind."

CHAPTER TWELVE

As Brick drove back to D.C., he thought a lot about what Fred Stewart had shared. He appreciated Stewart's candor, especially since he was obviously conflicted by his decision to follow Blancato's order. Brick wasn't about to criticize Stewart's actions. Were he faced with that set of circumstances, he may have done the same.

Fucking Blancato. The poster boy for political patronage. A good supervisor brings out the best in his subordinates. Blancato did the opposite. How many careers were derailed because he made decisions based on how it could best benefit himself? Brick and Stewart weren't the only casualties. And it was accepted that vacancies within the squad were filled with his choice of ass-kissing yes men. The new revelations ratcheted up Brick's interest in the case, but it seemed less appropriate for a group of students to investigate. Brick blew by an SUV and realized he was going way above the speed limit. He eased off the gas. Why had Blancato instructed Fred Stewart to do what he did? Did others in the department know about it and turn a blind eye? That thought didn't sit well with Brick.

It was after three o'clock when Brick pulled into the Shell station on M Street. Before getting out of the car, he looked around and observed who else was pumping gas. Given carjackers' fondness for self-service stations, he made sure no one was just hanging out in the immediate area. Hyper-awareness or paranoia, sometimes Brick found it hard to tell the difference.

This desirable piece of real estate hadn't always been a gas station. Twenty years ago, it had been a convenience store run by immigrants from Ethiopia. As a rookie cop assigned to the Second District, Brick had stopped there many times to buy lottery tickets. But nothing he learned at the Academy could prepare him for the carnage he saw late one summer evening. Three adults and two kids, all from the same family, gunned down in what the media dubbed "an apparent robbery gone bad." That characterization infuriated Brick. What defined a robbery gone good? Nobody dies and the perp gets away with the money? His anger at the senselessness of the crime motivated him. He knew, without a doubt, he wanted to be a homicide detective. Ten years later, he was.

After topping off the tank, he got back in the car and headed north on Connecticut Avenue. Already traffic was heavy. He turned left on Calvert Street and parked in a reserved spot behind Boland's Mill.

"Hey, look who's back." Rory groaned as he bent down and used a box cutter to slice open the top of a shipment of Bushmills. "My knees are barking today. Do you need a drink?"

"No, I have to meet someone so I'm not staying." Brick set Rory's keys on the bar. "Thanks for letting me use your car. Seems to be running okay since you replaced the battery."

"Good. Kelly and I are all set for this weekend." He set a couple of bottles of whiskey on the bar. "The last thing I need is for the feckin' car to break down."

"Reservations at that place in Charlottesville?"

"Yeah. And we're going antiquing, too."

The look of disdain on Rory's face made Brick laugh. "Maybe you'll find something worth a fortune and end up on the *Antiques Road Show.*"

"Oh, I'm sure that will happen." Rory rolled his eyes before filling a glass with ice and pouring himself a Coke. "I just want to shag and if that's what it takes, point me in the direction of the feckin' flea market."

"You might want to show a little more enthusiasm."

"Think so?" Rory seemed pensive. "Hey, maybe that's what you should do, dating coach for . . . gobshites like me."

"Good idea. I'll add your name as a reference on my resume." Brick checked his watch. "See you later."

"Wait a second. There's something I need to ask you." The serious look on Rory's face gave Brick pause. "If Kelly says yes, will you be my best man?"

"Of course." Brick and Rory exchanged a fist bump. "Good luck!"

*　*　*

The Starbucks barista called Brick's name and handed him a tall green tea. While he waited for Lieutenant Hughes at the corner table he had often shared with Ron, he checked his phone for text messages. He hoped there would be one from Nora. There wasn't. He slipped his phone into his pocket when he spotted the lieutenant crossing Indiana Avenue. As she approached the table, Brick stood up to greet her.

"What can I get you?" Brick asked.

"Gin and tonic, heavy on the gin." She pulled out a chair and slumped against the backrest. After brushing an errant lock of hair behind her ear, she glanced toward the list of coffee drinks displayed behind the counter. "Nitro cold brew with sweet cream. If I'm not having booze, might as well have sugar."

Brick got in line behind a couple of uniformed officers and waited his turn. After placing the drink order, he dropped the change he was handed into the tip jar and moved down the line.

"Tough day?" Brick handed Hughes the cold brew and a couple of napkins.

"Death by a thousand paper cuts." She took a sip of her drink. "Technology is supposed to make our lives easier, right? Well, between the computers crashing and—" Before she finished, her cell phone rang. "See what I mean, there's no escape." She reached into her bag and retrieved her phone. After checking the caller ID, she shrugged. "That can wait." She set the phone down on the table. "How was your meeting with Fred Stewart?"

Brick knew what he was about to say would only add to the lieutenant's already shitty day. "Raises more questions than answers."

"How so?"

"According to Stewart, first and foremost, it was a hit that turned into a hit-and-run."

"He's saying this college kid was targeted?" Hughes set her coffee down. "That sounds a bit far-fetched."

"That was my thought exactly until Stewart mentioned diplomatic immunity."

"Oh God, the two words we never want to hear." She picked up her coffee and drank slowly as she appeared to be collecting her thoughts. "Well, that would explain why the case was open and shut, but why would Yang be in the crosshairs of a high-ranking foreign official?"

"Or a member of the official's family or staff?"

"Good point."

"Stewart told me he wanted to investigate based on the eyewitness account, but he was told by Blancato to bury it."

"Why am I not surprised." Hughes leaned forward. "Forget I said that, but this does not sound like something a bunch of graduate students should be looking into."

"Or anyone else for that matter?"

Hughes didn't answer immediately. "Let me think about that. I know you have a history with Blancato but I'd hate to—" Again her cell phone rang and this time she answered. The conversation was brief, but even hearing one side, Brick could tell Lieutenant Hughes was upset by whatever was going on. "I need to leave." Hughes pushed back her chair and stood. So did Brick.

"Thanks for taking the time to meet with me," Brick said.

"Obviously, you didn't get my undivided attention and for that I apologize. As you may have heard, I've faced down three-hundred-pound gangbangers without being intimidated, but I'm off to wrestle the car keys from the hands of a tiny, eighty-eight-year-old woman. The very thought is as stressful as anything I've had to do on the job."

"Your mother?"

Hughes nodded. "I feel like I'm cutting off her legs. But the thought of her behind the wheel is keeping me awake at night. It's really tough when the child becomes the parent."

"I know." It wasn't a platitude. Brick was speaking from what he had experienced at a much younger age. As his mother's depression became more and more debilitating, he made sure she took her meds on time, did the grocery shopping and laundry, and wrote the checks for her to sign so the bills were paid. Responsibilities most teenagers never have to face until they leave home and live on their own.

"I will get back to you soon." Hughes picked up the cold brew she had hardly touched and headed toward the door.

CHAPTER THIRTEEN

WITH THE INFORMATION Grace Alexander had provided and an internet search, Brick was able to locate Henry Yang's former roommate. After speaking with him, the timing of the call turned out to be fortuitous. Brick wasted no time heading to the nearby N Street address. At the three-story vintage building he entered the intercom code he'd been given and identified himself when Drew Edwards answered.

The door to Apartment 202 was opened by a bearded young man in a light gray Lincoln U. tee shirt. Sweat stains darkened the shirt in a couple of places.

"Come on in." Drew Edwards extended his right hand to shake. In his left was a full bottle of Fat Tire.

Brick stepped inside the apartment and picked up on a pungent locker room smell. Moving boxes were stacked against the living room wall and it appeared a wardrobe carton was being assembled. A sofa was encased in plastic and stacks of books and some sports equipment littered the floor.

"Excuse the mess and the smell. Moving's a bitch and, of course, the A/C died yesterday. Murphy's Law, right." Drew wiped the back of his hand across his forehead. "Hey, do you want a beer?"

"Sure."

Drew set his beer on the table, retrieved another from the fridge, and handed it to Brick. The two men sat opposite each other at a well-worn table that reminded Brick of one he had purchased at IKEA many years ago for his first apartment.

"Finally, a break. First I've taken all day." Drew stifled a yawn. "Packing books is the worst."

"Looks like you still have plenty to do."

Drew nodded. "And the clock is ticking since the movers will be here tomorrow. I'm staying on for a few days, then it's D.C. in the rearview mirror."

"More school or a new job?"

"Job. I'm a systems engineer and will be working with NASA at the Johnson Space Center in Houston."

Brick raised his beer bottle in Drew's direction. "Congratulations, that's impressive."

"Thanks, it's a start. Being an astronaut is my goal."

For a moment, Brick envied Drew's youth and enthusiasm. Knowing what you want to do with your life and focusing on that goal—been there, done that, Brick thought. "An astronaut—that's awesome. Do you know what Henry was planning to do when he graduated?"

"He was studying accounting. Forensic accounting? I'm not positive, but I think that's what he called it. He wanted to be an FBI agent, but he was worried about being able to pass the physical requirements. That's why he started working out and jogging."

"Was Rock Creek Park his usual destination?" Brick asked.

"Yes, same time, same place, seven days a week. One thing I can tell you, he was a creature of habit."

"Sounds like you knew him well."

"Not really. I mean he was a good guy, always paid his fair share, but we didn't have much in common. He lived here for about a year and a half, maybe a little longer, but back then I was spending most of my time at my girlfriend's place. After Henry died, I actually found out stuff about him that surprised me."

"For example?"

"He didn't have any family. His father died when he was a little kid and his mother died just after he started his first year at Lincoln U. No brothers or sisters." Drew took a sip of beer. "Made me feel bad when I found out. I mean, if I had known, I would have invited him to spend holidays with my family. My mother would have loved it. The more, the merrier is her philosophy."

"So since Henry didn't have any family, except for the one box you mentioned on the phone, what happened to his other belongings?"

"I think it was his faculty advisor who took care of everything."

"Do you remember their name?"

Drew hesitated. "Give me a second." He closed his eyes for a moment. "Damn, it's on the tip of my tongue. Ask me another question."

Brick understood the technique of thinking of something else and letting your subconscious go to work. "Okay, why did they leave this one box?"

"It was shoved back in the hall closet behind the vacuum cleaner and ironing board, so it was easy to overlook."

"Those things didn't get a lot of use?" Brick smiled as he anticipated the answer.

"More like none." Drew laughed. "Hey, if you need a vacuum, it's good as new. By the way, that's the box over there and you're welcome to take it." Drew pointed to a white banker's box next to a tennis racquet. "Baez."

"Excuse me?"

"The guy, the faculty advisor, I remember his name was Baez."

"Are you sure?" Brick asked.

"Yeah, I can't remember his first name, but my mother is a huge '60s music fan and she's always playing songs by Joan Baez. I'm sure that's why I remembered, although now I'll have one of those folk songs in my head like an earworm."

"Not a fan?"

"Ah . . . no. I prefer Lady Gaga."

"I can see why." Brick took another sip of beer. "Is there anything else about Henry that I should know?"

Drew shook his head. "I can't think of anything off the top of my head, but to say I'm a little distracted is a huge understatement."

"Understood. It's obvious you've got a lot going on, but if you do think of anything, you have my cell phone number." Brick finished his beer. "I'll get out of here so you can get back to work."

Drew looked around the room. "I didn't think I had much stuff until I started packing and I've still got a way to go."

Brick shook hands with Drew before picking up the box of Henry's belongings. "Thanks for your time and the beer. Good luck with the move and your new job."

"Thanks. And good luck with your investigation. Like I said earlier, Henry was a good guy; he didn't deserve what happened. No one does. It really pisses me off whenever I think about the driver. I mean what a coward—man up when you make a mistake. That's how I was raised."

Brick had no reason to doubt that or anything else Drew had said.

*   *   *

It was after six when Brick got back home. He was anxious to start exploring the contents of the box but decided to put it off until after dinner. He fixed a plate of leftover Chinese food and crossed his fingers as he placed it in the microwave. This time the food was heated quickly and evenly. Maybe the microwave didn't need to be replaced after all.

While he was clearing the table, a phone call from Nora caught Brick off-guard with an invitation. All that stood between him and a last-minute weekend in Chicago was a plane ticket. He logged on to Expedia.com and hoped for the best.

Four seats were left on a 10:00 a.m. American Airlines flight to O'Hare. After entering his credit card information, only three seats remained. The box of Henry Yang's stuff would have to wait until he returned.

Although Brick was definitely attracted to Nora, he was keeping his expectations in check. She had made the terms of his visit very clear by offering to make a reservation for him to stay in the guest suite at her apartment building. As he carefully folded a gray cashmere sweater, he smiled as he recalled her words. "You seem like a perfectly nice guy, but I've watched plenty of episodes of *Forensic Files*. It takes more than one dinner date to know someone." He couldn't argue with her logic given the number of instances where a victim is clueless about someone they've known for years. He double-checked the items in his suitcase and was satisfied he had packed enough. All that was left were a few things for his toiletry bag and a quick trip to CVS provided those. Dial soap, a travel toothbrush and toothpaste, dental floss, mouthwash, deodorant, and a Trojan Pleasure Pack—all the essentials a perfectly nice guy might need.

Meeting women had never been a problem for Brick, but at forty-two, dating was different than it had been when he was younger. In his late twenties and thirties, women never questioned that he hadn't been married, but now his extended single status often required explanation. A broken engagement with a long-term girlfriend usually earned enough credibility points that he wasn't immediately disqualified. He didn't know how Nora would react but felt confident that she would communicate exactly what she was thinking. He liked that trait when he was interviewing witnesses and the same thing could be said for the "getting to know you" phase in the dating game.

CHAPTER FOURTEEN

BRICK TEXTED NORA when his plane landed and again as his cab merged onto the Kennedy Expressway. About twenty-five minutes later, the cab passed Wrigley Field. The streets around the ballpark were filled with Cubs fans and teeming with activity even though first pitch was still a few hours away. Halsted, Broadway, Pine Grove. Brick made a mental note of the street names they passed. Being able to pinpoint his location was a holdover habit from his early days in uniform. At Lake Shore Drive, the cab turned right from Addison and traveled south past a mix of vintage and modern high-rise residential buildings. The cab driver pulled into a circular driveway in front of a mid-rise building at the corner of Belmont and Sheridan Road. Brick retrieved his suitcase and closed the trunk.

"Welcome to Chicago." Nora kissed him lightly on the cheek.

"Glad to be here." Brick realized something about Nora was different. "Your hair is much shorter than I remember."

"You're right. Decided it was time for a new style."

"Looks great. Has anyone mistaken you for Enya?"

Nora laughed. "No one here, but two guys at Shannon asked me for my autograph. When I signed 'Nora Breslin,' one was annoyed but the other appreciated my sense of humor."

Brick picked up his suitcase and Nora pressed the button for the side door to open. "So, does this mean I get to be arm candy for an Irish singer doppelganger?"

Nora nodded. "No worries, you'll get used to it."

At the security desk in the lobby, Brick signed in and was given the key for the guest suite. He and Nora took the elevator to the eighth floor. The studio apartment was tastefully decorated with a queen-sized bed, desk, a two-seater sofa, and an overstuffed chair. Two high-backed barstools in front of a counter extending from the kitchenette provided dining space. Brick set down his suitcase and stepped over to the window.

"Quite a view. Does one of those yachts belong to you?"

"I wish." Nora laughed. "I could use a floating party room. Some of these never leave the harbor until the end of the season when all the boats disappear for the winter."

"Do we have time to take a walk by the lake?" Brick asked.

Nora checked her watch and nodded.

Just as they were about to leave, Brick's cell phone rang. He checked the caller ID, hoping it was spam, but instead saw Lieutenant Hughes's name.

"I need to take this." The conversation was brief and one-sided with Brick listening more than commenting. He slipped the phone back into his pocket and smiled at Nora. "Good news. The cold case I was telling you about, well, the lieutenant has decided it warrants looking into. Not from a group of college students but from an experienced detective."

"And you're the detective, I take it."

"Right. She found money in the budget so looks like I have a job when I return."

"Congratulations. I'm not surprised. I said I would put in a word with St. Cajetan." Nora stepped toward the door. "Maybe I'm your lucky charm."

Brick appreciated Nora's offer to say a prayer to the patron saint of the unemployed and there was no mistaking he was charmed by her. Later he was definitely hoping to get lucky, but at least for now, decided those thoughts were best kept to himself.

* * *

After crossing Sheridan Road, Brick and Nora walked past an equestrian statue. Brick stopped to read the plaque on the base identifying Civil War General Philip Henry Sheridan who led a campaign to defeat Confederate troops in the Shenandoah Valley.

"Glad he was on the right side," Brick said as he bent down to read the last line on the inscription. "And in 1871, he maintained law and order during the Great Chicago Fire."

"Commendable," Nora said. "But if the Cubs ever win the World Series, he'll probably be replaced by whoever is managing the team at the time."

"Think so?"

Nora laughed. "Just one of the reasons I love Chicago enough to divide my time between here and Galway."

The sun shone off the shards of glass and mirrors decorating the colorful mosaic mural lining the wall leading to the harbor. A couple of bicyclists who appeared to be training for the Tour de France zipped by. In the opposite direction, several joggers and dog walkers passed.

Brick and Nora followed a concrete path beyond the yacht club house and sailing school to an area of terraced steps leading from a grassy area down to the lake. A flock of Canada geese flew in formation overhead and dragonflies darted about. It was so much like the ocean with one major exception—the lake provided the city and several surrounding counties with drinking water.

After a few minutes they retraced their steps and headed north, stopping briefly to watch a Jack Russell terrier and black Lab puppy chasing each other around a patch of sand identified by a posted sign as Dog Beach. The underpass at Waveland Avenue was damp and smelled musty, but it provided a way to cross Lake Shore Drive without becoming roadkill.

The earlier activity around Wrigley Field had intensified. Several vendors selling hats and tee shirts were set up on the sidewalk across from Murphy's Bleachers. Brick took Nora's hand as they crossed Sheffield and stopped in front of the statue of Harry Caray to take a selfie.

Before going inside the ballpark, Brick was thinking back to the very first time he attended a baseball game. He was seven years old and his mother had taken him to Yankee Stadium. It became their annual summer tradition. For the next ten years, they never missed their mother-and-son trip to New York City even though his mother was intimated by crowds. It was still painful to think about the House that Ruth Built being torn down, especially now as he was about to enter one of the two remaining ballparks that thankfully hadn't fallen prey to the wrecking ball.

"Brick, here's your ticket."

"What . . . oh, thanks."

"Are you okay?"

Brick laughed. "I'm fine, just taking it all in. I've been to a lot of ballparks, but there seems to be a different vibe here."

"Think I know what you mean, but I'm not sure if it's optimism or insanity."

"Maybe a little of both."

The concourse was narrow and crowded, but Brick observed that no one seemed to mind. The mood was festive even though it was a foregone conclusion the Cubs would end the season at the bottom of the National League Central Division. A victory today against the Cardinals would give fans bragging rights, at least until tomorrow's game. Brick and Nora started up a series of ramps, stopping once to pick up hot dogs and a bag of peanuts at a concession stand before finding their seats behind home plate. The unobstructed view gave Brick goose bumps. Instantly, he understood why this team and this place earned the loyalty of generations of fans. Maybe the song that mentioned "magic in the ivy and the old scoreboard" was on to something, he thought.

The early innings were a pitchers' duel and then back-to-back home runs brought the Cubs fans to their feet in the bottom of the eighth inning. Three outs and the "W" flag was raised so riders on the "L" would know the Cubs had won. Brick felt his heart beating faster as a chorus of "Go Cubs Go" filled the stands.

"Now you can check Wrigley off your bucket list." Nora smiled at Brick. "I get the sense it didn't disappoint."

"Not at all. I envy you being able to walk here and experience this place. This is what baseball should be—no tee shirt toss or racing oversized costumed presidents, just baseball."

"Yeah, Wrigley's a tough act to follow, but . . ." Nora reached into her purse and pulled out two tickets. She handed one to Brick.

"No way! I mentioned them once—how did you remember?"

"How could I forget? It's not everyone who's a fan of the Dropkick Murphys."

Brick still seemed taken aback. "What are the odds they'd be performing here tonight."

Nora took Brick's hand. "I told you, I'm your lucky charm."

CHAPTER FIFTEEN

THE #22 CLARK Street bus stopped in front of the Women and Children First bookstore in Andersonville. Nora pointed out that the area was originally a Swedish settlement. Now, it's a diverse neighborhood with independently owned shops and ethnic restaurants. After considering several possibilities, she suggested Lady Gregory. Named for the cofounder of the Irish Literary Theatre and Abbey Theatre, it reminded Brick of Gaffney's, the restaurant in Galway where he and Nora had had dinner.

"I recommend the salmon," Nora said without looking at the menu.

"Sounds like you're a regular."

"Not here, but at Wilde. It's their other restaurant on Broadway in Lakeview."

"Wilde', as in Oscar Wilde?" Brick asked and Nora nodded. "All right then, I trust your recommendation. Salmon it is."

After the thunderous atmosphere of Wrigley Field and before what could be an earsplitting concert, Brick welcomed the opportunity to have a quiet conversation. He was curious to learn more about Nora, but there wasn't any urgency. They had the whole weekend ahead of them. For now, he was enjoying hearing her perspective on Irish authors and playwrights.

*   *   *

It was after midnight when the Uber pulled up in front of Nora's apartment building. A picture-perfect afternoon at Wrigley Field and seeing the Dropkick Murphys in person made for a day Brick was sure he would remember for a very long time. And thankfully, the acoustics of the Aragon Ballroom spared him damage to his hearing. After walking Nora to her door, he kissed her good night and took the elevator to the eighth floor. As he headed down the hallway, it occurred to him he had been in Chicago for just over twelve hours, but he felt totally comfortable in a city that bore little, if any, resemblance to Washington, D.C.

An early morning text from Nora woke Brick from a sound sleep. She suggested he meet her on the roof sundeck in a half hour. He stumbled out of bed and headed for the bathroom feeling like he was still asleep. He stepped into the oversized shower, turned on the water, and immediately understood the popularity of rain shower heads. Something so simple was so soothing. He lingered a bit longer letting the warm water wash over him as thoughts of sharing this experience with Nora filled his head. Maybe tomorrow morning.

Brick took the elevator to the roof and saw Nora was already there gazing out toward the harbor. He called her name rather than run the risk of startling her. She turned and smiled.

"Good morning. Did you sleep well?" Nora asked.

"Slept the sleep of the knackered."

Nora laughed. "I didn't know you're bilingual."

"Very limited. Just vocabulary I've picked up from hanging around Rory at Boland's Mill and a couple of phrases from my time in Ireland."

"So, you can swear in two languages, I'm guessing." Nora pointed toward a small round table. "There's a thermos of Barry's Tea and some pan dulce from Artemio's, the local Mexican bakery." She checked her watch. "The sun should be up in about twenty minutes."

Brick helped himself to the sweet bread and poured a cup of tea. He settled into one of the chairs facing east toward the lake. A few bands of orange and pink were visible on the horizon. He took a deep breath and exhaled slowly. The last time he remembered feeling this relaxed was when he was on Inishmore.

Nora took the chair next to Brick's and ran down the activities she had in mind for the day. "This morning, we have reservations for an architectural boat tour on the Chicago River. And for the afternoon, you get to choose—the Art Institute or a Chicago Crime and Mob Tour."

"So, it's the Impressionists versus the Untouchables?" Brick thought for a minute. "It's not that I don't appreciate fine art, but I can't pass up a chance to see the Biograph Theater. Let's do that." Brick reached for another piece of pan dulce. He figured carbo loading was necessary in order to keep up with Nora.

After a couple of hours of hopping on and off the tour bus and walking around Lincoln Park, Brick was happy to spot a Starbucks near 2122 North Clark Street, the address where the St. Valentine's Day Massacre took place. A cold drink was appealing but even more appealing was sitting down and taking a break. Nora welcomed his suggestion. While she found a table, he got their drinks.

"A vanilla latte for you." Brick handed Nora her drink. "And an iced green tea for me, although I'm thinking a Red Bull is really what I need."

A concerned look crossed Nora's face. "Have I overdone the tour?"

"No." Brick smiled as he shook his head.

"Good." She picked up her drink. "I figured if we found out we weren't compatible, at least you'd enjoy spending a weekend in Chicago."

Brick laughed as he took Nora's hand. "Going out on a limb here, but I think we're compatible."

Nora nodded. "I'm not surprised, but then again, I think I have an advantage and know more about you than you know about me."

"Really, how so?"

"I Googled your name and found the *Washington Post* story about the Delgado case. I was impressed by your determination to find the truth despite the obstacles you had to overcome and the price you ultimately ended up paying." Nora paused and set down her cup. "I get the sense I'm embarrassing you."

"The article . . . what can I say? It makes it sound like I acted single-handedly. That wasn't accurate. If the reporter had spent more time interviewing me, rather than some of the others involved in the case, it might have been clear that I owe a lot to my former partner. And not just while I was trying to find the killer, but afterward when I was dealing with the consequences."

"So, when I met you in Galway, it wasn't an extended vacation to celebrate your retirement?"

"No, it was my way of recovering from the events you read about. Probably better that we met at the end of my trip than the beginning. And I should warn you, I'm still a work in progress."

"Aren't we all." Nora glanced at her watch. "There is one more Chicago-centric experience you have to have."

An image of the glass boxes Brick had seen jutting out from the side of the Willis Tower popped into his head. "If you're thinking about The Ledge or whatever that thing is called, that's where I draw the line . . . ain't happening."

"Fear of heights?" Nora asked.

"More like distrust of architects and construction workers."

Nora laughed. "Actually, I'm thinking deep dish pizza. To leave Chicago without experiencing Lou Malnati's would be like going to New Orleans and not having beignets at Café du Monde. Or going to . . ." Nora seemed to be struggling for another example.

"It's okay, I don't need convincing," Brick said. "You had me at pizza."

By arriving just after five, the wait for a table at Lou Malnati's was short but long enough to stimulate Brick's appetite. He feared the aroma of garlic and oregano may have him drooling like Pavlov's dog. Brick studied the menu, but once again was willing to defer to Nora.

"What do you suggest?" he asked.

"That's easy. The Chicago Classic—sausage, extra cheese, and to-mato sauce. What's not to like?"

"I'm beginning to think that's a question I should ask you about this city."

"Let's see . . . what not to like." Nora didn't respond immediately. "The crime, for sure. Taxes, corrupt politicians, questionable police practices—pretty much the same issues facing all major cities." Nora set down her glass of Stella Artois and gave their pizza order to the server. "Oh, and there's the weather. Don't be fooled by the past two days. Most years we only have three seasons—cold, colder, and hot." Nora shrugged. "But despite all that, from day one, this city felt like home, even when I was staying in hotels between flights. So when the Shannon-to-O'Hare route became my permanent assignment, I decided to get a place of my own since I'm sometimes here for a week or two at a time."

"That makes sense," Brick said.

Nora raised her glass of beer in a toast. "Here's to the City of Big Shoulders."

Brick raised his glass, as well. "I think that's preferrable to "Hog Butcher for the World."

Nora tapped her glass against Brick's. "Agreed."

Preparation of deep-dish pizza took longer than thin crust, but as soon as Brick took his first bite, he was convinced the wait was worth every second. He smiled at Nora. "This may ruin me for all future pizzas." He took another bite, savoring the buttery crust.

"Just so you know, they ship all over the country."

"Great, next time you see me, I'll have gained fifty pounds." Brick finished his first slice and was about to reach for another when he noticed the TV mounted on the wall behind Nora. Subtitles scrolled across the screen as a CNN reporter appeared to be standing in front of a single-family home. The house looked vaguely familiar and there was no mistaking the distinctive red markings and blue lettering on the side of the D.C. Metropolitan Police cars parked in front. Brick leaned forward to get a better view so that he could read what was being reported.

D.C. police are asking for the public's help since yesterday's disappearance of the wife and infant twins of a homicide detective. Callers may remain anonymous.

Brick dropped his fork as he stared at the TV screen.

"Brick, are you all right?"

After reciting the telephone number for the police tip line, the reporter had moved on to another story. For a few seconds, Brick found it hard to believe what he had just seen. He grabbed his phone and located the story on the CNN app. Rather than try to explain, he handed his phone to Nora. "Here, read this."

"Oh my God, do you know the detective?"

"Ron Hayes . . . he was . . ." The words seemed caught in Brick's throat. With a shaking hand, he picked up his water glass and took a drink. "He was my partner."

"Oh Jesus, Mary, and Joseph." Nora crossed herself and appeared to say a prayer.

Brick stood up and glanced around the restaurant. "I need to make a call and it's too noisy in here."

The cab ride back to Lakeview provided Brick with the quiet place he needed. The first call he made was to Ron's cell phone. He wasn't surprised when it went straight to voicemail and he got a recording saying the mailbox was full. He thought about who he should try next and remembered yesterday's call from Lieutenant Hughes. Her number was at the top of his "recents." He tapped it and silently prayed that she would answer. She did, but was unable to provide any more information than he had learned from the CNN report.

It wasn't until Brick was sitting at the gate at the airport that he had a chance to reflect on what had transpired over the past couple of hours. After talking with the lieutenant, he made the decision to return to D.C. as quickly as possible. While he packed up his stuff, Nora managed to get him a ticket on the last flight out to Reagan National. She didn't have to ride along to O'Hare, especially at this late hour, but she did. Even though the weekend had ended abruptly, he felt sure he would see Nora again. He thought about how it is easy to be with someone when things are going well, but the real test is when things go south. And as far as he was concerned, Nora had passed the unscheduled test with flying colors. Perhaps her training and years of flight attendant experience helped her react calmly in a crisis. But Brick suspected it was as much a part of her DNA as her dark hair and blue eyes.

When his group was called, Brick boarded the plane. He made his way down the aisle and located his window seat over the wing. After stowing his weekender bag in the overhead bin, he sat down and with concern for what may lie ahead in D.C., Brick fastened his seat belt.

most of his diet, not exactly heart-healthy but Brick justified his choice rationalizing that the benefits from olive oil would counteract the damage done by the salami and provolone. Magical thinking, but Angelo was living proof that something was working.

"Take it easy, Angelo."

Angelo raised a small cup that may have contained espresso. His hand shook slightly. "You do the same and don't be a stranger."

CHAPTER SIXTEEN

WHEN IT COMES to air travel, Brick didn't consider himself a nervous flyer but neither would he say he was a relaxed one. It all came down to being in a situation in which he wasn't the individual in control. And truth be told, he envied the frequent flyers who managed to sleep soundly from takeoff to landing while he was feeling uneasy over the slightest bit of turbulence, anticipating it will only get worse. But this flight was different. Preoccupation with thoughts of what may have happened to Jasmine and the twins and imagining what Ron was going through made him oblivious to his surroundings. In what seemed to be record time, he saw the illuminated dome of the Capitol and felt the wheels of the plane touch down on the tarmac.

It was close to one thirty in the morning when Brick arrived at Ron's house in the Shepherd Park neighborhood of Northwest Washington, D.C. Unlike the rest of the darkened houses on the block, Ron's was brightly lit. As Brick walked up the stairs leading to the front door, he recognized a detective from the Missing Persons Unit walk past the window. Brick knocked and Lieutenant Hughes opened the door. Even though he was expecting her to meet him at the house, he almost didn't recognize her. Used to seeing the lieutenant in dark, tailored pantsuits, she was dressed in jeans and a Washington Wizards sweatshirt. With her blond hair pulled back in a ponytail, she looked ten years younger than the consummate professional responsible for supervising a group of homicide detectives.

Brick had been to the house only once a few months before but noticed the living room looked very different now. The sofa had been moved against the wall and in its place, a large folding table. A couple of yellow legal pads were scattered on top next to the laptop computers and cell phones.

"Hey, Brick." After setting a plate of food on the table, Michael Taylor, the detective Brick had seen walk by the window, shook hands with him. "Good to see you, just wish it were different circumstances." Brick nodded and was introduced to Carrie Dixon, the other detective at the table. She looked up briefly before she resumed typing on the laptop in front of her.

"Where's Ron?"

"He's upstairs. Hopefully, he's asleep," Lieutenant Hughes said.

"How is he?" Brick asked.

"About what you would expect, he's a wreck. Other than an hour here or there, he hasn't slept in two days." Hughes was holding a coffee mug. "I need a refill." She headed toward the kitchen and Brick followed. A tray of sandwiches from Subway was on the counter alongside a box of donuts. "There's sodas in the fridge. Help yourself if you want anything."

Brick did. He unscrewed the cap on a bottle of Pepsi and took a drink before taking a seat at the table across from Hughes.

"Guess I should start at the beginning and bring you up to speed." Hughes set her coffee mug down. "Ron worked midnight-to-eight on Friday and then had a pre-trial conference at the U.S. Attorney's Office. He said it was close to noon when he got home, and he was surprised that Jasmine and the twins weren't there. Immediately, he called her, but the call went straight to voicemail. He left an urgent message for her to call him." Hughes stopped to take a drink.

"Had he called or texted earlier in the morning?" Brick asked.

"Ron told me he had texted her twice. Once before the meeting and then afterward to let her know he was on his way home. Jasmine didn't respond, but he said he wasn't concerned. He figured she was napping along with the twins."

Brick knew next to nothing about taking care of kids, especially babies, but that sounded reasonable. While Hughes selected a glazed donut from the Krispy Kreme box, he waited for her to continue.

"From what Ron has said, her car and car keys were gone along with her purse and a diaper bag, but nothing in the house seemed out of order. He immediately called Jasmine's mother and sister and checked with neighbors, but no one had seen or talked to her." Hughes pointed to a calendar hanging on the refrigerator. "He told me Jasmine had been seeing a therapist, but since another appointment wasn't scheduled until next week, he ruled that out as a possibility as to her whereabouts."

Brick thought about what Hughes had said while she ate her donut. "So given Ron's shift and the pre-trial meeting, it's possible Jasmine had been gone for up to twelve hours at that point."

Hughes nodded as she rinsed her hands at the sink.

"And he was the last one to see her?" Brick asked.

"No. Jasmine's sister had spent most of the day with her to help with the twins. She stayed late and Ron gave her a ride home on his way to work. Detective Taylor verified this with Jasmine's sister."

"Good." Brick was relieved to hear this detail and it probably showed on his face.

"I know. I've heard about the Johnson case and it was the very first thing I thought of. Were you working Homicide then?"

"Narcotics, but it shook every one of us to the core. No cop ever expects to go home and find his kids drowned in the bathtub and then be falsely accused of doing it."

"That's for sure. Divorces can be messy, usually are, but always a better option than killing your family. Anyway, when Ron called and told me the situation, I immediately put out an APB on her car."

"How did Ron sound?"

"Clearly, he was upset, but given all he had already done, he was also proactive. At that point, still very much in cop mode. He even wanted to do more, but I convinced him the best thing he could do was to stay put, at least for a while, and make a list of her family, friends, doctors, and any place where she might go." Hughes finished her coffee. "I had a meeting that ended around five. As soon as I could, I headed over here. I was hoping it would be like most missing persons, resolved with nothing worse than some embarrassment. Since that wasn't the case, we issued an Amber Alert for the twins and notified the FBI."

"And now, it's been close to forty-eight hours," Brick said.

"Right, and we all know what that means." Lieutenant Hughes sighed. "I don't need to tell you, I'm worried. Really worried."

Brick nodded. "I take it there hasn't been any activity on her debit or credit cards?"

Hughes shook her head. "We've been monitoring those—nothing. And I'm seeing that as a positive. At least, no one else is using her cards."

Brick thought the lieutenant might be grasping at straws but wasn't about to voice his opinion.

"Since the news media picked up the story, we've been getting plenty of tips, but none of them panned out."

"Has Ron made a statement to the media?"

"No and I've advised him not to even though the media will read whatever they want into that."

"Damned if you do, damned if you don't. And in cases like this, they'll always assume the husband or boyfriend is responsible," Brick said.

"True. My worry is that Jasmine is a danger to herself and the twins. I'm trying not to betray a confidence, but Ron told me Jasmine is struggling with postpartum depression."

Brick nodded. "I know, he mentioned it to me when we had lunch a few days ago."

"Good. He hasn't expressed his concerns in so many words, but I'm sure the thought has crossed his mind."

"Has he talked to the therapist Jasmine is seeing?"

"Tried to but got a recording that she's attending a conference in Minnesota or Michigan, somewhere in the Midwest." Hughes shrugged her shoulders. "And given HIPAA regulations, I'm not sure how forthcoming the therapist would be anyway."

"Ironic, isn't it, lawmakers pass legislation to safeguard privacy, and you can still find almost everything about anyone on the internet." Brick was about to tell Hughes how easily he had located Henry Yang's college roommate, but just then he heard footsteps on the stairs.

CHAPTER SEVENTEEN

RON SEEMED TO do a double take when he shuffled into the kitchen and saw Brick.

"What . . . what are you doing here? I mean I thought you were out of town."

"I was but I decided to come back early when I heard the news."

Ron pulled out a chair and slumped into a seat at the table. "Oh, thanks, man." There was no enthusiasm in his voice, but Brick didn't expect there would be. Ron avoided making eye contact; instead, he stared at his hands as he twisted his wedding band. He stopped and rubbed his eyes. "I've never felt like this before. I can't sleep, but I don't feel like I'm awake either. It's like being in the Twilight Zone with weird thoughts and crazy images cycling over and over through my head."

Although never in this situation, Brick was no stranger to trauma. He understood the emotional reactions Ron was describing. Some emotional responses seem to be universal. "The unknown is torture, isn't it, partner?" Brick deliberately used the term to reinforce the bond he still felt for his former protégé, although his just being there spoke volumes. "Ron, what do you need from me?"

Ron appeared to consider what Brick had asked, but it was as if he couldn't find the words to express what he was thinking. He shrugged his shoulders. "I don't know, man . . . I don't know." Tears ran down his cheeks and suddenly gave way to sobs that rocked his body.

Without saying a word but communicating with a tilt of her head, Lieutenant Hughes left the kitchen. Brick appreciated her sensitivity to the situation and allowing them some privacy. He gave Ron a couple of minutes before he handed him some paper napkins.

Ron wiped his eyes and blew his nose. "I've been racking my brain trying to think of anything Jasmine has said that could be a clue, but I got nothing. Nothing, man." Ron kept twisting his wedding band. "I know she loves the twins. I've never doubted that for a minute. She'd step in front of a moving train to protect them and yet I'm worried . . ."

Brick waited for Ron to continue, but it seemed as though he couldn't bring himself to say out loud what he was thinking. It was the kind of reaction Brick had seen many times when talking to the family and friends of victims.

"You're worried she might harm herself or the twins." Brick felt like someone needed to address the elephant in the room and he took the initiative.

Ron nodded as a single tear slowly rolled down the side of his face.

"When we had lunch, you said Jasmine wasn't taking any medication. Is that still the case?"

"Yeah. Just the other day I said to her, why don't you talk to your doctor about getting something for your mood swings. I figured there must be something she could take that would still be safe for the babies." Ron looked down as he shook his head. "She wouldn't consider it. I know I should have insisted, but she was already upset, and I didn't want to make it worse." Ron sighed loudly. "I figured it was just messed-up female hormones and they'd get straightened out eventually."

Brick would never claim to be an expert on the subject of female hormones, but just after joining the Homicide Squad he gained a new perspective while investigating a case where a mother smothered her three-month-old infant. What seemed like baffling human behavior started to make sense when a psychiatrist explained that while it was common for new mothers to experience "baby blues," some developed postpartum depression. In rare cases, this can transform into a severe psychosis, which could have tragic results. Brick had seen that firsthand, and it was something he would never forget. Had Jasmine's depression progressed to psychosis? It was a thought weighing heavy on Brick's mind but something he intended to keep to himself, at least for now. The only way to know for sure was to find Jasmine, and every hour that passed with her still missing raised the stakes.

Ron wiped his nose and sniffled. "I haven't washed in two days and I know I stink." He pushed back his chair and stood. "I'm going to take a shower. I'll leave my phone with you . . . just in case."

When Ron headed up the stairs, Lieutenant Hughes returned to the kitchen. "I thought it was better to give Ron a chance to talk to you without me being present."

"I figured as much. He went upstairs to take a shower."

Brick's grumbling stomach reminded him that a bag of peanuts on the plane was his last meal. He helped himself to one of the subs. Just as he closed the refrigerator door, the kitchen seemed to explode with the sound of Darius Rucker singing "Wagon Wheel."

"What the . . . oh, it's Ron's phone." Brick dove across the table and grabbed the cell phone and hit *accept*. Lieutenant Hughes looked on anxiously as Brick listened to what turned out to be a recorded message. He hung up and set the phone aside. "Buybuybaby is having a sale this weekend. Twenty-five percent off on strollers and car seats."

"Oh my God, robocalls should be outlawed."

Brick agreed as he unwrapped a ham and Swiss cheese sandwich. "I wasted perfectly good adrenaline on that. What I was about to say before the country music concert is that it's really tough to see Ron like this. I get the sense he feels guilty for not taking her depression more seriously."

"That's understandable, but he shouldn't beat up on himself." Lieutenant Hughes opened the Krispy Kreme box and reached for another glazed doughnut. "I can't speak from personal experience, but I think it would be easy to minimize or overlook things while concentrating on caring for two babies. Plus, Jasmine and Ron are first-time parents—everything is new. Right now, it still looks like Jasmine left on her own, but we don't know that for sure, and we can't rule anything out."

"True. Kidnapping is unlikely given Ron and Jasmine aren't high-profile or wealthy, but a carjacking can't be overlooked as a possibility."

"Or she could have been involved in an accident," Hughes suggested. "Maybe ran off the road in a remote area."

"Although from what Ron has said in the past, Jasmine limited her driving to trips to the store, doctor appointments, or visiting her mother and sister. He said she hated driving on the Beltway and I-95."

"I don't blame her for that. My idea of hell is circling the Beltway for eternity."

Brick wished the lieutenant hadn't said that just as he took a bite of his sandwich. He started to laugh and almost choked. Joking at a time that might seem inappropriate was typical among the cops Brick had worked with. It was what kept them sane. He just didn't expect it from the lieutenant.

"We've notified all the emergency rooms in D.C., Virginia, and Maryland in case she shows up, but so far, nothing." Lieutenant

Hughes lifted the lid on the box of donuts but stopped and closed it before choosing another one. "The last time I worked a missing persons case was four or five years ago and I've forgotten how frustrating it is. My way of coping—junk food."

"Healthier than cigarettes."

"Good point. Hope my lungs appreciate my choice, even if my hips don't." She reopened the box and chose the last jelly donut.

"This is tough. At least working a homicide, you have a definite starting point and a protocol to follow," Brick said. "Here it's a waiting game and it's like every minute is an hour."

"Speaking of which, I have no idea what time it is." Lieutenant Hughes checked her watch. "Whoa, I have a meeting at headquarters in four hours and I probably should change my clothes. Maybe even grab a power nap beforehand. Can you stay with Ron for a while?"

Brick nodded. "Sure, I'll think of it as other duties as assigned."

Lieutenant Hughes looked confused. "What do you mean?"

"You can add that to the Memorandum of Understanding covering the cold case."

"Oh, of course, the cold case project. For a minute, I was actually thinking you were still with Homicide. Brain fog, probably from all the sugar in my system. See why I need a nap?"

She headed toward the door just as her cell phone rang. Lieutenant Hughes reached into her pocket, retrieved the phone, and held it up to her ear. The serious look on her face gave Brick an uneasy feeling. A minute or two later, she slipped her phone back into her pocket and turned in Brick's direction.

"They've found Jasmine's car."

CHAPTER EIGHTEEN

FINDING JASMINE'S CAR was, without a doubt, a very significant development, but Brick resisted the temptation to bombard the lieutenant with all the questions rolling around in his head. The two detectives from the Missing Persons Unit stopped what they were doing. Three pairs of eyes were trained on Lieutenant Hughes.

"Okay, this is what I know and it's not much. Jasmine's car was found in the long-term parking lot at BWI Airport. Maryland State Police have responded."

Michael Taylor leaned back in his chair and shook his head. "Fuck me. Oh, sorry, Lieutenant, but nothing good happens in long-term parking lots. I don't like the sound of that."

"The sound of what?"

Brick turned when he heard Ron's voice coming from the kitchen. A second or two later, Ron joined the others in the living room. He was barefoot and had changed into a pair of jeans and a wrinkled Washington Nationals tee shirt. "I said, the sound of *what*?"

Lieutenant Hughes didn't sugarcoat what she had to say. "Jasmine's car has been found at BWI, the long-term parking lot."

Ron's legs trembled as he reached for the edge of the sofa and sunk down onto one of the cushions.

"What about Jasmine . . . the twins?"

The panic in Ron's voice sent chills down Brick's spine. Several possibilities ran through his head and none of them were good.

Lieutenant Hughes moved a sofa pillow and sat next to Ron. "I wish I had more information, but I don't. The Maryland State Police are investigating, and they'll need to get a search warrant."

"And that takes time." Suddenly Ron jumped up. "I'm not going to just sit here and wait. I need to be there."

"Ron, listen to me. There's no point in you going to BWI." The irony of the current role reversal wasn't lost on Brick. He understood his former partner's anguish because he'd been in a similar situation and not that long ago. At that time, Ron was the one thinking clearly and providing a sensible approach for what needed to be done. Brick was trying to reciprocate accordingly. "The Maryland Police aren't going to tell you anything and they're not going to let you anywhere near the car."

"Brick's right." Lieutenant Hughes spoke but at the same time appeared to be scrolling through something on her phone. She got up and walked over to the table where the two detectives were seated. "I need your computer for a minute." Carrie Dixon got up and Hughes took her place. With no one saying anything, the only sound in the room was the clicking of the keyboard as the lieutenant typed quickly, stopping only to make notes on a slip of paper. "Okay, I've found what I was looking for." She picked up the paper and her phone and headed to the kitchen, closing the door behind her.

"BWI . . . what the hell? Why would she go there? The only time Jasmine and I have been to that airport was when we went to Miami on our honeymoon."

"Ron, does Jasmine have a passport?" Detective Taylor asked.

"No."

"Are you sure?"

"I'm her husband. If anyone would know . . . it would be me. Right?"

Brick had spent enough time with Ron to know his outburst was out of character. It really wasn't directed at Taylor; he just happened to be the convenient target. If the roles were switched, Brick may well have posed the same question. There was no mistaking that nerves and emotions were raw, and Brick suspected things might get a whole lot worse. If he had learned anything from his years of being a cop, it was that no matter how well you think you are prepared to handle a situation, you may not be at all. And this one had all the makings of a challenge he'd never imagined being part of.

"Ron, I'm not trying to give you a hard time, it's just we have to think of every possibility," Detective Taylor said.

Ron turned in Taylor's direction. "Yeah, I know, sorry, man. I don't have a passport and as far as I know, she doesn't either, but what the hell do I know. I'm not sure of anything anymore."

* * *

"Okay, here's the plan." Lieutenant Hughes emerged from the kitchen looking confident. "I've talked to a contact at Baltimore PD and he called in a favor for me." She pointed toward Detectives Taylor and Dixon. "I need you two to head up to BWI and observe. Obviously, we don't have jurisdiction, but the state police will know who you are and why you're there. And, of course, you'll let me know everything ASAP."

What Brick saw wasn't all that different from his meeting with the lieutenant at Starbucks just over a week ago. Then the dutiful daughter had to handle a family crisis. Now, another crisis and in many ways, it seemed the lieutenant considered the detectives she supervised like extended family. This was quintessential Lieutenant Sonia Hughes. Her reputation for taking charge and grace under pressure was well earned. The two detectives picked up their laptops and were about to leave.

"Wait a minute." Ron turned and faced the lieutenant. "If all they're going to do is stand around and watch, then there's no reason why I can't go along."

"Ron, there's lots of reasons why that's not happening." She signaled to Taylor and Dixon to leave. "You may not agree with me, you may be angry with me, but you need to trust me. I know what's best for you right now."

Ron ran his hand through his dreads and appeared on the verge of breaking down again. He shrugged his shoulders. "Okay." His voice was barely louder than a whisper. "The waiting is killing me. And it's the empty cribs. Every time I walk past the nursery and see them, it's like—" Ron squeezed his eyes shut. "It's like a knife stabbing me in the heart."

Until now, Brick hadn't said much but felt compelled to speak up. "Ron, can you remotely monitor when someone is at your front door?"

"Yeah, I have an app on my phone."

"Then there's no reason you have to stay here, is there?"

Ron smirked. "Only that I don't have any place else to go."

"No family nearby?" Lieutenant Hughes asked.

Ron shook his head.

Brick knew what he had to do. "You can stay at my place. Granted it's small and not exactly the Mayflower Hotel, but there's a pull-out sofa bed in the den so you'll have a place to sleep and some privacy."

Ron seemed to consider the offer before nodding his head. "Yeah, okay for a day or two." He stood up. "I need to pack some stuff."

"Just a second, Ron. There's one other thing," Lieutenant Hughes said. "For the time being, I'm placing you on administrative leave. I need your badge and gun."

CHAPTER NINETEEN

As they left the house just before sunrise, Ron handed his car keys to Brick. While he drove, Ron called Jasmine's family. Keeping them informed was something that absolutely had to be done, but Brick knew it was tough delivering news that would only add to their anxiety. Ron seemed to handle the call to his mother-in-law calmly and reassuringly, but speaking to his sister-in-law sounded like it was trying his patience.

"Yes, Tanisha. For the third time, I've told you what I know and as soon as I hear anything else, I will call you." Without saying "goodbye," he took the phone away from his ear but continued holding it in his hand as if expecting an incoming call any minute.

At a red light, Brick glanced over and saw that Ron had leaned back against the head rest and closed his eyes. It was obvious he didn't want to talk and the silence suited Brick as well. He had been up for over thirty hours and was glad that once he turned onto Connecticut Avenue it was just over two miles to his place. Ten minutes later, he pulled into his reserved parking space behind his condo building, a four-story, bay-windowed brownstone on a quiet, tree-lined street.

Brick stopped to check his mailbox before he and Ron headed up the three flights to his apartment. No mail, which could mean one of two things: he really didn't have any mail or what he should have received hadn't been delivered. It was an all-too-common occurrence lately.

Brick hadn't expected to have a house guest, and in the past when he did, it was a woman sharing his bed. Ron would be the first one to sleep on the pull-out sofa bed in the den. Given his height, his feet would probably hang over the end of the mattress, but Brick figured it wouldn't matter. For now, having a place to stay without being surrounded by painful reminders everywhere he looked was what did matter.

"Ron, help yourself to anything in the kitchen. There's a new set of sheets in the den closet, along with blankets and pillows. Towels are in there as well. If you need anything, let me know, but for now I have to get some sleep."

Brick lowered the blinds in his bedroom in an attempt to block out the morning sun. He pulled back the bedspread, stripped down to his boxers, and crawled between the sheets. He closed his eyes and tried to conjure up the peaceful feeling he'd experienced walking along Lake Michigan with Nora. He wasn't successful at first, but eventually, he drifted off into a fitful sleep.

*   *   *

The sound of the phone jarred Brick awake and for a minute he wasn't sure where he was. Getting his bearings, he grabbed the phone from its place on the nightstand and hit *accept* before checking the caller ID.

"Here's what I know."

Lieutenant Hughes. Hearing her words plus seeing Ron standing in the doorway sent Brick's heart rate soaring. Still, as he listened, he managed to maintain the neutral expression that had served him well when he testified in countless cases at Superior Court.

"Okay, I'll tell him." Brick set the phone down. "Ron, this much is good. The car is empty and there's nothing obvious to indicate any foul play. The cops got a search warrant, so they were able to open the trunk. The spare tire and a folding double stroller were the only things they found." Ron nodded slowly as Brick continued. "And it's been on the lot since the day Jasmine went missing."

"What about the car seats?" Ron asked.

"Just about to mention that. There was one installed in the back seat."

"But there should be two." Ron shook his head. "Why would there only be one?"

Brick knew the question was rhetorical. "The lieutenant said the car is being towed to the police impoundment lot so the crime scene techs can do forensics on it. Airline passenger lists are being checked, both domestic and international, and Jasmine's photo is being shown to TSA officers who were working security check-in."

"Okay, whatever." Ron turned to walk away but stopped. "Back when I was with the Fifth District, I worked a missing kid's case. I didn't have a clue what the parents were going through, and I remember telling them to try to stay positive. I realize now how stupid I must have sounded."

Although this was not the time to critique how Ron had handled the situation, Brick didn't agree that Ron's comment to the parents sounded stupid. Easier said than done but staying positive was often the only thing that got terrified family and friends through the day, or even, the next hour. And as far as not having a clue, Brick knew Ron well enough to know that wasn't true. Being able to maintain professional distance, but at the same time having empathy, was something Ron brought to the job every day.

*   *   *

By the time Brick took a shower and got dressed, it was close to noon. He regretted the day was half over and the gray, cloudy sky matched his mood as he headed to Boland's Mill. He asked Ron to join him but wasn't surprised that he declined. Knowing that Rory usually worked the lunch shift, Brick wasn't expecting to see Eamonn behind the bar.

"Guinness?" Eamonn asked as Brick draped his jacket over the back of a barstool.

"No, never a good idea on an empty stomach. I'll have tomato juice and the Irish breakfast. Where's Rory?"

"He's at the dentist." Eamonn started to laugh. "He and Kelly went away for the weekend. While they were having dinner, he bit into some crusty bread and his veneer popped off."

"Hope he didn't swallow it." By the look on Eamonn's face, Brick knew he had. He didn't mean to laugh at Rory's misfortune, but he couldn't help it and he wasn't alone, Eamonn joined in. "Guessing that made for an expensive weekend."

"Indeed. Although he wasn't upset since Kelly said yes, provided he gets his missing tooth replaced."

"That's great."

"Yeah, but speaking of weekends, I thought you'd still be in Chicago."

"So did I."

"Sounds like things didn't go so well."

"You're right but not for the reason you're probably thinking." Brick filled Eamonn in on why he cut his trip short.

"Aw, Jaysus. I saw something about that on the news, but I didn't make the connection to your former partner. His wife and babies missing . . . life can be so feckin' unfair. Weren't you just at the baptism?"

"Yes." Brick wondered if Eamonn's comment about life being unfair was referring to more than Ron's situation. Eamonn cared about his employees and the horrific murder of Jose Delgado had affected everyone who had known him but especially Eamonn. And it occurred to Brick that for all the years he had known Eamonn, he really knew little about him before he came to the States and settled in D.C. Had something unfair in his life been the motivation for him to start over in a new place?

"How's he doing?" Eamonn asked.

"What . . . oh, Ron? Not good. He's staying with me right now because being in the house was more than he could handle."

"Understandable." Eamonn placed a coaster on the bar in front of Brick. "He shouldn't be alone, not at a time like this. I'll go place your order." After doing so, Eamonn returned to Brick's end of the bar and set a large tomato juice in front of him. "I shouldn't ask, but—"

"Ron has an alibi."

"Thank God for that. He seems like a decent guy, but I watch the news and too many of those true crime shows. I'll never understand why those eejits do what they do when they could just get a divorce. They all think they're so feckin' smart." Eamonn reached under the counter. He retrieved a place mat and silverware wrapped up in a napkin. He set them in front of Brick. "I hope this doesn't turn into one of those media shit shows."

"That makes two of us." Brick felt his cell phone vibrate. Unlike the serious texts from Nora inquiring about Jasmine and the twins, this one made him smile. She sent a photo of the lamb stew dinner she was having at Gaffney's. When Eamonn returned with a plate full of eggs, sausages, baked beans, tomatoes, and mushrooms, Brick followed suit by taking a picture and sending it to Nora.

"Good news?" Eamonn asked with a hint of optimism in his voice.

"What?"

"The way you're smiling, I'm hoping you got some good news."

"Just catching up with Nora . . . the woman in Chicago."

"Well, at least I don't need to ask how things went before you had to leave. Good on you." Eamonn poured himself a cup of tea. "Enjoy your breakfast."

*　　*　　*

Brick returned home and juggled the bag he was carrying as he unlocked his door. Once inside, he could hear Ron talking on his cell phone. From the exasperation in his voice, Brick wasn't surprised to hear Tanisha's name mentioned.

In the kitchen, Brick started unpacking the containers of food Eamonn insisted on providing for Ron. He claimed it was the least he could do then quickly corrected himself by adding he'd pray for a quick and safe return for Jasmine and the twins. Brick knew Eamonn well enough to know he was a devout Catholic who attended Mass several times a week. He also knew Ron believed in the power of prayer. When Ron walked into the kitchen, Brick conveyed the message from Eamonn and pointed out the comfort food.

Ron grabbed a plate from a cabinet over the sink and unwrapped a corned beef sandwich before sitting down at the table. Brick put the potato soup and shepherd's pie in the fridge and reached for a couple of cans of Coke. He handed one to Ron and sat down across from him. For a few minutes, neither spoke. Brick simply watched as Ron inhaled half of the sandwich. During the year they worked together, they had shared many meals but never had Brick noticed Ron wolfing down his food. The ten-year age difference between the two men was never an issue while they were partners but now it seemed like a generation gap. Brick had never felt more like a parent.

"When's the last time you ate?" Brick asked.

Ron shrugged his shoulders as he picked up the other half of the sandwich. "Don't know." Before continuing, he took a bite and chewed more slowly. "I got a couple of calls while you were out. Helps to know my coworkers, at least some of them, have my back and the other was from one of Jasmine's Bible study friends. They want to have a prayer vigil at the church."

"How do you feel about that?" Brick asked as he took a swig of Coke.

"Okay, I guess. Even though Jasmine and I never wanted to be the center of attention, I'm willing to do whatever it takes."

"Did Jasmine's friend mention when they want to do the vigil?"

"Soon, maybe the day after tomorrow. She's been talking with Jasmine's mother and sister to make arrangements."

"How are things between you and your mother-in-law?"

Ron winced as he set down his can of soda. "As good as it can be with someone who expresses her displeasure with the husband choice her daughter made."

"Seriously?"

"Not in so many words to my face. But if they gave an Oscar for passive-aggressive behavior, she'd win." Ron put his plate in the dishwasher. "I'm going to try to get some sleep."

Brick reflected on Ron's movie industry reference and for a split second he recognized the typical behavior of the guy who had constantly challenged him with movie trivia. In most cases, Brick was clueless but occasionally he'd surprise Ron with the right answer. Was that kind of banter a thing of the past? It was impossible for

Ron to experience what he was going through without it affecting his personality. The ultimate outcome would, no doubt, determine how everything might change. Brick knew the drill—prepare for the worst but hope for the best.

Brick picked up his jacket and hung it in the hall closet. As he did so, he noticed the box of stuff belonging to Henry Yang. For a moment, he was taken aback. Just a few days ago, that had been his focus. He was all set to go through the contents of the box before he was lured away by an invitation to Chicago. Maybe today it would provide a much-needed distraction as the waiting game continued. He picked up the box and set it down near the dining room table. As cold cases go, three years wasn't very long, and if luck was on his side, he'd find some contacts who knew Yang. Brick started sorting through the items but didn't get very far. His cell phone pinged and he glanced at the text from Lieutenant Hughes.

New development. On my way to your place.

CHAPTER TWENTY

BRICK WASN'T SURE if Ron was sleeping, but if he was, there was no reason to wake him until Lieutenant Hughes arrived. As nerve wracking as the wait was for him, it would be that much worse for Ron. Meantime, while waiting, Brick tried to organize the stuff he had received from Henry Yang's roommate, but he couldn't concentrate. Instead, he was speculating as to what the lieutenant meant by new development.

Finally, Brick's cell phone pinged with a text indicating Lieutenant Hughes had arrived. When he opened the door, the expression on her face confirmed what Brick feared. He took a deep breath and braced himself for how bad the news might be. Without saying a word, she stepped inside the apartment just as Ron emerged from the den. With the groggy look of someone waking from a deep sleep, he yawned and rubbed his eyes.

"Lieutenant? What . . . what's going on?"

Hughes set her purse on the hall table and pulled her phone out of her jacket pocket. "Ron, I don't have any specific information on Jasmine or the twins, but some potential evidence was found floating in the harbor in Baltimore." She hesitated before continuing. "There's no easy way to show you this, but can you identify the infant car seat?" She handed her cell phone to him.

It only took a second for Ron to respond even though the words seemed to catch in his throat. "It looks like Jamal's."

"Are you sure?" Hughes asked.

Ron nodded. His hand shook as he gave the phone back to the lieutenant. He glanced toward Brick and looked as if he was about to say something. Before he did, he bolted toward the bathroom. There was no mistaking the sound of puking reverberating throughout the apartment followed by a toilet flushing, once and then a second time.

Brick exchanged a concerned look with Lieutenant Hughes. "I'll check on him, but for now he needs a few minutes."

"Definitely."

"Can I see the photo?" Brick asked. Hughes handed her phone to him. By enlarging the image, Brick noticed something significant. "That looks like blood splatter."

"I know. And I don't have to tell you how horrible that makes me feel. I keep thinking about *Sophie's Choice*. I pray to God I'm wrong. Anyway, Baltimore PD is running forensics but since it was in the water, I'm not optimistic they'll find much."

"Do you know where it was exactly?"

"From between the Inner Harbor and Fells Point. One of the water taxi drivers spotted it and called the Harbor Patrol."

Hughes's phone rang and Brick handed it back to her.

"It's my contact at Baltimore PD."

While she took the call, Brick headed toward the bathroom to check on Ron. Even though the door was ajar, he knocked before pushing it open. Ron was sitting on the edge of the tub with his elbows on his knees, his head in his hands.

"Are you okay, partner?" Brick asked. Ron managed a slight nod. Brick opened the medicine cabinet. On the bottom shelf was a bottle of mouthwash. He poured a generous amount into a paper cup and handed it to Ron.

Ron stepped over to the sink and rinsed his mouth. When he finished, he splashed water on his face. "Did you see the photo?"

"Yes."

"The blood splatter?"

"Yes."

Ron lowered the lid on the toilet and sat down. "What does it mean, man?"

"I wish I knew." As soon as the words were out of his mouth, Brick realized he was just saying something, anything, to fill the void. When he and Ron were working a case, this would be a time for brainstorming. Trying to do that now would only cause Ron more pain and most likely wouldn't help the situation at all.

"We went there a lot."

Brick wasn't sure what Ron meant. "Went where?"

"The Inner Harbor. Jasmine loved it. Even talked about how when we have kids, we'd take them to the Aquarium. And there was a place in Little Italy . . . a small family-owned restaurant." His words trailed off, replaced with a sob. After a minute or two, Ron grabbed a wad of toilet paper and blew his nose. "I've tried to convince myself that Jasmine wouldn't harm herself and she'd never hurt the twins, but I gotta tell you, I'm scared. I've never been so damned scared in my life." Ron stood up. "I have to call Tanisha. Awful as it is, they need to hear this from me." He left the bathroom, went back to the den, and shut the door.

"How's he doing?" Lieutenant Hughes asked as she slipped her phone back into her pocket.

"I'm guessing he'll never eat a corned beef sandwich again." Brick sat down on the La-Z-Boy recliner across from the sofa where the lieutenant sat. "Sounds like he's now convinced that Jasmine has harmed herself and the babies."

"Since we don't know, I can't reassure him that he's wrong, so it's best I say nothing." Lieutenant Hughes stood and buttoned her jacket. "I need to get back to headquarters. Detectives Taylor and Dixon will let me know if there's anything else that I should know about."

"They're still in Baltimore?"

"Yes. And one other thing, a reporter from Channel 7 was on the scene when the car seat was recovered."

"Great . . . that will be all over the news tonight."

Lieutenant Hughes nodded and headed toward the door. "Do your best to keep him away from the TV."

"I'll try, but that might be the toughest assignment I've ever had."

CHAPTER TWENTY-ONE

RATHER THAN WATCH the news on TV, Brick logged onto his computer and streamed Fox. It wasn't his normal source for news, but he was curious as to what the host of *And Justice for All* was saying about Jasmine and the twins.

Stella Owen opened her show holding the picture that had been shown on CNN. In her Southern drawl, she implored viewers to take a good look at the picture. The camera moved in to get a close-up.

"Her name is Jasmine Hayes and she is the mother of six-month-old twins, a boy and a girl. She and the babies are missing." Owen stared into the camera and raised her voice. "They are missing." She held up the picture again. "People don't just disappear. Something happened to this woman and her babies. Her car was found at BWI Airport in the long-term parking lot. Did she and the twins get on a plane and jet off to some tropical island for vacation? Are they soaking up the sun on a sandy beach in the Caribbean? I hope so, but I doubt it. Especially since the very next day, an infant car seat was pulled out of the Inner Harbor in Baltimore." Owen's lip quivered as if she were about to cry. "Blood stains were found on the car seat . . . blood stains."

It took a moment for Owen to regain her composure. "We have reached out to Jasmine's husband, but he has not returned our call. Why am I not surprised?" She paused for dramatic effect. "And guess what her husband does for a living . . . he's a cop. A homicide detective. I'm sure he's learned plenty from investigating lots of murders." She looked directly at the camera and rolled her eyes. Again, she held up the photo of Jasmine. "One more time, people, look at the photo of this beautiful woman, this young mother. If you know anything about her disappearance, please call our tip line. As always, you can remain anonymous."

Stella Owen glanced down at a folder on her desk. "And in a suburb of Atlanta, a seven-year-old girl—"

Brick had heard enough. He logged off the computer.

Brick knew it was inevitable. For armchair sleuths, a case where an attractive young mother and her six-month-old twins are missing and the husband and father is a homicide detective has the kind of elements they find tantalizing. Stella Owen made a name for herself turning true crime into a real-life game of Clue. As long as the ratings were high, it didn't matter if she played fast and loose with the facts. She usually did, and there was no mistaking her reference to Ron being a homicide detective was a deliberate attempt to implicate him without specifically saying as much.

It made Brick angry for several reasons, not the least of which was Owen's disregard for a family's anguish and pain while turning their circumstances into entertainment for crime voyeurs. But there was no recourse unless she crossed the line into slander territory. For now, Ron was in her crosshairs and whatever he said or didn't say would be scrutinized. The upcoming prayer vigil worried Brick . . . a lot.

* * *

For the first time in several hours, Ron emerged from the den. He grabbed a Coke from the fridge and slumped onto the sofa.

"Everything is set for the vigil tomorrow night." Ron took a swig of soda and belched.

"You know the media will be all over it," Brick said.

Ron shrugged. "What the hell, I know what they're saying. They've already decided I'm responsible for whatever they think happened."

Brick hated to see his former partner look so defeated. "Ron, I think it would be in your best interest to talk to a lawyer."

"Come on, Brick, you know what D.C. lawyers cost. The little savings that Jasmine and I had, we've spent since the twins were born."

Brick wasn't surprised. He knew babies are expensive, especially when you need to buy two of everything. He couldn't help but wonder if money issues added to Jasmine's depression. "I hear you and I'm not saying you need to hire someone at this point. What I am suggesting is getting some advice about how to handle the immediate situation."

"I don't know." Ron got up and headed toward the den.

Brick called after him. "There's a former Assistant U.S. Attorney who specializes in damage control. She's been responsible—"

"I told you I can't afford a lawyer. What part of that don't you understand?"

Brick ignored Ron's sarcasm and wasn't going to give up that easily. "Just hear me out."

* * *

Despite the circumstances, Brick was looking forward to seeing Amy Pennington. Occasionally, he had seen her interviewed on TV, most recently representing one of the Washington Wizards falsely accused of rape, but it had been a number of years since he had seen her in person. Brick and Ron took the elevator to the eighth floor of the newly constructed K Street building where a receptionist invited them to have a seat. A few minutes later, Amy led them back to her well-appointed office.

Brick looked around before taking a seat. "A little fancier than your office at Superior Court."

"You really think so? You mean the one I shared with Barry what's-his-name. God, he was obnoxious. Remember the time you told him not to open the evidence bag?" Brick nodded. "Obviously, you knew how bad dried blood smells, but he didn't listen."

"Maybe, if I had gone to Harvard . . ."

"Exactly. Because of Mr. Law Review, we had to close the office for several hours and have it fumigated at taxpayers' expense. Oh, those were the days." Amy laughed before offering Brick and Ron something to drink. They both declined.

"Okay then, let's get started. Ron, just to be clear, I'm not a defense attorney. What I do is advise clients on how best to present themselves during a difficult time and/or help them restore their reputation, if necessary. I've seen the news reports and I'm sorry for your situation. I probably don't need to tell you that every time you walk out your door, you have to navigate a mine field. Even if you aren't confronted by a reporter, there very well may be someone observing every move you make. From what Brick told me, I understand there's going to be a vigil. I can give you some guidance—"

"I'm sure you can, but there's a problem." Ron shifted in his seat. "Plain and simple, I can't afford you."

"I should have explained. I base my fee on several factors, such as complexity of the situation, a client's ability to pay—"

"I'm not a charity case."

"I wasn't implying that you are. If I had finished, I would have added professional courtesy. If it weren't for guys like your former partner, I wouldn't be where I am." She smiled at Brick. "Freeway Phantom case, right?"

"Okay." Ron shrugged. "What do I need to do?"

"Be honest with me. If you're not, we're both wasting time and there's no point in you being here."

Brick was seeing the attorney he remembered from her days prosecuting felony cases in Superior Court where she was known for her cut-to-the-chase style. He knew she wouldn't back away from the questions that needed to be asked. But whether he would be privy to the responses wasn't certain.

Amy Pennington reached for a yellow legal pad. "Ron, before I ask you any questions, do you want Brick to leave?"

"No . . . he's family."

"Brother from another mother?" Again, Amy smiled in Brick's direction. "Works for me." She turned back toward Ron. "Do you have any knowledge as to what has happened to your wife and children?"

"No."

"How long have you and Jasmine been married?"

"Almost nine years—our anniversary is in November."

"How did you meet?"

"College, University of Maryland."

Brick noticed a fleeting smile cross Ron's face. He suspected the question had triggered a happy memory from their college days.

Amy made a quick note before continuing. "How would you describe your marriage?"

"Strong. We have our ups and downs like any couple, but we work things out. We love each other and respect each other."

Brick was glad he didn't hear "perfect." Instead, what he heard was what he would consider an honest answer. Even though he was here as Ron's support system and not a detective, he couldn't turn off years of experience analyzing responses. He paid close attention to what Ron said and how he said it.

"Was Jasmine's pregnancy planned?"

"Not exactly." Ron seemed slightly embarrassed. "What I mean is, we both wanted kids and figured if it was God's will, it would happen. And when it did, we got twins."

"How did that change your relationship?"

"It's a big adjustment." Ron took a minute before continuing. "Lots of unexpected expenses and Jasmine's dealing with postpartum depression."

"Is she taking medication?"

"No. She's been seeing a therapist . . . a psychologist."

"Have you spoken to her therapist?"

"No, I tried but when I called her office, I got a recorded message that she's attending a conference."

"Even though you're the spouse, there's confidentiality issues." Amy made a few more notes before setting down her pen and looked directly at Ron. "Have you ever cheated on Jasmine?"

"No."

"Do you have any reason to think Jasmine may have cheated on you?"

"No."

Amy checked her notes before continuing. "We're almost finished. One last thing to cover. Does Jasmine have a life insurance policy?"

"Yes."

"What's the value?"

"Half a million."

"Are you the beneficiary?"

"Yes."

"When was the policy purchased?"

"After the twins were born."

"Okay, I have the information I need. Do you have any questions?"

Ron seemed to think for a moment then shook his head. "No."

"Again, Ron, I'm sorry for your troubles and hope your family is back home soon. As to the vigil, my advice is show up just before it starts and leave as soon as it's over. The less you say, the better. And remember, everyone has a phone with a camera. As to any calls from the media, let them go to voicemail. I can't say it enough, do not engage with the media." Amy handed her business card to Ron. "I'm here if you need a spokesperson."

CHAPTER TWENTY-TWO

ATTENDING SEARCHES, VIGILS, and funerals for victims was something Brick had done many times during his tenure as a homicide detective. On a few occasions, the perpetrator attended as well. Tonight, it was possible that someone responsible for Jasmine's disappearance could blend in with the crowd. With that in mind, Brick had to walk the fine line between being a participant and an observer. In order to do that he needed to keep his emotions in check and that would be a challenge.

It had been an unseasonably warm late September day, perhaps a harbinger of a brief return to summer following last week's frost, and the threat of a thunderstorm couldn't be ignored. Depending on the timing, it might be to their advantage by forcing the vigil to be brief. Brick agreed with Amy Pennington, the less Ron was on display, the better.

At Ron's request, Brick gladly accepted the role of designated driver. As he pulled into a parking space, he noticed the vans from two local news stations parked in front of the AME Zion Church.

"Ready?" Brick asked

Ron shook his head. "No, but I don't have a choice." He unfastened his seat belt and opened the car door. Together, he and Brick joined a group of men and women gathered on the steps of the church. "There's Jasmine's mother and sister." Brick saw the two women handing out candles as Ron walked over to greet them.

It didn't go unnoticed by Brick that Jasmine's mother's reaction to Ron was indifferent at best. Jasmine's sister hugged him half-heartedly and handed him several candles to distribute. Brick was about to move up a couple of steps when he felt a tap on his shoulder. He turned and saw Lieutenant Hughes. Standing next to her was a younger woman Brick had never met.

"Lieutenant." Brick extended his hand in her direction.

"Brick, this is Holly Beltran, our newest member of the team."

Brick recalled Ron mentioning a female detective had joined the Homicide Squad and that she looked like Central Casting's idea of a made-for-TV detective. Ron hadn't exaggerated. With her high-lighted long blond hair and wearing form-fitting jeans, it was hard not to stare. She smiled in Brick's direction.

"So nice to meet you. Not under these circumstances, of course." The wind had blown her hair and she brushed it out of her eyes. "I was so shocked when I heard the news after I got back from a short vacation to Rehoboth." A toss of her head sent her hair away from her face. "I still can't wrap my head around what Ron must be going through." She turned back toward Lieutenant Hughes. "I'll get a couple of candles for us." As Holly walked away, several heads, including Brick's, turned and watched.

Brick figured his time to speak privately with Lieutenant Hughes was limited. "Anything new?"

"No, they're testing the blood on the car seat. Fast tracking, so we may have results in a day or two." She pointed toward a reporter standing in front of a cameraman and holding a microphone. "We knew they'd be here. How's Ron handling it?"

"He's ignoring their calls. And as far as I can tell, they haven't figured out where he's staying."

"That's good to hear. Still, it might be in his best interest to hire a spokesperson at some point. I know that's expensive, but a ruined reputation is costly too."

Brick didn't feel it was his place to mention Ron had already spoken to Amy Pennington, but it was reassuring to know he had led him in the right direction. The wind had picked up and more people were gathering. Brick glanced around and estimated the crowd to be around fifty or sixty strong. He felt someone brush his arm and when he turned, Holly handed him a candle. Her fingers touching his in the exchange.

"I've heard lots of good things about you, mostly from Ron, but others as well." She stepped a little closer to Brick. Her smile showed off teeth that were either a testament to enviable dental genes or the work of a skilled orthodontist. "You're a legend around the squad."

The comment caught Brick off guard. He thought about how to respond but didn't get a chance. Ron had joined them on the steps and Holly turned her attention to him. It struck Brick as odd that Ron hadn't stayed with Jasmine's mother and sister. Despite what may be his in-law issues, the appearance in public of a united front with Jasmine's family would have been in Ron's best interest. Before Brick had a chance to point that out to him, a deep male voice called out, asking for everyone's attention.

"Good evening, everyone, and on behalf of Jasmine's family, thank you for being here. I'm Isaac Jackson, the Assistant Pastor here at Southeast AME Zion Church. Please join me in prayer."

Before bowing his head, Brick caught a glimpse of the pastor. This was not the minister who officiated at the twins' christening; the one who appeared to be consoling Jasmine afterward in the church parking lot. He looked around but didn't see the other pastor among the attendees. He made a mental note to be sure to mention it to Ron.

"Our Heavenly Father, we call upon you in this, our hour of need. We pray that our sister Jasmine Hayes and her babies, Jayla and Jamal, are safe and will come home soon. We also pray for Jasmine's family—her husband, Ron; her mother, Pearl; and her sister, Tanisha. Give them strength to see them through this difficult time. We ask this in the name of our Lord and Savior, Jesus Christ. Amen."

A chorus of *Amen* followed. The pastor stepped back from the microphone. A young woman took his place.

"Please join me."

In a voice that gave Brick chills, she sang an a capella rendition of "Amazing Grace". When she finished, he noticed several attendees wiping away tears.

Pastor Jackson returned to the microphone. "Thank you, Chantelle. Does everyone have a candle?" He looked around and seemed satisfied that everyone did. "Jasmine's mother will start by lighting her candle and that flame will in turn light the candles each of us holds."

If the attendees hadn't noticed that Ron wasn't standing with Jasmine's family before, they'd be aware of it now. And, to Brick's way of thinking, the husband and father should be the one leading the candle lighting. Too late now.

It took a few minutes as everyone participated and shielded their flickering candles from the occasional gust of wind. Brick heard a faint rumble of thunder in the distance.

Pastor Jackson held his candle in his outstretched hand.

"We send this message to Jasmine. Follow the path this candlelight symbolizes. Come home to the people who love and miss you. Amen."

After a minute or two of silence, he blew out his candle. "Thank you for joining Jasmine's family and friends. Please keep them in your prayers."

The rain had held off, but now the threat seemed imminent. A loud clap of thunder sent people rushing to their cars, although Holly didn't seem to be in a hurry as she and Ron continued their conversation. Brick was about to interrupt when big drops of rain mixed with pea-sized hail started falling and saved him the trouble.

CHAPTER TWENTY-THREE

FOLLOWING THE VIGIL, Brick had some questions for Ron but delayed asking them on the drive back to his apartment. For now, he needed to concentrate on driving as the torrential downpour challenged the windshield wipers to keep pace. A downed tree at the corner of Connecticut Avenue and Kalorama forced him to take a detour. The trip took twice as long as it normally would even in afternoon rush-hour traffic. The rain continued along with deafening claps of thunder and streaks of lightning illuminating the dark sky. After pulling into the parking lot behind his building and his assigned space, Brick checked the AccuWeather app on his cell phone.

"Looks like the storm is right on top of us, but it's moving fast. Might as well wait it out."

"Whatever." Ron adjusted his seat to a partially reclining position.

"Are you okay?" Brick asked.

"I'm exhausted." Ron rubbed his eyes. "I know Jasmine's friends meant well and I want to believe the vigil will help, that prayer works ... but, I don't know anymore. I mean, I was raised to go to church." Ron yawned before continuing. "Not this church, this is Jasmine's, but I guess it's mine now. Maybe I should say, ours. I'm trying to keep the faith, but it's hard, man."

The response was more than Brick expected. In some ways, it sounded as though Ron was thinking out loud. Brick thought for a couple of minutes, processing what Ron had said, as well as things he had observed at the vigil.

"Ron, I didn't see the pastor who officiated at the twins' christening. Was he there tonight?"

"You mean Marcus Walker. I thought he'd be the one in charge, so I was surprised when Tanisha told me he had to go out of town. She wasn't sure why but thought it was either some kind of religious retreat or a family emergency."

"Is he married?" Brick asked.

"No, but I know he's from North Carolina and has family there."

Ron adjusted the seat again bringing it fully upright. "There's something you don't know."

Brick figured there was probably a lot he didn't know. He waited for Ron to explain.

"For a while, Jasmine and Marcus dated."

"Before you two met?"

"No, we had been dating for over a year, but we had a fight about something." Ron shrugged. "I don't even remember what and it doesn't matter. We broke up for a while. During that time, she started dating Marcus."

"Was he at Maryland, too?"

"No, he's about seven or eight years older than me. He had just moved to D.C. to take the job of assistant pastor at AME Zion. That's how he and Jasmine met."

"How long did they date?"

"A couple of months, I guess. Then she and I worked things out and got back together."

"How's your relationship with Marcus?"

"It's cool."

"Was it awkward when you first started attending the church?"

"Not really. I mean, it's not like he was the reason that Jasmine and I split. Besides, I was dating during that time, too. A couple of girls." Ron hesitated before continuing. "The only one who seemed to have any problem with Jasmine and me getting back together was her mother."

Brick heard some bitterness in Ron's voice. "How so?"

"She's made it known that if Jasmine kept dating Marcus, she might be married to a minister now, instead of a cop. And from her perspective, that's a far better choice."

What Ron had revealed explained a possible reason for the strained relationship with his mother-in-law he had previously mentioned to Brick. But knowing Jasmine and Marcus had some history made Brick wonder if there was more to the interaction he had seen between the two of them after the christening.

"Has Marcus contacted you since—"

Ron didn't wait for Brick to finish. "No and I gotta say it's pissing me off. Even if he couldn't be here to attend the vigil, he could have at least called me. But then again, I don't know how long he's been out of town."

"Maybe he doesn't know what's going on."

"Yeah, I guess that's a possibility if he isn't watching the news . . . whatever."

Brick let it drop for now. In the morning, he would text Lieutenant Hughes. One of the detectives from the Missing Persons Unit should follow up on Pastor Walker's whereabouts.

"Looks like the rain has let up." Brick reached for the door handle. "Let's make a run for it."

* * *

Once inside the apartment, Ron headed straight for the den. Brick understood. For both of them, it had been another long, stressful day and the conversation in the car was enough. After changing into a pair of sweatpants, Brick went to the kitchen and opened the refrigerator. He considered having a beer but instead grabbed some ice cubes from the freezer, dropped them in a glass, and poured a couple of jiggers of Jameson. He settled on the sofa, picked up the remote, and channel surfed until landing on ESPN. He watched a few innings of a game between the Yankees and the White Sox. It wasn't surprising that anything associated with Chicago made him think of Nora. He grabbed his phone and started to text her but remembered she was back in Ireland. With a five-hour time difference, receiving a text at three in the morning might not be appreciated.

The lopsided score in the Yankees' favor meant Mariano Rivera wouldn't be called upon to work his magic. As far as Brick was concerned, if the future Hall of Famer wasn't going to take the mound, there wasn't much point in watching the rest of the game.

Before going to bed, Brick headed to the bathroom. When he finished brushing his teeth, he noticed light coming from under the door of the den and he heard Ron's voice. Brick stood by the bathroom door and listened.

"Yeah, I know. Still, it means a lot to me hearing it from you." Ron paused before continuing. "You're right, but I'm sure you know that without me telling you."

Brick didn't know if Ron had placed or received the call, but especially given the hour, he was curious as to who he was talking to. He stayed by the door.

"Thanks, I will. You do the same, okay? Good night, Holly."

CHAPTER TWENTY-FOUR

BRICK CRAWLED INTO bed, turned off the light, and after twenty minutes was still wide awake. Too many questions were swirling around in his head. The late-night call between Ron and Holly—what was that all about? Brick recalled Amy Pennington asking Ron if he had ever cheated on Jasmine and the response was an emphatic "no." But was he telling the truth? Normally, Brick wouldn't be giving it a second thought, simply because it wasn't his business what Ron or anyone else did. But with Jasmine and the twins missing, it couldn't be dismissed as possibly being a factor in their disappearance. Having met Holly, it was easy for Brick to see how Ron could be tempted, especially if he felt Jasmine was ignoring his needs. It wasn't unheard of for a first-time father to resent the attention newborns demand.

A few more minutes passed. Brick recognized the futility of lying awake with his mind racing. He turned on the light and glanced at the stack of books on his nightstand. He picked up a worn paperback copy of *The Deep Blue Good-By*. Maybe Travis McGee would be the distraction he needed tonight. A few pages into the fourth chapter, the book slipped from his hand and hit the floor.

* * *

While Ron was taking a shower, Brick turned on the morning news. As he expected, there was coverage of the vigil, but it wasn't the lead story. A multi-vehicle accident on the Beltway had turned rush hour into a commuting nightmare. When the segment on the vigil aired, it focused briefly on the candle lighting and then displayed a photo of Jasmine and a contact phone number for the Missing Persons Unit. Brick was relieved that the separation between Ron and Jasmine's family wasn't obvious although that didn't mean Stella Owen wouldn't notice. It was likely she'd have her flunkies scrutinizing the news footage for anything she could use to keep viewers tuning in to hear her nightly update and commentary.

Brick turned the TV off and headed to the kitchen. He put a bagel in the toaster while he waited for a cup of tea to steep, three minutes for Irish breakfast. He was still thinking about the brief conversation he'd overheard last night. He couldn't help but wonder about the relationship between Ron and Holly, but he was hesitant to come right out and ask. At least for now.

"Hey, Brick." Ron was looking down at his phone and didn't make eye contact when he walked into the kitchen. "Did you see the text from the lieutenant?"

Brick patted his pants pocket and realized he'd left his phone in the bedroom. "No, what's up?"

"She wants to see us ASAP."

"Any indication—"

"No."

Brick sensed the anxiety Ron must be feeling. He finished chewing his bagel. "Okay, give me ten minutes."

*   *   *

Taking an Uber to Judiciary Square saved the time of trying to find a parking space. As they had done many times in the past, Brick and Ron climbed the steps of Police Headquarters together. Once inside, they passed through the metal detector and took the elevator to the Homicide Squad offices on the third floor. As they exited, Lieutenant Hughes made her way down the hallway from the direction of the break room. She had a bag of Cheetos in one hand and a can of Dr Pepper in the other.

Brick held the door leading to the reception area and motioned for the lieutenant and Ron to enter.

"Jenny Craig can go to hell." Lieutenant Hughes smiled at Brick but still had the guilty look of a kid caught with a hand in the cookie jar.

Brick and Ron followed Hughes to her office where the two detectives from the Missing Persons Unit were seated at the conference table.

"Have a seat, guys." Lieutenant Hughes poured her soda into a glass and took a sip. "Okay, Baltimore PD Crime Lab ran tests on the infant seat they retrieved from the harbor. Turns out what appeared to be bloodstains were fake. The kind of theatrical stuff used at Halloween and, I don't know, zombie walks."

"What kind of bullshit is that!" Ron reared back in his chair. "Oh, sorry, Lieutenant."

"No need to apologize—my reaction was a whole lot stronger. Although once the reality set in, I was encouraged that it isn't human blood. This was a ruse, and I can come up with some possible explanations. Sorry, Ron, the one that makes the most sense to me—and I know this is hard to hear—is that this was deliberately staged to send you a message which would inflict as much pain as possible."

Ron blurted, "What do you mean?"

She continued, "Since the birth of the twins, has Jasmine's behavior been erratic?"

Ron didn't answer immediately. He shifted in his seat. "Sometimes, in fact often, she definitely seemed overwhelmed and sad, but I wouldn't say erratic."

"Did she ever talk about or even threaten to take the babies and leave?"

"No . . . never."

Lieutenant Hughes glanced around the table. "Any ideas?"

Detective Dixon from Missing Persons spoke up. "We sometimes see this sort of vindictive stuff in nasty divorce and child custody cases. One spouse trying to hurt the other."

"That doesn't sound like Jasmine." Ron shook his head. "She just wouldn't do something like that."

Brick kept his thoughts to himself. It was easier for him to be more objective than Ron, and he didn't share his certainty that Jasmine wasn't responsible. Over the years on the job, he had seen too many things he never would have imagined committed not by strangers, but by people who vowed to love and honor each other. There were questions he wanted to ask Ron and something he needed to reveal but not in front of the group assembled here.

"Does anyone have anything else to discuss?" Lieutenant Hughes glanced around the table.

"I do." Detective Taylor leaned forward in Ron's direction. "Does Jasmine have her own bank account?"

"Yes. We both contribute to a joint household checking account. At least Jasmine did when she was still teaching. And we have a joint savings account, not that there's much in it now. We also have our own accounts."

"So far, there's been no activity on her credit cards. Have you noticed anything on the joint bank accounts?"

"No."

"Okay, is your name on her personal account?"

Ron shrugged his shoulders. "I'm not sure."

"Can you check with the bank? If your name is on it, with your permission, we can access the account. Otherwise, we'll have to subpoena the records to see if there's been any activity."

As far as Brick was concerned, hearing that there hadn't been any activity on Jasmine's credit cards could be significant. If she had been abducted, it wouldn't be surprising for the perpetrator to start using her cards or sell them on the black market. And if she left on her own, it was likely she would eventually need to use the cards herself. Mastercard may provide a break the investigation desperately could use. There were, of course, other possibilities. She wouldn't need cash or credit cards if someone else was footing the expenses. Not good for any future relationship with Ron, but a better scenario than the obvious explanation Brick didn't want to consider.

"Excuse me, Lieutenant." Hughes's secretary stepped into the room. "There's a call for you on line two."

"Thanks, I'll take it at your desk." She left the room for a few minutes. By the look on the lieutenant's face when she returned, it was apparent to Brick that she was not pleased about something. "Okay, guys, that's all I have for now. Baltimore PD has been good about sharing information. So, I trust they'll keep me informed. What I know, you'll know."

CHAPTER TWENTY-FIVE

"HOW ABOUT IF I pick up a couple of sandwiches." Brick handed Ron the keys to the condo as he closed the door to the cab. "An Italian sub?"

"Yeah . . . sure, whatever." Ron turned and walked away, his head down and eyes focused on the sidewalk. He kicked at some leaves covering his path.

Brick crossed the street and headed north on Connecticut Avenue to a small strip of mixed-used businesses. Located next to a Kinko's was a family-owned sandwich shop. Brick had discovered Dino's Deli twenty years ago when he was a rookie cop. Even though the third generation of the Palladino family was now in charge, the family patriarch was usually there. Today was no exception.

"Hey, Brick." Angelo sat at a small table in the corner. "Long time, no see."

Brick stopped in front of the table and shook hands with Angelo. Close to ninety and bearing a striking resemblance to Uncle June on *The Sopranos*, his grip was surprisingly strong. "Angelo, how have you been?"

"So so, but still above ground. Can't complain."

Brick and Angelo talked Nationals baseball for a few minutes before Brick stepped up to the counter and ordered two subs. Like most of his diet, not exactly heart-healthy but Brick justified his choice rationalizing that the benefits from olive oil would counteract the damage done by the salami and provolone. Magical thinking, but Angelo was living proof that something was working.

"Take it easy, Angelo."

Angelo raised a small cup that may have contained espresso. His hand shook slightly. "You do the same and don't be a stranger."

*　*　*

After lunch, Brick decided it was time to tackle the questions that he had postponed asking. Over the years, Brick had interviewed hundreds of witnesses and suspects. No matter how personal or intrusive the questions, it was possible to maintain professional disinterest when talking to a total stranger. This was different. Already before asking the first question, it felt awkward. He knew he had to maintain a neutral position so he didn't influence how Ron responded. For the moment, he decided to hold off mentioning Holly.

"Ron, still nothing from Marcus?"

"Not a word. I can't believe he hasn't talked to someone from the church who would have told him about the vigil. I mean, even if he's at some kind of religious retreat, it's not like he'd be locked up in an isolated monastery. It's his church, man, and he's the head honcho. I don't get it. When he's away he's got to stay in touch with his staff."

"One would think." Even though Brick agreed, it occurred to him that Ron was ignoring what seemed like an obvious possibility. Then again, Ron hadn't seen what Brick did in the church parking lot. "Ron, this didn't seem significant at the time, and maybe it isn't now, but on the day of the twins' christening, I was crossing the parking lot and saw Jasmine crying."

A muscle in Ron's jaw started to twitch. "Was she by herself?"

"No, she was with Marcus. It appeared he was comforting her. Like I said, I didn't think much about it, but then you said they had dated and now—"

Ron shook his head. "No, no way. Okay, Jasmine had reason to be pissed at me, but no, she wouldn't turn to Marcus . . ."

Brick waited but Ron didn't finish his thought. "I remember Jasmine seemed upset when she couldn't find the babies' pacifiers. Is that really what she was pissed about?"

Ron rolled his sandwich wrapper into a tight ball. "No." He pushed back from the table and got up. He stood in front of the window, his back toward Brick.

"Ron, I know this is hard, but you've got to consider every possibility. C'mon, talk to me."

Ron started pacing in front of the dining room window. "The night before the christening, we had an argu . . . well, actually, Jasmine had a meltdown."

"Over what?" Brick asked.

Ron sat back down. "A text."

Brick grabbed another Coke from the fridge. He had a feeling this was going to take a while. He poured half of the soda into his glass and offered the rest to Ron.

"It was late." Ron took a swig from the can of Coke. "I was asleep when my phone pinged. Jasmine was awake so she picked it up." Ron gripped the soda can and avoided eye contact with Brick. "You met Holly, right?"

Brick nodded although Ron probably didn't notice. "Yes, at the vigil."

"Okay, the text, well actually it was a photo, and it was from Holly . . . but it wasn't meant for me." Ron swallowed hard. "She meant to send it to her boyfriend." He shifted in his seat. "Holly is into Comic Con and this was a costume she was thinking of wearing. I don't know much about what goes on at those conventions, but her outfit was definitely X-rated." Ron took a deep breath, then another before continuing. "Jasmine went ballistic. I tried to calm her down, but she wasn't having it. She was yelling at me and woke up the twins. Jayla and Jamal started crying so she went to check on them. On the way out of the room, she threw the phone at me."

Brick waited as Ron finished the can of Coke and tossed it in the direction of the recycle bin, missing by several inches.

"I picked up my phone and texted Holly asking why she sent me the photo. At first, she didn't know what I was talking about. When she realized her mistake, she was so embarrassed and kept apologizing."

Brick thought about what Ron had said. He could easily relate to sending a text to the wrong person. He'd done it himself; more times than he liked to admit. But had this really been an innocent mistake? And what about last night's overheard phone call?

"That definitely explains why Jasmine was upset. What happened next?"

"Not much. She spent the rest of the night in the babies' room. Slept in the rocker. The next morning, she barely spoke to me until we got to the church. Then we tried to act like nothing was wrong. Except for the incident with the pacifiers, I thought we pulled it off. Guess I was wrong."

"Ron, you know the old saying about 'hell hath no fury like a woman scorned.' It's easy to understand why Jasmine was angry."

"But I tried to explain that Holly made a mistake. It wasn't a big deal until Jasmine turned it into one."

"C'mon, Ron. If the situation were reversed and Jasmine got a dick pic from a coworker by mistake, you'd be cool with that? Not the least bit suspicious?" Brick waited for a response, but Ron said nothing. "No doubt, Jasmine figured it was late-night sexting intended for you. Is it any wonder she felt betrayed?"

"I'm telling you, it wasn't my fault. I can't control how Jasmine responded and now from what you said, sounds like she didn't waste any time turning to Marcus for comfort."

Brick heard the disdain in Ron's voice but wasn't sure whether it was directed at Marcus or Jasmine. Most likely both.

"What more could I do? If only she would have listened to what I was saying, maybe none of this would have happened."

"Level with me, Ron. What's your relationship with Holly?"

"Coworkers . . . friends."

"Friends with benefits?"

Ron shook his head. "It's not like that."

"Is that a denial?" Again, Brick waited for a response but didn't receive one. "Ron, last night I came out of the bathroom around midnight. I overheard you talking on the phone to Holly." Brick deliberately paused and tried to read Ron's reaction, but his expression hadn't changed, revealing nothing. "Look, I don't know who called who and I don't care. I don't care if you were screwing Holly every hour on the half. But I want to make myself perfectly clear, I do care if you're lying to me."

Ron locked eyes with his former partner and mentor. "Fuck you, Brick!"

CHAPTER TWENTY-SIX

CONSIDERING THE NUMBER of times Brick had dropped an f-bomb, it would have been hypocritical to be offended by someone else's use of the expletive. Still, hearing the word directed at him, not by a surly suspect in handcuffs, but instead by Ron, caught him off guard, and it stung. There was no mistaking Ron's anger, but was it because Brick had questioned his integrity or was Ron being defensive when it came to Holly. Although Brick's encounter with her had been brief, there was something about it that had been off putting. There was more to be said, but not until cooler heads prevailed. Brick grabbed his jacket, sunglasses, and keys and left his apartment.

Boland's Mill was his original destination, but when Brick got there, he changed his mind before going inside. He wasn't in the mood to be sociable. He continued north on Connecticut Avenue until he reached the entrance to the National Zoo. It had been several months since he had watched the Sumatran cubs playing under the watchful eye of their mother. On the way to see them, he passed the Reptile House without stopping. When it came to snakes, he shared the sentiments of Indiana Jones.

Brick replayed in his mind what Ron had revealed. There was a time when he felt more confident in his ability to read people. All that changed with one case—the last case he worked as a homicide detective. Now, just like then, the stakes couldn't be higher. Lives were hanging in the balance.

Was Ron telling the truth? As a friend, Brick wanted to believe him. As a former detective, he wasn't sure. But he was sure that Ron's explanation to Jasmine didn't convince her that Holly had made an innocent mistake. Had she really turned to her current pastor and former boyfriend for comfort? Were the two of them and the twins hiding out somewhere? Or given Jasmine's fragile postpartum mental state, did her belief that Ron was cheating send her over the edge? To punish Ron and inflict as much pain as she possibly could, did she harm the twins and herself? That thought gave Brick a sinking feeling in the pit of his stomach.

"Excuse me!"

Brick didn't realize how distracted he was until he almost collided with a stroller, earning a dirty look from the woman pushing it.

"Oh, I'm so sorry." Brick stepped aside and let the woman and stroller pass. He glanced around to get his bearings and followed the arrow pointing in the direction of Tiger Hill.

The three cubs had doubled in size from when Brick last saw them. He recalled that afternoon back in April and ironically Ron had met him here with a confidential file he had surreptitiously copied. Most likely the file was gathering dust, but Ron could have gotten into serious trouble for what he did. Still, he didn't hesitate when Brick needed the favor. Two of the cubs wrestled while the other was stretched out soaking up the late afternoon sun. Brick took a couple of photos and texted them to Nora. With all that was happening, it seemed like the Chicago trip had been weeks ago when it really had only been a few days.

Brick checked the time. Watching the cubs had provided a respite from the confrontation with Ron and he had spent longer at the zoo then he had realized. The thought of a Guinness was appealing, but happy hour was already in full swing, and he still wasn't up for socializing. A noisy bar, even Boland's Mill, wasn't cutting it tonight.

As Brick approached his building, he wasn't sure what to expect. It was possible Ron had packed up and left. Before going inside, he checked the parking lot. Ron's car was where Brick had parked it last night. When he opened the apartment door, Brick heard the voice of Jim Vance, the longtime news anchor on WRC-TV, and the acrid smell of burned popcorn filled his nostrils. Ron was sitting on the sofa, remote in hand.

"I think I ruined your microwave." If ever a six-foot-four adult male looked like a guilty little boy, it was at this very moment. "It started making weird noises and then one big bang. I'm really sorry, man."

Brick started laughing. "No worries, it was here when I bought the place and that was over ten years ago. I was about to get a new one anyway."

Ron looked up, directly facing Brick. "That's not all I'm sorry about. I owe you an apology. I was way out of line."

"Frankly, Ron, I wasn't sure you'd still be here and I'm glad you are." Brick took a seat on the opposite end of the sofa. "I want to be supportive. Just as you were there for me, I want to be here for you. To see this through."

Ron nodded. "I appreciate it. God knows I wish Holly hadn't sent that photo to me, but what I told Jasmine and what I told you is the truth."

"Do you think it really was a mistake or did Holly actually want you to see that photo?"

"I guess it's possible that she did it on purpose, but I didn't consider that at the time. She talked about her boyfriend a lot. Enough that it sounded like they have a serious relationship. Plus, she's met Jasmine and even babysat for us. As far as I'm concerned, I just never thought she was hitting on me, but I have to say if I was single, I would have been thrilled if she was. We're friends, that's all."

What Brick heard from Ron rang true. As to the old "can men and women just be friends" debate, he would argue that it is possible, especially between coworkers. But with a woman as sexy as Holly it can be complicated. Any guy who wouldn't want more than friendship, even if they didn't act on it, probably wasn't interested in women to begin with.

"Is Holly's boyfriend a cop?" Brick asked.

"No, he manages an Outback Steak House in Fairfax County." Ron hesitated. "At Holly's suggestion, that's where I took Jasmine for our date night." He made a sound that was a cross between a laugh and a sigh. "What really sucks is that even though I didn't betray Jasmine, it doesn't matter. She believes I did. And for all I know, she turned to her old boyfriend. I mean, she's gone . . . he's gone. A coincidence? I don't think so."

Brick thought it was too early to draw a conclusion, but he also didn't believe in coincidences. Even though he had mentioned the pastor's absence to Lieutenant Hughes, he asked if Ron had as well.

Ron nodded. "She's having one of the detectives from Missing Persons look into locating him. And what do I get to do . . . sit on my ass and wait. It's killing me, Brick." Ron stood up and stretched. "By the way, Jasmine wasn't the lead story tonight. I saw on the news that a Senate staffer was found strangled."

"Where?"

"Her Capitol Hill apartment, a couple of blocks from Union Station."

"Any arrests?"

"No. Looks like Travis Allen is working the case. When they showed the victim's building, I caught a glimpse of him standing outside talking to one of the Mobile Crime guys."

Just the mention of Travis Allen's name brought back memories of the ass-kissing relationship Allen had with Blancato over the years. Still, Brick would be the first to acknowledge Allen was a competent detective. For a moment, he missed the feeling of new-case adrenaline most detectives experienced as a photo of a beautiful dark-haired young woman filled the TV screen. She appeared to be in her mid-to-late twenties. Immediately, Brick thought of Chandra Levy. Would this case turn into a full-blown political scandal? Time would tell, but Brick would bet the rent that Stella Owen was already salivating at the prospect.

CHAPTER TWENTY-SEVEN

"I'M GOING TO Starbucks. Do you want anything?"

It was just after seven and Brick was surprised to see Ron was up and dressed. "No thanks, I've already had breakfast."

Brick heard the door close as he put his cereal bowl in the dishwasher. It was the first time Ron had left the apartment by himself. Maybe he was just tired of instant coffee, but as the days dragged on with no major developments, he had seen changes in Ron's demeanor. It was obvious he was on an ever-changing emotional roller coaster and at the moment, he seemed motivated by anger. Even though it was unknown if Jasmine had run off with Marcus, it had to be considered as a very real possibility. Had one of them parked her car at BWI, splashed fake blood on the infant car seat, and then dumped it in the Inner Harbor? Thinking about that was enough to make anyone angry. And in some ways, Brick thought it was better for Ron to be angry than paralyzed by fear and grief.

About twenty minutes after he left, Ron was back. "Wait 'til you hear this, partner." Brick noticed that Ron seemed wired and unless he had chugged the contents of his grande cup, caffeine probably wasn't the reason. "Got a call from Jasmine's sister. Seems the accountant at the church discovered money missing from two different accounts."

"Did she say how much?" Brick asked.

"Just that it was a lot." Ron lifted the top off his cup and took a sip. "Damn, how convenient is that?"

Brick knew it wasn't a question needing an answer.

Ron picked up his phone and appeared to text a message. When he finished, he reached for his cup. "I don't know if Jasmine ran off with Marcus. If that's what she did and that's what she wants, I'll survive. But they're not getting my kids . . . no way, no how." Ron picked up his coffee, spilling some of the still steaming liquid on his hand. He didn't seem to notice as he headed in the direction of the den. Brick heard the door slam.

Brick fixed a second cup of tea, sat down at the table, and thought about Ron's reaction to what he had learned from Jasmine's sister. He could have cautioned Ron about getting ahead of himself, but that would have been counterproductive. Given what he knew as far as missing church funds, an out-of-town incommunicado minister, and the disappearance of his former girlfriend and her kids, coming up with a scenario where all were linked was reasonable. Besides, it allowed Ron to have hope that Jasmine and the twins were alive. Brick didn't see any harm in that even though he considered it as only one possibility and not necessarily the most likely. Jasmine's photo and story had been local and national news. Unless she and Marcus had a well-organized plan to disappear, it's a safe bet they would have been spotted somewhere. A couple with infant twins checking into a hotel makes an impression and draws attention in a restaurant. Still, Brick would admit, he'd been wrong before. Maybe it would play out that Jasmine, feeling betrayed, turned to Marcus and maybe he was more than willing to provide the comfort she sought. As much as Brick hoped Ron and Jasmine would reconcile, if that didn't happen, knowing she and the twins were safe would be poignant consolation.

From this horrendous experience, Brick had a renewed appreciation for the suffering of the families and friends of victims waiting for news of their missing loved ones. He had no intention of mentioning what he was thinking to Ron, but in the back of his mind was a nagging thought—what if they never find out what happened to Jasmine and the twins. Even, God forbid, if the outcome was bad, knowing would be preferable to living in limbo. A place Brick knew all too well. He thought about his father, Patrick Kavanagh, who he only knew through old photographs and stories from his mother when she was still alive. Two months after Brick was born, she got the devastating news that her husband, a Green Beret Army captain, was missing-in-action in Vietnam. All these years later, his status had remained unchanged. As he had done many, many times, Brick shook off the emptiness he felt. He reached for the box of Henry Yang's possessions.

Brick had gone through most of the items, but there were a few he hadn't examined. He reached for a black-and-white marbled composition notebook. When he picked it up, a couple of photographs fell out. The first one Brick saw tugged at his heartstrings. A much younger Henry was standing next to a petite, smiling Asian woman with her arm around his shoulder. In the background Brick recognized the Baseball Hall of Fame in Cooperstown from when he had been there as a kid. Another photo showed Henry in a graduation cap and gown squinting in the bright sunshine and holding his high school diploma. Standing next to him was the woman from the other picture. She looked painfully thin in a flower print dress and appeared to be wearing a wig, but her smile was identical. The last photo showed Henry wearing a Lincoln U. sweatshirt while handing out a bag of food. A banner for So Others Might Eat, a D.C. nonprofit providing services to the poor and homeless, hung in the background. Henry was clean shaven and sporting a crew cut. For a guy aspiring to a career as an FBI agent, he was interview ready. Brick opened the notebook. He flipped through several pages of entries recording dates, distances run, and times per mile, along with a countdown of days to the Marine Marathon. It appeared Henry was following a strict training schedule.

For Brick, the image of Henry Yang was no longer limited to a set of autopsy photos. He placed the pictures back inside the notebook and was about to put it back in the box when he spotted a thumb drive partially hidden under an empty file folder. Brick booted up his computer and inserted the storage device into the USB port. He double-clicked on the label listed. Five files with names that didn't give a clue as to their contents immediately piqued Brick's curiosity. He clicked on the first file listed, hoping it would be readable. It was. A spreadsheet with alphanumeric codes and dates displayed. The other files were similar. Brick figured this data had significance for Henry but whatever that may be wasn't obvious. He printed copies he intended to share with Grace Alexander.

After taking a break to stretch and work out the kinks in his shoulders, Brick looked for the professor's business card. He dialed her number and on the third ring, a receptionist answered. Brick identified himself and asked to speak to the professor.

"One moment, please." The receptionist put Brick on hold. He figured he had made it through two of Vivaldi's *Four Seasons* before the receptionist came back on the line.

"Ms. Alexander is no longer affiliated with the University."

CHAPTER TWENTY-EIGHT

FOR A MOMENT, Brick stared at his phone as if it would somehow provide an explanation for what he had just been told. "Son of a bitch."

"Are you talking to yourself or talking to me?" Ron asked.

"What?" Brick set the phone aside and looked up. "No, I didn't even realize you were standing there." He went on to tell Ron what he had just found out. "Two weeks ago, she's offering me a job and now it's, 'Ms. Alexander is no longer affiliated with the University.' Their words, not mine. It doesn't make sense."

Ron pulled out a chair and plopped down across from Brick. "Man, if you ask me, nothing makes sense anymore."

"I can't argue with that." Brick double-checked the business card Grace Alexander had given him. The only phone number listed was the one he had just called. And the .edu email address was obviously her professional account at the university. Brick regretted having turned off the computer after he finished printing the spreadsheets. He tapped his fingers on the table while he waited for his computer to boot up again.

"That took a while," Ron said. "How old is your computer?"

"I don't know, six or seven years. Maybe older."

"When you go to Best Buy to check out microwaves, you might want to check out computers, too . . . just sayin'."

Brick shrugged. "It's slow, but it works."

"So did the microwave until I blew it up." Ron still looked guilty and didn't crack a smile, but Brick did.

"Good point. I'll check it out."

Brick entered the professor's name to start a Google search. Several images of women sharing the same name appeared. None of them looked like the Grace Alexander he was seeking. He added "Washington, D.C." to the search criteria and tried again. A bunch of website addresses popped up. He scrolled through a couple before clicking on the first one listing a phone number and address. Although there was no photo, Brick knew he had hit on who he was looking for. The profile information listed her place of employment as Lincoln University. Only one way to find out if the phone number was current. He picked up his cell phone and tapped the number listed. After four rings, he was expecting to hear a voicemail recording. Instead, he heard a tentative "hello." The voice didn't sound familiar.

"Grace Alexander?"

"Yes."

"It's Brick Kavanagh." He waited for a response but didn't get one. "I called your office this morning and was surprised to hear you're no longer—"

"You're surprised—I'm shocked." Brick sensed she had started to cry. "I can't believe they're accusing me of plagiarism, it's total bullshit. I never—"

He waited a minute to give her time to compose herself. "Are you okay?"

Brick heard her sniffle before she responded. "No."

"I don't mean to pry, but is there someone . . ."

"No and I don't mean to sound like a drama queen." Another sniffle. "I'll be okay."

The flat affect in her voice didn't sound convincing and Brick was concerned about her. "Grace, I know what it's like to suddenly be unemployed. Talking can help. How about if you join me for lunch, my treat."

"Thanks for asking, but I . . . I don't think so."

"Help me out. I'm trying to pay it forward." That wasn't the only reason. He was also trying to move forward with the Yang investigation and wanted to ask her about the spreadsheets. Brick heard a loud sigh before she responded.

"Well, since you put it that way." Another sigh. "Give me an hour."

"Boland's at noon?"

"Okay."

Brick set his phone down and turned the computer off.

"Achieve your goal?" Ron asked.

"Sort of. Whether she'll be interested in the spreadsheets remains to be seen. From the way she sounded, she may be too distracted right now by her own situation. At least I know how to get in touch with her."

"Technology, man."

"Yeah, can't tell you how thrilled I am to think how easy it is for some mope I arrested to track me down." Brick wrote Grace Alexander's phone number on the back of her card and placed it in his wallet.

"Doesn't always work," Ron said. "I've been searching for Jasmine's therapist and other than her website, haven't found a thing. Thought I hit on something, but it turned out it wasn't her."

"Well, that's reassuring. I'll sleep a little better knowing I might not be one click away from some asshole packing heat showing up on my doorstep."

* * *

Brick took a seat at the bar and ordered a Guinness while he waited for Grace Alexander.

"There you go." Eamonn set the pint in front of Brick. "Any news on the disappearance?"

Brick shook his head as he picked up his glass. It was the easiest way to evade the question. It hadn't been revealed publicly that the blood on the infant car seat was fake, and even though Brick trusted Eamonn as a confidant, he couldn't share this latest development.

"It's hard to believe, Eamonn, a couple of weeks ago I was having a pint at a pub in Galway. After all that had happened earlier in the year, it was behind me. Mentally, I was ready to come home and figure out the next chapter in my life story." Brick took a drink. "I never thought it would be this."

"Ahh, it's good we don't know the future."

There was something in the way Eamonn spoke those words that again gave Brick pause. For as long as he'd known Eamonn, he knew little about his life before he came to Washington and opened his namesake pub. In all probability, in Eamonn's seventy-plus years he'd had to deal with plenty of things he never anticipated. And his point was well taken.

Eamonn started to wipe down a section of the bar. "The waiting—that's got to be the worst." He stopped what he was doing and made eye contact with Brick. "Let's hope and pray that's the worst." He wadded up the bar rag and set it aside. "Need anything else before I head to the kitchen?"

"I'm good." Brick glanced at his watch. A few minutes past noon. Had the professor changed her mind? It wouldn't be the first time he had been stood up, but at least this wasn't a date. Even though he tried not to take those times personally, he usually did. Although, like most guys, he'd never admit it. Another ten minutes passed. He set down his half-empty glass before turning and glancing out the window fronting on Connecticut Avenue.

Turns out he wouldn't be having lunch alone after all.

"Sorry to keep you waiting." Grace Alexander pulled out the barstool next to Brick and sat down. "While I was emptying my trash, I locked myself out of my apartment. Then I had to wait for the office manager who was off somewhere in the building. Finally got back in and I would have texted, but I realized my cell phone needed to be charged and when I picked up the charger, it fell apart." She managed a smile. "I feel like I have reverse Midas touch."

"Everything you touch turns to . . . something other than gold?"

"Sounds like you know the condition."

"Absolutely." Brick picked up his glass. "Something to drink?"

"Think I'd better pass. I had a week's worth of wine last night so no more for a couple of days."

"I understand." Brick handed her a menu. "Let's order then move to that table." Brick pointed to one adjacent to the fireplace, which would provide the privacy he figured the professor would prefer.

Grace removed her jean jacket and draped it over the back of her chair. "Thank you for suggesting lunch. Otherwise, I'd probably stay in my pajamas all day and binge-watch episodes of *Downton Abbey* that I've already seen." She stirred a packet of sugar into her glass of iced tea. "I know that sounds like a cliché, but like a lot of women it's the indulgence I've resorted to when dealing with stress."

"I don't think it's a gender thing, except for the *Downton Abbey* part. I'll admit to watching *Field of Dreams* on a continuous loop without moving from the sofa."

Grace smiled sheepishly. "Good to know." She unwrapped a straw and stuck it in the glass. "Walking over here I had an epiphany. The pity party has lasted long enough. I can't waste another minute feeling sorry for myself. I have to find out who filed these false allegations and why they would do it."

"The allegations being plagiarism?"

"Right, and it's infuriating that my accuser can remain anonymous." Grace added another packet of sugar to her drink and took a sip. "Whoa, that's really sweet. Guess I doubled up on sugar."

Brick laughed. "You did. I can get you a new one."

"Thanks, it's fine as long as I don't start speaking with a Southern drawl and get mistaken for being Stella Owen." She set the glass down. "I'm sure you've heard the expression 'publish or perish.' Well, I've published several papers, and everything is one hundred percent my original work."

"And you can prove that?" Brick asked.

"I don't have a choice; I have to prove it. Bad enough this has derailed my tenure track, but I will not let it ruin my reputation. An accusation like this could follow me for the rest of my career." She took a deep breath. "Victim is not a role I play well."

"Good for you. That's the right attitude," Brick said. "Can you think of anyone who would want to sabotage your career?"

"No, that's what I find so strange. I've always gotten along with everyone in the department. And my boss was supportive of the cold case project I proposed. According to him, it showed 'thinking outside the box.'" She used her fingers to make air quotes around the overused expression. "That's why I was so surprised when the funding was denied."

"Was that before or after I found out about the diplomatic immunity aspect?" Brick asked.

Grace thought for a moment. "It was after because once we knew the Yang case wasn't appropriate, I mentioned we needed to find one that was. I explained that shouldn't be a problem based on what Lieutenant Hughes had said."

"You're sure?"

"Yes. Why is that important?"

"I'm not sure it is, but soon afterward, you were accused of plagiarism and forced to resign or be fired."

"Right." Grace took a sip of iced tea. "Are you implying there's a connection?"

"Not implying. It's too soon for that, but it's something to consider."

"Really?" Grace seemed skeptical. "It's probably just a coincidence."

Brick resisted mentioning he didn't believe in coincidence. That could be a later discussion. "Think about it, Grace. From what you said, jobwise everything was fine. You suggested looking into the unsolved hit-and-run death of a student and at first, it was well received. Then you mention the reason why the case isn't appropriate. Suddenly, you're dismissed on false allegations."

"Well, in case there is a connection, seems like I should spend some of my time looking into this stuff even though it's not my project and never really was."

"Consider all possibilities. That's what I would have told the grad students," Brick said.

Grace nodded. "Guess I wasn't thinking 'outside the box.'" The air quotes again. This time followed by a laugh.

"It's hard to think objectively when you're too close to a situation. It's my job to do that." Brick cleared his throat. "Or, I should say, it was my job."

"You miss being a cop, don't you?"

"I miss being a detective."

CHAPTER TWENTY-NINE

I MISS BEING a detective. It was the first time he had actually said the words aloud and he had surprised himself when the words came out of his mouth. As Brick headed home, his admission to Grace played over in his head like the repetitive lyrics of an annoying song. For now, working on the Yang case and supporting Ron took up most of his waking hours. But neither was likely to last indefinitely. Sooner or later, he would have to figure out what to do to fill the void created when he impulsively walked away from the job. Ten years spent investigating homicides would be a tough act to follow.

Brick stopped to check his mail for the first time in a couple of days. The usual monthly bills—Pepco, Comcast, Mastercard, and one thing he wasn't expecting. He was tempted to leave that envelope in the mailbox. When he entered his apartment and saw Ron seated at the table, he waved it in his direction. "500 Indiana Avenue."

"Pretty good idea what that is," Ron said.

Brick tore open the envelope and unfolded the paper inside. "Jury duty."

"When?" Ron asked.

"End of the month." Brick shrugged. "Odds are I won't make it through voir dire."

"Prosecutors would be glad to have you."

"And the defense will treat me like I have bubonic plague. Guess I'll catch up on reading since I'll end up spending my days in the jury lounge."

"Got to do your civic duty, man."

"After twenty years on the job, I think my dues are paid . . . in full."

Brick picked up the box containing Henry Yang's stuff and placed it on a chair. Rather than make a list of the items he planned to leave with Grace, he took a photo of each with his phone. He had already made duplicate copies of the spreadsheets that were on the thumb drive. There was one more thing Brick needed, the notebook where he recorded a few things Yang's roommate had shared with him. He slipped it into his pocket.

"I need to drop this stuff off to Grace. Can I borrow your car?"

"Sure. The keys are on the table in the hall."

The address of Grace's apartment didn't ring a bell with Brick, but as soon as he turned onto Adams Mill Road, he recognized the circa 1940s building. He had been here years before investigating a double murder and suicide that shocked homeowners on this upscale residential street. As so often happened, long after the yellow crime scene tape had been removed, in his mind's eye, Brick could still see it cordoning off the designated area. He stepped up to the door, entered the code he had been given on the keypad, and waited for Grace to respond.

Although the building exterior retained its pre–World War II architecture, it appeared the interior had been rehabbed. Even so, he wasn't expecting what he saw when he stepped inside Grace's unit. Highly polished hardwood floors, an exposed brick wall, and plenty of afternoon sunlight from large windows facing west. Brick set the box next to a golden oak and brass coat tree. As he glanced around the spacious living room, his eyes were drawn to a wall covered with floor-to-ceiling bookcases. A rolling ladder provided access to the books on the upper shelves. The opposite wall displayed posters of vintage *Vogue* magazine covers. Mid-century modern furniture blended with a few antique pieces. Not that he was a subscriber, but Brick had seen enough issues to know that Grace's apartment was *Architectural Digest* worthy.

"I have to say, I've been in a lot of apartments all over this city and this may be the nicest."

"Thanks." Grace smiled broadly. "In the divorce settlement, I got the house in Potomac. I wasted no time selling it and moving here."

In that one sentence, she had revealed a lot but left Brick wondering if there were other houses besides the one in a very affluent suburb. At any rate, the look of satisfaction on Grace's face gave the impression she had no regrets about her decision. She bent down and started checking out the contents of the box.

"This should provide a distraction for me, at least for a while."

Brick nodded. "I also found a thumb drive and printed the files I retrieved. Copies are in the manila envelope. The spreadsheets didn't provide anything that made sense to me, but maybe you'll find something significant."

"Let's hope because there's not much here. I was expecting more."

"Actually, we're lucky to have what we have. If Henry hadn't shoved this back in the closet behind the vacuum cleaner and if his former roommate wasn't moving and found it, we probably wouldn't have anything at all. According to Drew Edwards, a professor from the University took care of Yang's other belongings."

"An unenviable task, but someone always has to do it. So sad that Henry didn't have any next of kin."

Brick opened his notebook and flipped to the page where he had written a few notes. "Drew recalled the professor's name was Baez."

"Alphonso Baez?" Grace sounded skeptical.

"He didn't remember the first name."

Grace stood up and faced Brick. "That's really interesting. As far as I know, the only Baez at Lincoln U. is Alphonso Baez. He isn't a professor, he's the University's Chief Financial Officer."

* * *

As Brick drove to the local Giant, he thought about Grace's reaction to learning Baez had taken care of Henry's possessions. After she had a chance to review the spreadsheets, he'd set up an appointment to speak with Baez. More than that, however, Brick found himself thinking about Grace. He was blown away by her apartment. But he was really impressed that her down-to-earth demeanor when they had lunch didn't give off the pretentious vibes so prevalent in a town where image is everything.

Brick realized he needed cash before heading to the grocery store. He stopped at the Chase Bank and observed the activity in the lobby before entering. Satisfied all was well, he stepped inside. At the ATM, he checked his account balances, drew out cash, and slipped the crisp, new twenties into his wallet.

Next stop, the Giant, where Brick grabbed a basket and walked past the fresh produce to the cereal aisle. A box of Cheerios, a quart of milk, and a six-pack of Heineken filled the basket. With his free hand, he picked up a package of store brand dishwasher pods. A quick check of his phone. Nothing from Ron so he headed to the express ten items or fewer checkout line where he stood behind an attractive, well-dressed woman who looked to be in her early thirties. As she placed her fifteenth item on the conveyer belt, she turned and glared at Brick.

"I see you watching me and I know what you're doing." She added a jar of olives to the items on the belt. "You're counting, aren't you." Brick didn't respond, thinking sometimes it's best not to engage. "I work at the Senate and I don't have time to stand around waiting in line." Her voice had raised a couple of decibels. "If you don't like it, that's your problem." She paid with a platinum American Express card, picked up her bag of groceries, and turned in Brick's direction. "Screw you, asshole!"

As Brick set his four items on the conveyer belt and stood opposite the cashier, he thought about this incident as proof of the balance in the universe or at least in D.C. For every Grace Alexander–type, there's someone with an inflated sense of self-importance. The cashier handed Brick change from his two twenties. "Thanks. Sounds like someone forgot to take her meds."

"D.C. personality disorder." The cashier laughed. "I see it all the time. Too bad it's so contagious."

Brick started the car and backed out of his parking space. Maybe the Giant incident would provide Ron with a much-needed moment of comic relief.

*   *   *

Any thoughts of regaling Ron faded when Brick called out to him and didn't get a response. Brick set the bag of groceries on the hall table and knocked on the door to the den. Still no response. Brick pushed the door open and saw Ron rigidly sitting on the unmade sofa bed staring into space as if in a catatonic state.

"Ron . . . Ron, what's going on?"

Slowly, Ron turned and looked at Brick. "I got a call from Lieutenant Hughes."

Brick braced himself for what he might hear next.

"They've tracked down Marcus." Ron tossed his cell phone aside like a hot potato. He's in Vegas . . . alone. Or, if not alone, not with Jasmine."

From Brick's perspective, the news could have been worse, but he understood why Ron found it disturbing. "How can they be sure?"

"One of the detectives from Missing Persons searched passenger lists and found his name on a flight from Reagan. Turns out it was a Vegas flight and hotel deal that led to Mandalay Bay. Lieutenant Hughes has a contact in the Vegas PD who interviewed him. Said Marcus was shocked to hear about Jasmine." Ron stood up. "Do you have any Tylenol?"

"In the kitchen, the cabinet to the right of the sink."

While Brick put the milk and beer in the fridge, Ron helped himself to two caplets and washed them down with a glass of water.

"The detective also talked to the hotel staff, and they confirmed Marcus checked in by himself. I'm sure they would have remembered a couple checking in with six-month-old twins. It's ironic, isn't it?"

"What do you mean, Ron?"

"I should be relieved Jasmine didn't run off with her old boyfriend, but instead it's like a gut punch. I'm losing hope, man. Hope that I'll ever see them again. The only thing that makes sense now is that she's harmed our kids and herself."

Brick didn't agree. There were other possibilities. Jasmine may not have harmed herself and the twins, but someone else may have. And even though it seemed her pastor could be ruled out, perhaps Jasmine was involved with someone else. With all the online ways to meet, companionship is just a click away for anyone so inclined. Although suggesting these scenarios to Ron, especially now, would only pour salt into an open wound.

"Ron, did Jasmine keep a journal?"

"If she did, she never mentioned it."

"Given her first pregnancy, maybe she wanted to remember how she was feeling. You know, emotions, thoughts, the kind of stuff women write about." Brick was actually thinking a journal could reveal more intimate details but didn't see a need to mention that.

"Maybe, I don't know." Ron didn't sound convinced.

Brick reached in his jacket pocket, retrieved Ron's car keys, and set them on the kitchen counter.

"If she did keep a journal, it might still be at the house." Ron sighed loudly. "Only one way to find out." He picked up the keys and tapped them against his palm. "I'm not in any shape to drive."

"No problem, give me the keys." Brick stuck out his hand. "If we leave now, we should be able to avoid rush hour."

CHAPTER THIRTY

AVOIDING RUSH HOUR turned out to be wishful thinking on Brick's part. Traffic on Connecticut Avenue was bumper-to-bumper thanks to a fender bender involving a Lincoln Town car with diplomatic plates and a Metrobus near the Van Ness Station. The fifteen-minute trip took at least twice that, and an awkward silence made it seem longer. Finally, Brick turned onto Ron's street and parked in a space directly across from the house.

"What the hell!"

It was the first time Ron had spoken since he had gotten in the car. Initially, Brick thought he was talking to someone on his cell phone but when he looked over at Ron, he realized the phone wasn't in his hand. It was then that he saw a woman rush up the steps of Ron's house.

"Who's that?" As soon as the words were out of Brick's mouth, he realized it was a question Ron was most likely incapable of answering. Unless there's something identifying, like a distinctive way of walking, recognizing someone from behind is difficult. From a distance, almost impossible.

"I have no frigging clue."

Friend, neighbor, reporter, Jehovah Witness—possibilities were running through Brick's head as the woman approached the door. Ron lowered his window to get a better view.

"Holy shit!" Ron unfastened his seat belt and opened his car door.

"Wait!" Brick was equally taken aback as he watched the woman unlock the door and step inside.

"I can't just sit here, man. A total stranger walked into my house like she owns the place. I gotta find out who she is and what the fuck she's doing."

Brick reached out and grabbed Ron's arm before he had a chance to get out of the car. "There's no telling what you might walk in on. There could be someone else already inside. You could step into some kind of trap. We need to sit tight."

"I can't do that, man. I feel like I'm going to jump out of my skin."

Given that Ron was younger, bigger, and stronger, if he decided to bolt, Brick knew he wouldn't be able to restrain him. "Listen to me, Ron. We'll give her ten minutes. If she's not out by then, we'll call 911." Brick checked his watch before training his eyes on the front door. He was relieved Ron had closed his door and, at least for now, was staying in the car.

"Check the app on your phone. See if you recognize her."

"Damn, I forgot about that." Ron looked down at his cell phone. "Shit, it's like she knew to keep her head down."

"Have you or Jasmine given anyone keys to the house?"

"No, no way I would and I'm sure Jasmine wouldn't. I mean, if she was going to give anyone a key, it would be her sister, and I know Tanisha doesn't have one." Ron glanced at his left wrist. "Forgot my watch. How long has it been?"

"Four minutes."

"Jesus, this is killing me." Ron was rocking back and forth in his seat.

"I hear you, but you need to be ready for when she comes out. You have a better angle to get a picture of her. And we need to decide what we're going to do."

"I know what I'm going to do—confront her. Whoever she is, she'd better have a damn good reason or I'm arresting her ass for trespassing. Even though I'm on admin leave, I'm still a cop." Ron opened the central console and removed a pair of handcuffs. "I'm ready."

It didn't surprise Brick that Ron had a pair of handcuffs. Lots of cops had an extra pair they kept in their car. Others, no doubt, in nightstands depending on their intended use. Brick understood Ron's inclination to confront the woman, but he wasn't convinced it was the best strategy.

"Following her may tell us more than confronting her right here. If she's on foot, she's not going to outrun you, but I'm guessing one of these cars belongs to her. Call in the plate and we'll have a good starting point."

"That's going to take patience I'm not sure I have."

Brick understood Ron's anguish, but he was unwavering in his conviction that following the woman made the most sense. He leaned forward and to the right, trying to get a better vantage point. "I think she just walked past the window. Too bad you don't have binoculars in that console."

"Yeah, well if I had—"

Brick didn't wait for Ron to finish. "The door's opening. She's coming out."

He was too far away to see her face but watched as the woman looked from side to side as if to see if anyone was watching her before she closed the door. She quickly turned around and briefly stood in front of the door before heading down the stairs. Brick recalled Ron had locked the door from the outside. Presumably, that's what she had been doing.

"Go time." Ron sounded determined as he slouched down and leaned as far out the open car window as he could without being seen. He held up his phone and started snapping photos as the woman approached a black, late model Honda Civic.

"Do you think she saw me?" Ron asked.

"No, she was looking straight ahead, not this way."

Brick fastened his seat belt and Ron did the same. He watched as the Civic pulled away from the curb and waited for the woman to turn the corner before he started following. Being on a residential street made it easy to keep the target in view, but also easy to be spotted. As he followed the Civic through the neighborhood, he heard Ron reciting the license plate number into his phone. Brick slowed as he saw the car approach a stop sign. The turn signal on the left tail light began to blink.

It had been a long time since Brick had tailed a car. Easy so far, but he knew that was about to change. A left turn meant the target was heading toward New York Avenue. Staying far enough behind the target to avoid being made, yet keeping it in sight on a busy road would be a challenge. After discouraging Ron from confronting the woman, Brick knew he owed it to him to follow her successfully to her destination, wherever that may take them. Another car, a silver Toyota, merged to the right and pulled in behind the target providing the separation Brick had hoped for. Up ahead, he saw the traffic light change from green to yellow. If she didn't stop, losing her was almost a given. Brick held his breath as the target approached the intersection. The car slowed and stopped just as the light turned red.

"That was too close for comfort." Brick's cheeks puffed up as he blew out his breath. He glanced over at Ron anticipating a response, but he seemed unaware that Brick had said anything.

Ron's fingers tightly gripped the cell phone he held to his ear. "Are you sure?" He repeated the license number. "Roger." He lowered the phone and turned toward Brick. "I don't believe what I just heard. The car is registered to a Lynn Reznick."

The name meant nothing to Brick. "Who's she?"

"Jasmine's therapist."

CHAPTER THIRTY-ONE

"MAN, WHAT THE hell is going on? Why would Jasmine's therapist have a key to my house . . . our house? Jasmine wouldn't even give one to her mother or sister."

Brick also wondered what was happening. "Just to be clear, we only know who the car is registered to. Most likely she's the one driving, but we can't be certain. Whoever she is, entering the house during daylight hours takes balls." It occurred to Brick that if Jasmine had been abducted, her captor or captors would most likely have access to her address and house keys. Then again, if she left of her own volition, she may have created a support system and freely given someone her key.

"Yeah, right." Ron shifted and adjusted his seat belt. "I've never met her therapist, so I don't know if that's her or not. What I do know is that whoever that woman is, she had no business being in my house. She's going to answer to me because whatever it takes, I'm getting to the bottom of this." Ron hit his hand against the dashboard. "Whatever it takes." He leaned forward and positioned the visor to block the sun. "Looks like she's merging onto Route 50."

"Guess we're heading toward Baltimore." There was no avoiding heavier traffic now, but it was possible it could work to their advantage. Brick hoped so. The slow crawl made surveillance easier but seeing the gas tank indicator arrow hovering between a quarter tank and "E" made him nervous. There was nothing he could do about it so, for now, he tried to ignore it and didn't mention it to Ron. Adding to his anxiety level that already appeared off the charts could only make the situation worse.

This stretch of highway was testing Brick's patience. A broken-down van forced vehicles to maneuver around it. Brick tried to keep only one car between him and the target, but a driver aggressively attempted to cut in front of him. With a wave, Brick signaled for the driver to go ahead. A two-car separation was preferable to provoking a road rage incident. Once past the bottleneck, the car directly ahead changed lanes and Brick closed the gap. At the interchange, the target merged onto the Baltimore-Washington Parkway and Brick followed. A quick glance at the gas gauge showed the arrow edging closer to "E." Were it not for the circumstances, Brick could have enjoyed driving the four-lane road with its wide, tree-filled median displaying the first hints of fall colors. Instead, he was laser focused on the target as they approached the junction for MD175. At the last possible moment, the target signaled and exited onto Jessup Road. Brick did the same.

He was in unfamiliar territory now on a two-lane undivided road but seeing a sign for Patuxent Institution gave him some perspective. Years ago, he had interviewed an inmate at the maximum-security correctional facility. Maintaining surveillance on this road without being observed would present new challenges. Brick and Ron were now directly behind the target. After traveling about a mile, the target turned into the parking lot of a 7-Eleven. Brick continued driving until he reached a nearby Super 8 Motel. He pulled into a parking space where he could still keep an eye on the target. He suspected she wouldn't be in the 7-Eleven very long, but even a brief break provided a respite from the stress of tailing the target. With both hands, Brick kneaded the tight muscles in his neck. A couple of shoulder rolls followed.

"Is this area familiar to you?" Brick asked Ron.

"No. I don't ever remember being on this road. And can't think of any reason why I would want to. This feels like the middle . . . hey, that's the target."

Brick looked past Ron and saw the woman leaving 7-Eleven carrying two plastic bags. He started the car as he watched her back out of her parking space.

"Hate to tell you this, Ron. We're running on fumes. If she gets back on the Parkway, we're screwed."

The target passed the Super 8, and Brick followed, keeping a three car–length distance. After traveling a mile or so, the target turned right onto a dirt road. A "No Outlet" sign provided the break Brick knew they desperately needed. He drove past where she had turned and pulled off onto the shoulder of the road. Even before he stopped the car, Ron had unfastened his seat belt.

"Ready?" Ron asked.

"Hold on. In fifteen or twenty minutes, it's going to be dark. That gives us an advantage."

"What the fuck, man. All we do is wait."

"I know, Ron, I know. But we've come this far, let's not blow it now. We still don't know exactly what we're dealing with."

These past few days, Brick had seen reactions and emotions from Ron that had never surfaced during the year they were partners. Everything from fear to frustration to anger and sometimes a combination. Brick tried to be the anchor, making decisions based on experience rather than on emotion. If only he had known that a short drive to Ron's house would morph into their current situation, he would have been prepared with a full tank of gas, binoculars, and a flashlight. Instead, the only thing he had to rely on was his cell phone and when he checked, no signal. Considering where they were, he wasn't surprised, but his stress level went up a couple of notches. Deserted country roads unnerved him in a way that city streets, no matter the neighborhood, never did. The sky had darkened, and Brick slipped the car keys into his pocket.

"It's time . . . let's go."

As they set out on foot, keeping up with a former track star, ten years his junior, was a challenge for Brick. He stepped up his pace and figured they had walked about half a mile. They stopped for a minute and in the distance saw three small bungalow-style houses. Two were dark but the lights were on in the one set back the farthest from the road. The Honda Civic was parked in the driveway on the left side of the house.

"Guess this is it," Ron said.

"Let me check it out. With what I'm wearing, I'm harder to spot." It wasn't as if Brick were dressed in camo but his dark shirt and jeans weren't as conspicuous as Ron's light-colored tee shirt and pants. And truth be told, Brick was considering factors besides which clothes would provide the best cover. He was concerned Ron's emotional state could impair his judgment and jeopardize their position.

"I think—"

"You need to trust me on this." Brick didn't wait for Ron to respond; he set off in the direction of the bungalow. Several trees and bushes provided coverage, but Brick feared poison ivy was concealed among the weeds. He'd know in a day or two if his fears were well founded, but for now he figured that might be the least of his concerns. His heart pounded in his chest as he approached the dusty driveway. He bent down and hid behind the car. Slowly, he made his way to the side of the house and crouched beneath a window. He raised up enough to peer inside. In the dim light, he saw a sparsely furnished bedroom. He continued around the corner and heard what sounded like a baby crying. He stopped, held his breath, and listened. Nothing.

Brick's legs were cramping as he edged along the side of the house toward the front door. He ignored the pain and pushed forward. Just before he passed another window, a light flicked on. He stayed where he was for a couple of minutes. Crouched under the window, he listened closely and heard a faint beep that sounded like it came from a microwave. Slowly, he raised up, keeping his body to the side of the window, and glanced inside. Since the sun had set, the temperature had dropped several degrees, but it was what he saw through the window that sent a chill down his spine.

CHAPTER THIRTY-TWO

WITH EVEN MORE adrenaline coursing through his veins, Brick made his way back around the house and across the driveway. He rushed back to where Ron was waiting.

"What . . . what's going on?"

"I don't know . . ." Brick was winded from running and needed to catch his breath. "I saw Jasmine. She was sitting at the kitchen table."

"Are you sure?" Panic had raised Ron's voice to a pitch Brick had never heard before.

"Yes."

"I . . . I have to get to her."

Brick grabbed Ron's arm. "Listen to me. We don't know if she's here by choice or against her will, but something very strange is going on in that house." Brick wasn't sure how to describe Jasmine's unkempt condition. "From what I could see, her hand was shaking as she attempted to raise a coffee mug to her mouth."

"All the more reason I need to get to her."

"You're right, but we can't do this alone."

"C'mon, there's two of us."

"Let's not waste time arguing. It's too fucking dangerous because they have the advantage of knowing what's going on. Plus, we're in the middle of freaking nowhere. No cell phone service and a car that's out of gas. You need to go back to the 7-Eleven and call the police."

"All right." Reluctantly, Ron took off jogging while Brick stayed behind, keeping watch on the house.

While he waited for Ron to return, Brick took a couple of deep breaths and exhaled slowly. It didn't help; his heart was still racing. Even though he had only seen Jasmine for a minute or two, it was long enough to really worry him. She had the vacant look of someone under the influence of some strong medication. Brick deliberately chose not to mention that he thought he heard a baby cry. He feared that if he had, there would be no stopping Ron.

After buzzing past his ear, a mosquito landed on Brick's arm and instantly helped itself to a snack. Brick slapped at another mosquito and this time he was the victor. He flicked the insect's flattened body parts off his arm and onto the ground. There was a reason he had dropped out of Boy Scouts after his first and last camping trip. His ten-year-old self was afraid his mother would be angry when she had to drive two hours to pick him up, but instead she seemed relieved that camping vacations weren't in either of their futures.

Brick leaned against the trunk of an oak tree. Questions were swirling around in his head and his imagination was in overdrive. What could possibly be going on in that bungalow with the peeling paint and the overgrown lawn? With any luck, they should know soon. Who was the other woman? If she was Jasmine's therapist, had their relationship crossed the line from professional to personal? It hadn't occurred to Brick before, but had Jasmine left Ron for a woman? Or was Jasmine being controlled in a Stockholm syndrome–like scenario? Brick had never encountered a case involving the phenomena but had studied it enough to know it was possible she had become the victim of mind control by her captor. And Brick couldn't dismiss the possibility that since Jasmine apparently believed Ron had betrayed her, she had simply chosen to take the twins and leave. The other woman, presumably her therapist, concerned that Jasmine may be in danger, assisted her with that decision. Occam's razor. He needed to call Lieutenant Hughes. It was beyond frustrating to be only five miles from downtown Baltimore and not have cell phone service.

When Brick saw the headlights of a vehicle approaching, he stepped behind the tree to conceal his location until he could identify the car. As it got closer, he was relieved to see the Maryland State Police shield below the window on the driver's-side door, along with the words "State Trooper" spelled out in large yellow letters. When the car stopped, a young, petite female officer and Ron got out. Brick was pleased that a female officer had responded. In these circumstances, she may be seen as less intimidating than a male officer. Gaining access inside the bungalow may be easier to accomplish.

"I'm Jennifer Clarke." She extended her hand in Brick's direction. "Detective Hayes has apprised me of the situation. Have you observed anything new?"

"No."

"Okay, we all know about this case from the APB we got last week, and I've seen the news coverage. I've already notified my supervisor and brought him up-to-speed. He's on his way. Wow, we haven't been involved in anything big like this in a long time."

Brick's first impression of Officer Clarke was that she seemed professional, but her excitement about being involved in a high-profile case caused some concern.

"Can you point out where you approached the house?" Officer Clarke asked.

Brick pointed out how he crouched along the side of the house until he reached the window where he saw Jasmine sitting at the table. "I'm not sure about this, but at one point, I thought I heard a baby cry."

"What . . . why didn't you tell me?" Ron's anger wasn't lost on Brick.

"Because I only heard it once and it could have been a stray cat out here."

"He's right." Officer Clarke backed up what Brick had said. "There's plenty of feral cats around here, but if I can get inside, I'll check it out." She went on to explain she planned to use a ruse that there had been a prison break. With the close proximity to a maximum-security facility, notifying nearby residents of a break and reminding them to keep their doors and windows locked and to call 911 if they saw anything unusual would be standard procedure.

Her plan sounded reasonable to Brick but going in alone wasn't without risk. "It's your call, but waiting for your backup might be—"

"I hear you," Officer Clarke said. "But the sooner we get a handle on the situation, the sooner we can take the necessary action. No worries, I've got this." She opened her car door. "I need you guys to just hang back here out of sight."

Brick hoped she was right. "Do you have a pair of binoculars we can use?"

"Sure." Officer Clarke got back in the cruiser, retrieved the binoculars, rolled down the window, and handed them to Brick.

Brick watched as she drove down the road and parked behind the Civic. When she got out of her car and approached the front door, he raised the binoculars to his eyes. He made the necessary adjustments, trying to get the clearest view possible despite the dim illumination from the porch light. He watched as Officer Clarke knocked on the door and stepped back. A minute or two elapsed. A curtain was pulled back from the window adjacent to the door and then the door slowly opened. Even with the limited lighting, it was obvious the woman wearing jeans and a green tee shirt was Caucasian. Brick handed the binoculars to Ron.

"See if you recognize her."

Ron held the binoculars up to his eyes. "No. She's white, looks to be mid-to-late thirties. That's consistent with what I was told was on Reznick's driver's license. But without a photo, no way to tell if that's really her." Ron lowered the binoculars and rubbed his eyes. Just as he turned to hand them back to Brick, a shot pierced the quiet September night.

CHAPTER THIRTY-THREE

THE BINOCULARS DROPPED from Brick's hand and hit the ground as he watched Officer Clarke stumble backward and fall off the porch. The front door of the bungalow slammed shut. For a split second, neither Brick nor Ron moved. Then without a spoken word, their first responder reflex kicked in and both guys sprinted toward the fallen officer. They didn't get far.

Headlights from an approaching vehicle stopped them and the driver rolled down his window. Brick shouted the two words no cop ever wants to hear.

"Officer down!"

"Fuck me!" The burly officer whose name tag identified him as Sergeant Thomas Doyle grabbed his radio and yelled as he jumped out of his vehicle, "10-999, 10-999."

Brick was grateful Officer Clarke had briefed her supervisor so there was no confusion as to who he and Ron were and why they were there. But for now, their priority had shifted. They needed to attend to Clarke who was lying motionless in front of the steps to the porch. Knowing there was an active shooter in the house meant timing was critical. They quickly strategized how to rescue Officer Clarke. Considering her petite size, Brick was confident he could drag her away from where she was lying, and at the same time, stay low to the ground to minimize being a target. Sergeant Doyle drove his vehicle onto the lawn and positioned it to provide as much coverage for Brick and Ron as possible. Using his opened car door for some protection, he trained his service revolver on the front door of the bungalow. It was easy to see that, if necessary, he was prepared to engage with the shooter.

The threat of more shots being fired was all the motivation Brick needed to move with warp speed. As he stayed crouched down, he got behind Officer Clarke and grabbed her under the arms.

Officer Clarke's eyes fluttered. "What happened?"

Brick was thrilled to hear her speak but didn't answer her question. He managed to drag her back to the side of the cruiser where Ron was waiting by the open back door. Together, they lifted her onto the back seat.

"My head hurts."

Again, Officer Clarke asked what happened as Brick checked her over for any injuries she may have sustained. Aside from a bump on the back of her head, nothing was evident. He checked both of her ears and was relieved not to see any bleeding. Although she looked okay, he suspected she may have a concussion. Given that her pulse was already rapid, he figured this wasn't the ideal time to tell her that her Kevlar vest had stopped a bullet that may have killed her.

"You fell and hit your head." Brick patted Officer Clarke's hand. "You're going to be fine. Help's on the way."

* * *

In response to Sergeant Doyle's 10-999 call, available units from Maryland State Police and Baltimore County responded with lights flashing and sirens blaring. A fire truck and two ambulances joined the assembled vehicles turning the dead-end road into a staging area.

While EMTs transferred Officer Clarke to one of the ambulances, Sergeant Doyle used a bullhorn to announce the house was surrounded. He encouraged the occupants to come out with their hands up.

No response.

Again, Doyle raised the bullhorn and this time it sounded to Brick as though he was attempting to de-escalate the situation by reassuring the shooter that the officer was okay. In a calm voice, Doyle explained that turning herself in now would prevent anyone else getting hurt.

No response.

Brick knew from experience that a standoff like this could go on for hours or end quickly in a hail of gunfire. Suicide by cop. Despite the impressive police response, he was worried it wasn't enough. Was shooting Officer Clarke an act of desperation? If so, what else was the shooter capable of doing? Sergeant Doyle's cruiser had become a makeshift command center and he motioned for Brick to join him.

"She's not responding and I'm worried time's not on our side. I've got to get some eyes on what's going on inside that house. What can you tell me about the layout?" Sergeant Doyle asked as he wiped sweat from his face.

"Not a whole lot." Brick pointed to the window where he had observed Jasmine. "That's the kitchen and around the back, there's a small bedroom. I didn't make it to the other side."

"Did you see a back door?"

"No."

"Fuck . . . I was afraid of that."

Brick stepped aside as Doyle signaled to a couple of SWAT officers. After being briefed, the two officers made their way along the outside perimeter of the house while Doyle continued encouraging the shooter to come out. Brick wasn't surprised the message didn't work, but it may distract the shooter and that, at least, could provide protection for the officers as they crouched near the windows. He watched as the officers, with their guns drawn, slowly worked in tandem to provide coverage for each other as they made their way around the side of the house. Temporarily, one of the officers disappeared from view.

Being a bystander was another source of frustration for Brick, and not being able to see the officer behind the house raised his anxiety level. The look on Ron's face told him he was feeling the same. Slowly, the minutes ticked by, and finally, the officer rounded the corner of the porch and made his way back to the sergeant's vehicle. Brick and Ron moved close enough to hear what he was saying.

"There's two bedrooms on the back side of the house. In one, I saw a crib with two babies, both about the same size. They were crying but otherwise looked okay. In the kitchen, there was a black woman seated at the table. She appeared out of it, drunk or on drugs. She put her head down on the table and looked like she passed out." The officer paused long enough to catch his breath. "The window to the other bedroom was wide open and the screen had been knocked to the ground."

Sergeant Doyle turned toward Brick and Ron. "You heard what he said?"

Ron nodded vigorously but seemed to be struggling to put words together. "That's my . . ." Brick placed his hand on Ron's shoulder. "That's my wife and kids. I've got to . . . got to get to them."

"Don't worry," Sergeant Doyle said. "We're going to bring them out. It's possible the woman you said was the shooter escaped out the window."

"Or she wants us to think she did," Brick said. "She could be hiding in a closet or under a bed, just waiting to ambush anyone who goes into the house."

"You're right and that's—" Sergeant Doyle stopped to listen to the dispatcher's call. Despite some static, Brick was able to understand the message.

"Any units in the area, respond to the 7-Eleven on Jessup Road. Possible carjacking in progress."

Even before the dispatcher went on to describe the alleged carjacker as a white woman, mid-thirties, wearing jeans and a green tee shirt, Brick and Ron exchanged a knowing look with Sergeant Doyle.

"Be advised, suspect is believed to be armed and dangerous."

CHAPTER THIRTY-FOUR

At Sergeant Doyle's direction, two officers returned to their cars and headed to the 7-Eleven. With the threat from the shooter removed, Doyle determined it was safe for other members of the SWAT team to enter the house. Removing Jasmine and the twins was now the highest priority but not without challenges. The officers had to ensure the house hadn't been booby-trapped in some way and considering Jasmine's presumed drugged condition, her reaction could be unpredictable and potentially violent.

After days of stress from not knowing if Jasmine and the twins were alive or dead, it all came down to this. Relief, for sure, but so many unanswered questions. Brick understood the need for caution and taking it slow, although for Ron more waiting was probably bordering on the unbearable.

"How are you doing, partner?" Brick asked.

"I don't know, man." Ron stopped pacing in front of Sergeant Doyle's cruiser and ran his hand through his dreads as he stood next to Brick. "I mean, it's what I was praying for . . . still, it feels surreal."

"I know, Ron, just hang on a little longer." Brick barely got the words out of his mouth when an EMT came out of the house carrying a baby. From a distance, it was impossible to tell if it was Jayla or Jamal. Ron bolted in their direction and may well have set a new track record. Although not moving as fast, Brick followed and got there just as Sergeant Doyle told the EMT it was okay to hand the baby to Ron. Even though he only got to hold Jayla for a couple of minutes before he was handed Jamal, the unmistakable joy on Ron's face brought smiles to everyone involved in their rescue. Both babies appeared healthy but would be transported to the hospital and checked out.

On a made-for-TV drama, the happy reunion scenario would probably continue when Jasmine was removed from the house. But this was real life and unscripted. She was flanked by two officers and her hands were cuffed in front. Brick wasn't sure why that was necessary but wouldn't be surprised if she had struggled with the officers who confronted her. On the porch, she was placed on a stretcher and strapped down. No longer a threat, the handcuffs were removed. Brick was close enough to see the blank expression on her face that didn't change when Ron approached, bent down, and touched her hand. It was as if he was a complete stranger. Brick turned away and tried to swallow past the lump in his throat as Jasmine was loaded into the ambulance with the twins. He needed a minute to compose himself and figured Ron could use the same.

"Bittersweet, man. Bittersweet." Ron wiped his eyes with the back of his hand.

* * *

Brick had lost track of time. He glanced at his watch and saw it was after ten. Crime scene tape was being unrolled to cordon off the area. A forensic team had arrived and was deployed to go through the house. No doubt they would be there for hours cataloging evidence. If they found any drugs Jasmine may have taken, reporting that information to the hospital would help in treating her. There was nothing more for Brick and Ron to do but three good reasons to go to Johns Hopkins. Aware of its stellar reputation, Brick was pleased when an EMT said that's where they were taking Jasmine and the twins. He waited for Sergeant Doyle to get off the phone.

"That was an update on Officer Clarke." Doyle smiled. "She's awake and alert. Has a few bruises and a concussion and the mother of all headaches, but otherwise she's okay."

"Thank God for Kevlar vests and that she was wearing one," Brick said.

"You're right about that. They're keeping her at Hopkins over-night for observation, but barring any complications, she'll be good to go tomorrow."

"Speaking of Hopkins, Ron needs to go there to check on his family, but we've got a problem—a car with an empty gas tank."

Doyle laughed. "With all the shit that's gone down tonight, that's an easy problem to fix." He opened the door to his cruiser. "The re-port I need to write up can wait. I'll drive you guys to the gas sta-tion." Doyle backed up from where he had parked on the lawn and maneuvered around several vehicles as the dispatcher's urgent mes-sage filled the silence.

"Carjacking suspect has abandoned her car. Threatening to jump from Bay Bridge. Proceed with caution, armed and dangerous."

"Ten-four." Doyle hit the siren and lights. "Sorry, guys, but as a trained negotiator—"

"It's okay, you got to do what you got to do." Ron's voice sounded calmer than Brick had heard in some time.

Brick was riding shotgun as Doyle turned onto Old Jessup Road. "It's what, about forty miles from here to the Bay Bridge?"

"Yup, forty miles, give or take."

Doyle slowed as he approached the ramp to Route 175. After merging onto the highway, he moved to the far-left lane and accelerated. Brick didn't need to see the speedometer to know they were traveling over ninety miles an hour. It seemed Doyle was skilled at high-speed driving. Still, Brick would have preferred to be behind the wheel than in the front passenger seat. He tightened his seat belt and reluctantly resigned himself to not being in control. At the speed they were traveling, at least it wouldn't take long to reach the bridge.

Flashing red and blue lights and a loud, high-pitched siren cleared the path for Sergeant Doyle. They had the left lane to themselves or so it seemed to Brick when, without warning, Doyle swerved onto the grassy median separating the east- and westbound lanes. Gravel flew, pinging off the side of the cruiser and hitting the windshield. It felt as though Doyle had eased off the gas as he yelled for Brick and Ron to hang on. Brick could see Doyle was struggling to steer the cruiser back onto the highway. It all happened so fast and unexpectedly. At first, Brick thought a tire had blown, but then he saw the flick of a deer's white tail. Buck or doe, he couldn't tell and didn't care. It crossed over to the shoulder of the road and disappeared into the woods.

"Motherfucking Bambi! They're usually out around dusk, not this late. Son of a bitch! You guys okay?" Sergeant Doyle asked as he continued driving in the left lane but at a much lower speed. Both Brick and Ron confirmed that they were. "Glad to hear it, 'cause I came dangerously close to browning my shorts."

From the back seat, Brick heard laughing. Nervous laughter, no doubt, but it sounded good, and he joined in.

CHAPTER THIRTY-FIVE

SEEING A SIGN indicating five miles to the Bay Bridge triggered feelings of relief and dread for Brick. Relief that the high-speed ride was about to end, but dread for what may take place at the bridge.

Like many who have crossed the Bay Bridge, Brick was aware of the reasons why it was considered one of the most dangerous bridges in the world. Its height, lack of hard shoulders along the spans, and the frequency of strong winds made for his own white-knuckle grip on the steering wheel whenever he drove across it. And with its low guardrails and lack of suicide barriers, it was a chosen site for men and women determined to end their lives.

As they approached the entrance to the bridge, Brick heard a helicopter and saw it circling overhead. The assembled police and emergency vehicles resembled the earlier scene on Old Jessup Road with one major addition—a news crew from WMAR-TV, the Baltimore ABC affiliate.

Sergeant Doyle parked behind a police car from Anne Arundel County. "If you guys want to stretch your legs, feel free. Just try to avoid getting into the middle of this clusterfuck." He put on his hat and opened his car door. "It's showtime."

Brick watched as Doyle joined a couple of officers from the Maryland Transportation Authority. He lost track of them as they gathered with a group of first responders approaching the west-bound span.

"I need some air, Ron. How about you?"

"Yeah."

Brick got out of the car and opened the back door, freeing Ron from the back seat usually reserved for someone under arrest.

"Thanks." Ron leaned against the cruiser. "At least it's happening at this end of the bridge. Driving across that thing gives me the hee-bie jeebies."

Brick had never heard Ron use that phrase, but it was an accurate description of the anxiety lots of people experienced on this span across Chesapeake Bay. Men and women of all ages and occupations routinely pay a fee and become a passenger while a professional bridge-crosser drives their car the four miles to the other side. Before Brick had a chance to respond, he felt his phone vibrate.

"Hey, Ron. I've got cell service. Check your phone."

The text message was a weather alert, which he deleted. He didn't need to be told it was windy and that the temperature had dropped into the forties. Even though it was close to midnight, he immediately called Lieutenant Hughes. He figured she'd rather be awakened and hear the news from him and Ron than be caught off-guard by a reporter asking for a comment. She answered on the third ring, sounding groggy, but quickly recovered when Brick started telling her all that had happened. When he finished with his update, he overheard Ron talking to Jasmine's sister. Mid-sentence, Ron asked her to hold on as Sergeant Doyle returned.

"Ten minutes too late. I'll never know if I could have talked her down, but I would have liked a chance to try."

"Have they recovered her body?" Brick asked.

"No, but they saw where she went in and it's at least thirty feet deep. Not survivable." Doyle cleared his throat as he opened the door to his cruiser and got in. "They're setting up lights, but it might be morning before they pull her out." Doyle adjusted his seat belt. "Ten goddamned minutes."

Even though arriving too late to prevent a bad ending was something most cops would experience at some point in their career, it was hard to accept. Brick heard the defeat in Doyle's voice and knew the hollow feeling he most likely felt. But it wasn't only Doyle who sounded defeated. Ron did, too, although understandably his concern was for questions that would probably go unanswered. Considering Jasmine's condition, there was no guarantee she would be able to fill in the blanks.

The uneventful drive back to Jessup took twice as long, for which Brick was grateful. It was after one thirty when Sergeant Doyle pulled into the Shell station on Old Jessup Road. Ron got out of the car and headed inside to purchase a gas can.

"I don't know how he's keeping it together," Doyle said. "I've got two boys. You got kids?"

"No."

"Mine are grown now, but just the thought of them going missing makes me weak in the knees."

"It's been rough, and Ron's had his moments, but somehow he's managed."

"I get the sense that you guys are close. How long were you partners?"

"Just over a year. He's a good cop and a good man."

"But he's the husband. Did you ever—"

"I know what you're going to ask. Yes, I always considered he might be responsible, but at the same time, I also considered he might not be."

"I hear ya. Let's face it, we're all capable of doing things we never would imagine doing. And it doesn't matter how long you've known someone; you never really know them. At least, that's been my experience."

Brick agreed but was too spent to get into a philosophical discussion. He was relieved to see Ron returning to the car.

"Okay, guys, we'll head back to your car and then you can follow me to Hopkins. My wife has worked there for years so I know the place like the back of my hand. I'll get you where you need to go with a lot less hassle."

That was an offer too good to pass up and Doyle delivered. Having him run interference proved to be invaluable. Brick and Ron were quickly led to a waiting lounge and told someone would speak with them as soon as possible.

"Okay, guys, guess this is it. At least for now." Sergeant Doyle extended his hand in Ron's direction. "I know you've been through a lot; I wish you the best, buddy. And if there's anything I can do, don't hesitate."

Ron shook hands with Doyle. "Thanks, I really appreciate that."

Doyle turned in Brick's direction. "The circumstances sucked, but it was great meeting you." He handed Brick one of his business cards. "Just so you know, the Maryland State Police are hiring, and experienced investigators have a leg up."

"Thanks, I'll keep that in mind." Brick's response was his tactful way of saying he wasn't interested. State police officers had to spend way too much time in their cars for the job to ever appeal to him.

While they waited for an update on the condition of Jasmine and the twins, Brick felt the pins and needles sensation of his left foot falling asleep. He walked to the end of the hallway and took in the view of downtown Baltimore. Seeing the warehouse of Camden Yards reminded him of the games he had attended there. The one that immediately came to mind, the Mariners at the Orioles on September 1, 2001, and one of the last chances to see Cal Ripken play.

Tickets were hard to get and expensive, but he and his baseball
buddy, an Army major assigned to the Pentagon, weren't going to be
denied. Ten days later, the major was a statistic. Brick turned away
from the window and saw a short, bearded, white-coated man heading toward the lounge. He followed behind.

"I'm Dr. Singh." He shook hands with Ron and Brick before
taking a seat. He set a laptop on the end table and looked directly
at Ron. "Both babies have been evaluated by Pediatrics and appear
to be doing well. Out of an abundance of caution, we're keeping
them on an overnight observation, but all indicators are they'll be
ready to go home tomorrow, or I guess I should say, later today.
Any questions?"

Brick could see Ron's shoulders relax before he responded. "No,
that's good news."

Dr. Singh checked his computer before continuing. "Regarding
Mrs. Hayes—her vital signs are normal. She is currently being given
an IV for dehydration. There are obvious indicators of substance
abuse—bloodshot eyes, dilated pupils, slurred speech, drowsiness.
We're running a tox screen and should have results soon. Does she
have a history of alcohol or drug abuse?"

Ron shook his head. "No, absolutely not. Before she was pregnant, she might have a gin and tonic or a margarita when we went
out. Occasionally, a glass of wine with dinner, but never more than
one drink. While she was pregnant and since the twins were born,
she doesn't even drink coffee or anything else with caffeine."

"What about any prescription or over-the-counter drugs?"

"Tylenol and Benadryl, but only when necessary."

"Understood." Dr. Singh typed a few notes before continuing.
"When were the twins born?"

"Six months ago."

"Any complications during her pregnancy?"

"Not really, although the last four or five weeks she was on bed rest."

"And the twins were delivered by C-section?"

"Right."

"Has she had any postpartum health issues?"

"Depression. That's why she was seeing a psychologist, Lynn Reznick."

"I'm sure our team will want to speak with her."

"Can't. She committed suicide tonight."

"Excuse me?" Dr. Singh looked from Ron to Brick. "Are you saying Jasmine's therapist killed herself?"

"Yes." Ron deferred to Brick to explain while he used the men's room. A few minutes later, he returned.

Dr. Singh shook his head. "I've got to say, I'm stunned." He leaned forward in Ron's direction. "What I can tell you, we have a very experienced team of professionals trained to deal with post-traumatic stress disorders. Your wife will be evaluated and provided the best care available."

"I hope so. Can I see her?"

"She was agitated earlier but is resting comfortably now. It would be better if you wait until later today. If you haven't done so already, just leave your contact information at the nurses' station. If anything changes, we'll notify you immediately." Dr. Singh stood and shook hands with Ron and Brick. "Try to get some rest. I'll meet with you again this afternoon."

CHAPTER THIRTY-SIX

IT WAS AFTER ten when Brick staggered out to the kitchen. Six hours of sleep was usually enough for him. Not this morning. Six hours felt more like six minutes. He yawned and rubbed his eyes before dropping a bagel into the toaster and heating water for tea. From the den came the sound of snoring. Deep, sonorous sounds that could easily match the decibels generated by a chainsaw. No surprise, it was probably the best sleep Ron had gotten since Jasmine went missing. Knowing that his wife and twins were alive and being cared for in a safe place seemed to be more effective than a double dose of Ambien.

Brick brewed and drank a second cup of strong Irish breakfast tea before taking a shower. Slowly, he was beginning to feel more alert. As he finished shaving, he heard Ron's cell phone ringtone. A few minutes later, Ron came out of the den with a broad smile on his face.

"That was the hospital. The twins will be ready to come home this afternoon. And Dr. Singh will meet with me at three."

"Good news."

"Yeah, it is except I'm worried about Jasmine and I will be until she's home, too." Ron took a deep breath and exhaled slowly. "At least it's a start."

Despite Ron's relief, Brick sensed he was feeling a little over-whelmed. He had no doubt Ron was capable of taking care of his kids on his own, but sometimes moral support isn't enough and this felt like one of those times. "Are you going to need help getting the twins?"

Ron shrugged. "I got this, but if you're volunteering . . ."

Brick nodded. "I am."

"Thanks, bro." Ron smiled but at the same time wiped away a tear before closing the bathroom door.

*   *   *

After a stop at a nearby Target to buy two infant car seats, Brick and Ron drove to Baltimore. It was just after noon and with a couple of hours before the appointment with Dr. Singh, there was plenty of time for lunch at the Inner Harbor. A choice between the Hard Rock Café or Phillips Seafood Restaurant was a no-brainer. A hostess led Brick and Ron to a table at Phillips overlooking the harbor. They both ordered the Hooper Island crab cake sandwich.

"Jasmine loves the Inner Harbor. We've been here lots of times." Ron leaned back in his chair. "Except for our honeymoon, when we first got married, we couldn't afford a real vacation, so we'd come to Baltimore for the weekend. Then it kind of became our anniversary destination."

"Nice."

Ron smiled mischievously. "Last anniversary, we stayed at one of those boutique-style hotels in Fells Point. Jasmine picked it out because they had a special romantic getaway package. Nine months later . . . twins." He took a sip of iced tea. Ron's smile faded, replaced by a somber expression. "Right now, I've got so many *what if* thoughts running through my head."

"Those will drive you crazy, Ron."

"I know, but I can't help thinking about what if you and I had gotten to my house a few minutes earlier or later, everything could have been different." Ron knitted his brow as he continued. "It's kind of like in the O.J. case. If Nicole's mother hadn't left her sunglasses at the restaurant, maybe Nicole and Ron Goldman would be alive today."

Brick understood Ron's thought processing. "Yeah, like the old saying, hindsight is 20-20. A seemingly insignificant event set off a series of actions like dominoes toppling one by one."

"Right. Had it not been for the fender bender causing the traffic backup, we wouldn't have seen Reznick walking into my house."

"But if we had gotten there sooner, we might have been inside the house and if she had the gun . . ."

"Well, there is that. And if you hadn't talked me out of approaching the bungalow in Jessup, I might have been the one taking the bullet."

"In a tee shirt, not a vest. Let it go, Ron. Don't waste energy thinking about all the scenarios that might have been. Save your energy for dealing with what actually happened. That's a big enough assignment."

The waiter's arrival with the sandwiches was well timed. Other than a few comments on the crab cakes, conversation ceased while Brick and Ron ate their lunch. Ron finished first. He wiped his hands and dropped the napkin on his empty plate.

"Brick, did you ever think I might be responsible for their disappearance?"

The question was unexpected and Brick took a minute to think about what he wanted to say. "You know the statistics as well as I do. Just because I'm retired doesn't mean I don't still think like a cop.

But I also had the advantage of knowing you and that erased most doubts. I know how much Jasmine and the twins mean to you."

"It's true. They mean the world to me, but I haven't been the husband or father they deserve." Ron shifted in his chair. "When I got so angry because I thought Jasmine had run off with Marcus, I was actually angry with myself. If she had, it was my fault."

"What do you mean?"

"It's hard for me to admit this, but I've felt ignored since the twins were taking up all of Jasmine's attention. And I should have been helping out a lot more at home, but instead I was spending extra time at work."

"Because of Holly?"

Ron picked at a hangnail on his left thumb. "Did I find Holly attractive? Yes. Did I cheat on Jasmine? No. If circumstances were different, could things have gotten . . . out of hand? Maybe."

"Sounds like you just cross-examined yourself."

"Yeah, well I needed to do some introspection and finally be honest with myself. Looking back, I was kind of a dick."

"Kind of?"

"Okay, I was a dick." Ron looked up and made eye contact with Brick. "I can always count on you to not cut me any slack."

Brick raised his glass of iced tea in Ron's direction. "That's what friends are for. So, what are you going to do differently now?"

Ron didn't hesitate. "Not squander a second chance to be the husband and father I should have been from the start. I just pray Jasmine gives me that chance."

Brick recognized Ron's need to say out loud the things he had been thinking in order to atone for his shortcomings and validate his intentions. He respected his courage for doing so. The mood lightened as they left the restaurant and stopped at Crabby Jack's

General Store. They left with two small stuffed teddy bears dressed in Orioles uniforms.

When Brick and Ron arrived at Johns Hopkins, they retraced last night's route and checked in at the nurses' station. They were directed to the same waiting lounge where they had been hours before. Within a few minutes, Dr. Singh joined them.

"First things first," the doctor said. "The twins are doing fine and charming the nurses." He pointed toward the infant car seats. "I see you're prepared to take them home."

"I am," Ron said. "I just wish their mother was going home, too."

"Understood." Dr. Singh glanced at notes on his clipboard. "Her condition is stable, but we detected a high level of antidepressants in her system. Of course, we don't know conclusively if she took them voluntarily or was drugged, but based on what you've told me, it probably wasn't her choice. Be that as it may, we need to get her off the meds but stopping suddenly is problematic. We need to do it gradually."

"How long will it take?" Ron asked.

"Every patient is different, but given the type of drug and in a clinical setting, in most cases, five to seven days."

"Can I see her?" Ron's voice cracked as he asked the question.

"Yes. Right now, she's sedated because she was experiencing some hallucinations."

"What? That sounds serious."

"It's a common reaction and not unexpected given the circumstances. Even though it's unlikely she'll be aware of you being there, it's possible she may be, so keep that in mind if you say anything."

While Brick waited for Ron to return, his thoughts turned to the Yang case. Soon, he'd be able to shift gears and focus on it full-time. Why had Blancato told Fred Stewart to deep-six it? Until that question was answered, it would bug the hell out of him. Yeah, it was personal given their history—everything involving Blancato was. And what was up with those spreadsheets on the thumb drive? They must have meant something to Henry Yang, but what? Hopefully, Grace Alexander would have a clue.

About twenty minutes had passed when Ron and Dr. Singh returned. Brick immediately noticed Ron's arms and legs swaying slightly as he entered the lounge. A quick thumbs-up from Ron indicated he was reassured by what he had seen.

They each picked up a car seat and followed Dr. Singh to Pediatrics.

CHAPTER THIRTY-SEVEN

ALTHOUGH RON HAD driven them to Baltimore, for the return to D.C. he was comfortably sitting in the back seat between Jayla blowing spit bubbles and a sleeping Jamal. As Brick exited the hospital parking garage, he glanced up at Ron's reflection in the rearview mirror. From the look on his face, there was no place on earth where he would rather be. Brick didn't quite share that sentiment. He was happy to help out, but the forty-five-minute trip seemed twice as long when Jayla started crying, woke Jamal, and the two engaged in what seemed like a contest to see who could cry the loudest and the longest. If asked to judge, Brick would declare it a tie.

With about five miles to go, both babies fell asleep and Brick could gratefully hear himself think when he turned onto the street where Ron lived. So much had happened in just over twenty-four hours since they were last here. With Lynn Reznick committing suicide, would they ever know why she had been inside the house. And considering Jasmine's condition, would she be able to explain or even remember what had happened during the time she was gone. At least for now, he'd shelve those thoughts for a more pressing concern. A news van from the Fox affiliate was parked across the street from Ron's house.

"Looks like you have company, Ron."

"Yeah, I see them . . . vultures. I don't want my kids on the news. Drive around the block and we'll go in the back way."

Brick wasn't sure the diversionary tactic would work but it was worth a try. Even though the twins were probably too young to be traumatized by what they had been through, protecting them at the moment was a priority Brick shared with Ron. He parked behind a shed at the end of Ron's property and looked around. So far, so good. Unless a reporter was hiding in the bushes, they were home free. As quickly as they could, Brick and Ron got the babies out of the car and into the house. Brick breathed a sigh of relief as he set down the baby carrier with a still sleeping Jamal. Ron was in charge of an animated Jayla.

To say that Brick's experience with babies was limited implied he had more experience than was the case. Without kids of his own or nieces and nephews, until six months ago he couldn't recall holding a baby. That changed when Ron's twins were born. And now, despite his novice status, even he could tell one of them was in serious need of a diaper change.

"Whoa." Ron waved his hand in front of his face to clear the air. "Can you keep an eye on Jamal while I take Jayla upstairs?"

"Sure." As if on cue, the moment Ron left the kitchen, Jamal woke up and started to howl. Brick picked him up and paced around the room making what he hoped were reassuring shushing noises. Apparently, Jamal didn't find them very comforting. Brick was about to try singing but was spared the effort when Ron returned with a smiling Jayla in his arms. As they traded babies, Brick got a whiff that smelled like lavender, a definite improvement.

"Got the feeling we're like a tag team," Brick said.

"Seriously, feel like I need four hands. I don't know how Jasmine does it."

"I do—women are the more evolved gender."

Ron nodded. "Did you hear that, Jayla? No pressure, but we're counting on you."

It still seemed the news crew parked across the street wasn't aware that anyone was inside the house. That would probably change. It was either take the risk and reveal their presence or stumble around preparing formula in the dark. Ron turned on the kitchen light and almost immediately, there was a knock at the door. They ignored it at first, but the knocking continued, louder and more insistent.

"I don't want to talk to them, but they're probably not going away."

Brick handed Jayla back to Ron. "I'll take one for the team."

"Thanks, bro."

Before opening the door, Brick looked out the small window in the door. As far as he could tell the woman was alone, but it was possible someone with a camera was lurking in the corner of the porch. He opened the door a crack, confirmed she was working solo, and stepped outside.

"May I help you?" Brick asked.

The well-dressed reporter in heavy makeup seemed slightly confused. "Is this the Hayes home?"

"Yes."

"Oh, good. I'm in the right place. I'm Stella Owen." She shook hands with Brick and paused as if expecting a reaction.

Brick didn't let on he knew who she was as he shook her hand.

"I'm the host of *And Justice For All* on the Fox station." Another pause, as if giving him a second opportunity to acknowledge her.

Brick responded with a shoulder shrug. "Okay?"

"And who are you?"

"Brian Kavanagh."

"What is your connection to the Hayes family?"

"Friend."

"Whatever." To Brick's ears, it sounded as though Stella wasn't happy to be speaking with someone other than Ron. Maybe her attitude was a slip. When she continued, her television personality seemed to emerge. She smiled and stepped a little closer. "I'm sure you're aware I've been following this story very closely. I know my viewers are so excited that Jasmine and those two precious babies have been found. I can only imagine that Detective Hayes is over the moon. An interview with him holding the twins would be so heartwarming."

Brick was so tempted to say, "Bitch, please, give me a break. A few days ago, you as much as accused Ron of being responsible for the disappearance of his family." Instead, he took the high road. "I'm sure you can appreciate this has been very traumatic and the family needs privacy at this time."

"Of course, but everyone loves a story with a happy ending. So many of my fans really get involved in the cases I cover, especially when children are victims. They worry and pray for them. They're invested, and in a way need and deserve closure."

Brick had heard enough of her sales pitch to promote her show and boost her ratings by exploiting Ron and his family. "If Detective Hayes wishes to speak with you, he'll be in touch."

"Just one more—"

Brick stepped inside and firmly closed the door.

"Looks like you have an invitation from Stella Owen."

"Are you shitting me?"

"Nope, that's who was out there. You rate, otherwise she would have sent one of her flunkies."

"Given what the bitch was saying about me on her show, she can hold her hand on her ass until the cows come home."

"What?" Brick couldn't stop laughing. "You're a city boy, where did that come from?"

Ron was laughing too. "I don't know, must be a line from a movie."

"Of course, I should have known. The movie trivia savant strikes again."

Ron continued to laugh as he finished filling two bottles with formula. "Are you up for a challenge?" He handed one of the bottles to Brick.

"As long as it doesn't involve chugging what's in the bottle."

"It does in a way. Take your pick, Jayla or Jamal?"

"Jamal and I'll follow your lead."

CHAPTER THIRTY-EIGHT

"I HAVE TO get a picture of this. Otherwise, I'll think I'm hallucinating." Ron pointed his phone in Brick's direction. After taking the picture, he checked the image. "You look like a natural, bro."

"Yeah, right. I'll add nanny to my multifaceted resume." Brick looked down at Jamal, comfortably nestled in the crook of his arm. Despite the self-deprecating response, there was something comforting in this moment after all the chaos. He held the bottle up to check its contents. "Almost gone."

"Same with Jayla. Good appetites, definitely a sign—oh, man, not again. That better not be another reporter." Ron patted the chair. "Shoot, I don't have my phone. Guess I'll have to check it out the old-fashioned way." Ron set Jayla's bottle on the end table and held her as he stepped over to the window. He stood behind the drapes and pulled them aside to see who was knocking. "Thank God, it's the lieutenant." He went to the door to let her in.

Lieutenant Hughes stepped inside carrying a bag from a nearby Jersey Mike's. "Thought you guys might be hungry. Here, I'll trade you."

"Thanks, I'll put that in the fridge." Ron handed her Jayla in exchange for the bag of sub sandwiches. "Brick is in the living room with Jamal."

"What do you say, Jayla, should we join your brother?" Hughes smiled as Jayla made a cooing sound. "I'll take that as a yes." She took a seat at the opposite end of the sofa from Brick, placing Jayla on her lap. "How are you doing, Brick?"

"That's a question you might want to ask Jamal."

"Really? You look like you've got everything under control."

"Fake it till you make it. This is a first for me."

"Seriously? So no kids of your own?"

"None I'm aware of."

Lieutenant Hughes laughed. "Nieces or nephews?"

Brick shook his head. "I was an only child."

"So was I but I earned my spending money from babysitting. I liked being a solo act then, but now I wish I had ten siblings to share the responsibility of elder care."

Ten may have been an exaggeration but Brick understood. For an instant, he thought about his own mother. Invariably, it always triggered emotions, some happy, some sad, and usually he couldn't predict which it would be. A gentle kick from Jamal as he shifted brought Brick back to the present.

Ron returned from the kitchen and picked up Jayla's bottle. "Lieutenant, there's still a little bit of formula for her; want to do the honors?" He handed her the bottle and turned in Brick's direction. "How's my boy doing?"

Brick held up the empty bottle. "Done."

"But you're not." Ron smiled. "Got to burp him."

"You're really enjoying this, aren't you?"

"Hey, it's easy. Just put him up on your shoulder and pat his back."

"Okay, let's give it a try." Brick positioned Jamal onto his left shoulder and gently patted the baby's back. Nothing. After a couple more pats with no results, a resounding burp caught everyone's attention. "Whoa, was there Budweiser in that bottle?" Feeling much more confident, Brick gave Jamal a few more pats. Another healthy burp followed and then Jamal turned his head. Without warning, projectile-regurgitated formula sprayed the front of Brick's shirt and the side of his face.

"Uh-oh, time for me to take over." Ron quickly stepped in and picked up Jamal. "Sorry about that." He handed Brick a box of Kleenex.

Brick wiped his face before looking down to survey the damage to his shirt. He grabbed a couple more tissues and rubbed away as much of the formula as he could. "No problem, my dry cleaner will take care of it." As he said that, he wrinkled his nose. "Smells kind of sour."

"I'll get you one of my tee shirts. Do you mind holding Jamal again?"

Brick laughed as he reached for the baby. "The damage is already done."

Ron gave his son to Brick and headed upstairs. He quickly returned empty-handed and stood in the doorway to the living room. His eyes darted from Lieutenant Hughes to Brick. "There's something up here you guys need to see."

With Jamal in his arms, Brick followed Ron, and Lieutenant Hughes carried Jayla up the stairs. At the end of the hallway, Ron directed them to step inside the master bedroom. Brick looked around. A king-size bed flanked by matching nightstands took up one side of the room. Across from it, a flat-screen TV was mounted on the wall. The only other piece of furniture was a narrow oak chest of drawers. On top of it was what appeared to be a wooden jewelry box. Nothing seemed out of place, but something had caused Ron's reaction.

Lieutenant Hughes spoke up after glancing around and expressed what Brick was thinking. "Ron, what am I missing, 'cause everything looks okay."

"That's what I thought until I went into the walk-in closet and opened my dresser drawer. Take a look." Ron stepped aside so the lieutenant and Brick could see what he was talking about. Brick noticed the second drawer on the right side of the dresser was opened halfway. An envelope with Ron's name hand-printed on it was lying on top of a stack of neatly folded tee shirts. He stepped back from the dresser and out of the closet.

"Well, that may explain why Reznick was in the house."

"That's what I'm thinking," Ron said. "I know for an absolute fact that envelope was not there when I packed my stuff to take to your place."

Lieutenant Hughes handed Jayla to Ron. "I'll go call the agent-in-charge."

Ron looked surprised. "When did the FBI get involved?"

"Early on when we suspected Jasmine had been abducted across state lines. And they've got resources we don't have to investigate Reznick's background. I'll take all the help I can get."

Brick and Ron followed behind the lieutenant as she left the bedroom. While she headed downstairs, they stopped at the nursery to put the twins down for a nap.

"There's no telling what kind of schedule they're on. Guess it will be trial and error until I can figure something out." Ron sounded worried. "Hope I can."

"If I can feed Jamal a bottle, you can figure out a sleep schedule."

"We'll see. Oh man, I forgot to get a clean shirt for you."

"Forget it, I'm used to the smell now." Brick shrugged. "Guess I've been initiated."

"You have, bro, you have." Ron laughed. "And for what it's worth, be glad it came from that end."

* * *

Within the hour, Agent Frank Harrison from the D.C. FBI field office arrived. Lieutenant Hughes introduced him to Ron and Brick.

"I think we worked a case together several years ago," Brick said. "A sting operation that caught an assistant U.S. attorney."

"Really? I remember the case, but I don't recognize you," Harrison said.

"I was undercover—dyed my hair black and faked a New York accent."

Harrison nodded as he ran his hand over his bald head. "At least you still have hair. As I recall, the prosecutor was selling information from grand jury testimony and the operation was shut down before he could do any more damage. Cast a wide net, you never know what you're going to catch."

"That's for sure. No one was expecting involvement from an Ivy Leaguer, respected by his peers and married with three kids. He threw it all away for a few hundred dollars and a couple of blowjobs from the hooker who dropped the dime."

"How did he fool so many—" Lieutenant Hughes waved her hand in a dismissive gesture. "Never mind. Some things defy explanation."

While Ron and Lieutenant Hughes took Agent Harrison upstairs, Brick checked his phone to see what the local news websites were reporting. The case was getting detailed coverage, but Jasmine and the twins weren't the lead story. Washington was abuzz with a breaking news story. Secret Service agents were caught entertaining prostitutes in Las Vegas when they should have been protecting the Vice President. A text message from Nora interrupted what he was reading. He was about to reply but slipped his phone back in his pocket when he heard footsteps on the stairs.

"Ron, I'm sure you're curious about the contents." The unopened envelope was secured inside a plastic evidence bag. Agent Harrison attached a label with the date and his initials. "As soon as we know anything—" Harrison stopped to check his phone. "Excuse me, I need to take this." He stepped out on the porch.

A few minutes later, Harrison rejoined the others in the living room. "Okay, two significant updates. The prints on file for Lynn Reznick don't match the fingerprints taken from the jumper."

"That's weird," Lieutenant Hughes said. "She wasn't in the water very long so that shouldn't be a factor."

"Right. I'm not saying the technician wasn't accurate, but I'm going to the medical examiner's office in the morning and run a set myself. Also, we heard back from our contact at ATF. They traced the gun that was found in the car Reznick stole. It's registered to you, Ron."

"What the hell!" Ron leapt from the sofa and headed to the hall, followed by Lieutenant Hughes and Agent Harrison. Brick stayed out of the way, but could see Ron's reaction when he yanked open the closet door.

"I don't fucking believe it!" He pointed to an empty space on the middle shelf. "The gun vault, you know, the strong box . . . it's gone. That's where I always kept the gun, along with my service revolver."

"So, that's missing, too?" Agent Harrison asked.

"No." Lieutenant Hughes spoke up. "Ron turned it over to me when I put him on administrative leave."

"Good. Ron, who knew that's where you kept your guns?"

"Jasmine. No one else."

"And, as far as you know, Reznick is the only one who's been in the house?"

"Yeah, I customized my alerts to get a notification when the Ring device spots a person."

"Sounds like she left something and took something. Also sounds like she knew exactly where the gun would be," Harrison said.

"Jasmine hates guns. I can't think of any reason why she would have told Reznick about my gun being in the closet. It doesn't make any sense."

"Maybe it will, eventually." Agent Harrison shook hands with Ron and Brick, then followed Lieutenant Hughes as she showed him out.

When the lieutenant returned, she picked up her jacket and purse. "Are you okay, Ron?"

"I don't know. Finding that envelope and then having the gun stolen. I just can't wrap my head around this."

The lieutenant stepped close to Ron, then stepped back. "My bad, almost gave you a hug, but after last week's kerfuffle . . ."

"Excuse me?"

"Oh, of course, that happened while you were out. We had to have mandatory sexual harassment/workplace sensitivity training. An incident with a mistakenly sent text sparked a firestorm." She stepped toward the door. "Enjoy the sandwiches and try to relax—"

"Wait a second, Lieutenant. Was the text a photo?"

"Yes."

"Of Holly in a sexy outfit and it was intended for her boyfriend's eyes only." Lieutenant Hughes nodded as Ron continued. "I don't know what her game is, but I know one thing for sure—that wasn't a mistake."

CHAPTER THIRTY-NINE

It was after ten when Brick arrived home. Changing into a clean shirt was his first priority. A cold beer, his second. He stretched out on the sofa and took a drink. Even before a Myers–Briggs evaluation during a college psychology class confirmed his personality type, Brick knew he was an introvert. Although he was glad to have provided a refuge for Ron, it was a relief to have the place to himself for the first time since returning from Chicago. He took another sip of beer, picked up the remote, and turned on the Nats game.

With the team playing in San Diego, there were a few innings to go, but Brick quickly realized his mind wasn't on baseball. Questions about Holly were bouncing around in his head. One major texting error should have been incentive to make sure it didn't happen again. Either she was chronically careless when texting or getting off on what she was doing deliberately. Who was the real Holly Beltran? The female equivalent of plenty of male cops Brick knew who routinely hit on women in the workplace? Maybe. Ron had said Holly was involved in what sounded like a serious relationship. Was that really the case? If so, why was she seeking attention from Ron and then, whoever else she "accidentally" texted? Was she trying to make her boyfriend jealous? Whatever Holly's endgame, she probably didn't intend to set in motion the series of events the likes of which no one could have imagined, but it seemed she had some ownership. Now that Lieutenant Hughes was aware of her modus operandi, she would undoubtedly be asking Holly the tough questions and demanding the answers.

Brick finished his beer and turned off the TV. He tossed the empty bottle in the recycle bin and turned off the lights. There were many nights when Brick bemoaned sleeping alone. This wasn't one of them.

As he pulled back the covers and crawled into bed, his thoughts shifted from Holly to Dr. Lynn Reznick. When more facts were known, her name might be added to his personal list of infamous women. One he had dated; the others he had arrested for crimes that shocked even veteran cops—not a good idea to dredge up these images as he drifted off to sleep.

*   *   *

The morning sun flooding Brick's bedroom jolted him awake from a fitful sleep. For a minute, he tried to remember the dreams that woke him a couple of times during the night. The jumble of disconnected images he could recall made so little sense he decided that trying to analyze their meaning wasn't worth the effort. An unexpected text from Grace Alexander suggesting a meeting provided the motivation he needed to get up and back to work on the Yang case.

While Brick ate breakfast, he looked over notes he had made. Nothing seemed to indicate Henry participated in what would be considered high-risk activities. If anything, the opposite seemed to be more characteristic. But if he had been the target of a hit, there had to be a reason. Sometimes, it was the quiet ones that totally fooled everyone. Brick set aside his notes. Maybe Grace had found something relevant in the stuff he had given her to review.

* * *

It had been over a year since Brick had been to Teaism in Dupont Circle, but he readily agreed when Grace suggested it. The unique neighborhood teahouse was perfect for quiet conversation and, in Brick's opinion, served the best chai in D.C. He stepped up to the counter, ordered a large and joined Grace at a small table for two. Before eyeing a rolled-up yoga mat leaning against the table, he noticed the form-fitting tee shirt crisscrossing her breasts.

Grace smiled warmly as Brick sat down. "Forgive my saying, you look exhausted."

It wasn't what Brick expected to hear, but in Grace's voice he heard caring, not criticism. "It's been a rough forty-eight hours." Steam rose as he removed the top of his cup and a faint scent of cinnamon filled the air.

Grace nodded. "I'm guessing there's more to the story than what I saw on the news."

"Definitely, some of which we still don't know and there's a chance we never will. Although for Ron's sake, I hope that's not the case."

"How's he doing?"

"Mixed emotions and a little overwhelmed." Brick took a sip of chai, pleased that it tasted the way he remembered. "Of course, Ron is overjoyed at being reunited with the twins but he's extremely worried about Jasmine."

"Sure. From what I read in the *Post*, it seems like she could be a victim of Stockholm syndrome."

"Too soon to tell, but the FBI is looking into Dr. Reznick. They're also considering the possibility she had a Svengali-like hold over Jasmine."

"Sounds to me like this could be a future episode of *Dateline*."

"Oh, please, don't go there. The last thing Ron wants is publicity. Getting Jasmine home and getting back to work, that's his goal now." After regaling Grace with the incident involving the night stalking deer that nearly caused an accident that could have killed them, Brick was ready to change the subject and focus on Henry Yang. He pointed at the folder in front of her. "Anything interesting in there?"

Grace opened the folder as a smug smile crossed her lips. "In all the commotion when I left, I forgot I made a copy of Henry's academic record." She removed a couple of pages. "As you know, Brick, he was an accounting major. Turns out, in his senior year he participated in a federal work-study program in the Financial Aid Office. Anyway, let's go over what you found on the thumb drive." Grace turned the spreadsheet in Brick's direction and pointed to the first column on the left.

"That's the student ID number. The ones starting with *U* are undergraduates and the ones with *G* are graduate students. The codes in the next column represent the type of financial aid." Grace identified grants and scholarships based on the entry before pausing to take a sip of tea. "Rather than go through each column, check out the highlighted data."

Brick scanned the page. "Looks like four full-scholarship recipients."

"Exactly, but there's a problem." Brick noticed Grace becoming more animated as she referred to the highlighted entries. "Those student ID numbers are invalid."

"Are you saying scholarships were given to nonexistent students?"

"Sure looks that way."

Perhaps Grace was correct, but Brick wasn't ready to reach that conclusion without more explanation. He looked across the table and locked eyes with Grace.

"Convince me."

Grace leaned forward and Brick picked up a scent of sandalwood. She pointed to the first entry on the spreadsheet. "At the time of acceptance, a student is assigned a unique identification number."

Brick glanced at the item Grace pointed to. "Okay, we know that one is an undergraduate."

"Correct."

Brick noticed Grace was sitting up straighter now and sounding like she had slipped into teacher mode.

"The first four numbers represent the student's birth month and day, followed by the last four digits of their Social Security number."

"What about international students who don't have Social Security numbers?" Brick asked.

"They're given a random computer-generated four-digit number." She pointed to the last digit in the ID. "That number identifies the specific school or college the student applied to. A '3' indicates the College of Arts and Science. The School of Public Affairs is a '5.'"

"So, with the exception of the highlighted IDs, were you able to confirm these are valid?"

"Yes." Grace slid her manicured index finger down the page and stopped midway. "That's Henry's ID indicating he was enrolled in the Sullivan School of Business. All of the highlighted IDs end in '8.' Every time I entered those numbers, I got an invalid entry message. Turns out there's a good reason—numeric codes for the schools and colleges end at '7.'" Grace brushed a strand of hair behind her ear. She looked up at Brick, raising her eyebrows as she did so. "Convinced?"

Brick thought for a minute or two. "Yes and no." Immediately he could tell by her reaction that Grace was disappointed. "As far as the IDs you highlighted, I'm convinced they're invalid, but that's not proof scholarships were given to nonexisting students." Brick leaned against the back of his chair. "Ron is a movie trivia savant and if he were here, he would quote a line from *All the President's Men.*"

"Follow the money?" Grace asked.

"You've seen the movie."

"More than once. I'm a huge Bob Woodward fan."

"Really? Are you sure Robert Redford wasn't the draw?"

Grace blushed as she laughed. "Guilty."

Brick nodded. "Anyway, what was a full scholarship worth at that time?"

"For undergraduates, between sixty-five and seventy thousand."

"Big bucks." Brick shook his head as he looked over the spreadsheet before continuing. "People have done stupid things for a whole lot less. Seems like an audit of the Financial Aid Office should have caught this."

"Maybe someone did and chose to ignore it. I hate to say this, but plenty of things that happen on college campuses are swept under the rug." Grace took a deep breath and exhaled slowly. "Lincoln U. is no exception and I wonder if Henry Yang may have stumbled onto this and recognized the potential for fraud."

Brick was wondering the same thing. He picked up his cup and finished his chai. "How familiar are you with the Financial Aid Office?"

"Not very, except that it comes under the supervision of the Chief Financial Officer." Grace flipped through several pages in the folder before removing one. She handed it to Brick. "That's a copy of the organizational chart for the Office of Finance and the Treasurer."

"Obviously, I need to talk to the CFO." Brick took a quick look at the chart. "What can you tell me about Alphonso Baez?"

Grace didn't answer immediately. "How can I put this tactfully? He knows how to work a room. At least that's the impression I have from the three or four times I've seen him at a faculty function. Rumor has it he's an A-lister on the Washington social scene, but I can't speak to that since I don't travel in those circles. Nor do I want to." Grace glanced at her watch. "Yikes, it's almost one; I need to leave."

"Yoga class?"

Grace nodded. "And it's a little out of character, but the Zen master gets really pissed if anyone walks in late." She stood and slung the strap binding her yoga mat over her shoulder. "If you're ever interested in taking a class, let me know; I have some guest passes."

"Thanks, I'll keep that in mind." Unlike when he had said that in response to Sergeant Doyle's employment suggestion with the Maryland State Police, this time he was sincere.

"*Namaste.*"

Brick returned her smile and watched as Grace hurried past the window. At the time she offered him the opportunity to work with her graduate students, he wasn't sure it was something he wanted to do. Now he regretted it was no longer a possibility. Working closely with Grace Alexander might have been an interesting experience. Maybe he would accept her invitation to a yoga class, Brick thought.

CHAPTER FORTY

One Week Later

"Lieutenant Hughes will be with you shortly."

"Thanks." Brick took a seat and waited. Even though he had been here a few times since he left the department, his mind wandered back to the day he resigned. Officially, he retired after twenty years on the job, but lately it felt more like quitting. He wasn't inclined to act impulsively and yet that's exactly what had happened when he had met with Blancato. He was glad when Lieutenant Hughes opened her door.

"Good morning, Brick, come on in." She motioned for him to take a seat at the conference table. "Ron texted he's on his way and Agent Harrison will be joining us shortly. I'm anxious to hear the latest on the Yang case." Before she continued, her cell phone rang. She glanced at the caller ID and rolled her eyes. "Excuse me." The conversation was brief and she laughed as she set the phone down. "Crisis averted."

"That's always a good thing."

Lieutenant Hughes continued laughing. "Since I moved my mother into assisted living, seems there's a crisis du jour. Today's involved someone sitting in someone else's seat at the breakfast table. I swear if I worked in a place like that, I'd end up shooting somebody."

Brick sensed he had seen a side of Lieutenant Hughes not everyone did. The role of dutiful daughter with the responsibility of caring for an elderly parent seemed to be weighing on her despite her comments making light of the situation.

"Lieutenant, Brick." Ron nodded as he entered the office. "Sorry, Metro had to offload at Rhode Island Avenue and the next train was packed. I don't get it. We can send astronauts to the International Space Station, but we can't rely on the Red Line to go a few miles without breaking down." Ron took a seat at the conference table next to Brick. "But if that's the worst I have to deal with today, it's a good day."

Lieutenant Hughes smiled at Ron. "How are the twins and Jasmine?"

"The twins are great. They're eating, sleeping, pooping; doing everything they should be doing. I saw Jasmine yesterday and she's made a lot of progress. They've got her off the antidepressants and the other drugs and the change is amazing. When I think about the condition she was in when the SWAT officers brought her out of that house . . ." Ron's voice drifted off as he seemed to relive that moment. "Anyway, I'm encouraged by the improvement I've seen. I know it's going to take time and she'll need outpatient therapy, but if things stay on track, she may be ready to come home next week."

"That's good news, Ron. And how are you doing?"

"I'm okay." Ron smiled mischievously. "Given the way Jasmine's mother is treating me now, I must be doing something right."

"Hasn't always been the case?" Lieutenant Hughes asked.

"Oh, no." Ron shook his head. "Not by a long shot. She's done a one-eighty. I feel like I'm a candidate for son-in-law of the year."

"Well earned I'm sure, Ron," Lieutenant Hughes said. "Agent Harrison should be here soon, but I wanted to update you on Holly Beltran. In light of the circumstances, she's been reassigned to Youth and Family Services Division, effective immediately. And, Ron, I think it would be in your best interest to not have any contact with Holly."

"No worries, Lieutenant. I know I'm not the smartest guy, but I've learned a lesson and I think Brick can tell you, I don't make the same mistake twice."

Before Brick had a chance to agree, the intercom on the lieutenant's desk buzzed. The secretary announced Agent Harrison had arrived.

Ron took a deep breath and exhaled slowly. "I'm anxious to hear what Harrison has to say, but it's kind of like waiting for the dentist to begin a root canal. I've been anticipating this for days and I just want it over."

Brick wasn't surprised by Ron's admission despite his upbeat demeanor. Hopefully, the more he learned about what happened, the sooner he and Jasmine would be able to put it behind them and move forward.

Before taking a seat next to Lieutenant Hughes, Harrison shook hands all around. As he opened a folder and removed several pages and a couple of photographs, he looked at Ron. "First, let's talk about the envelope you found in your dresser. Here's a copy of the note inside." He slid the sheet of paper across the table.

Ron picked it up and paused before reading aloud. "This is your fault. Are you happy now?" He sat up straight and shook his head. "No way . . . Jasmine didn't write that."

"Are you saying the printing doesn't look like Jasmine's?" Agent Harrison asked.

Ron studied the copy. "I'm not sure because she never prints; always writes longhand. But I am sure if Jasmine had written that note, she would have said a whole lot more than those eight words. It might have been eight pages by the time she listed everything I've ever done wrong—from not emptying the trash to forgetting to lower the toilet seat." Ron started to laugh, and the others joined in. "I'm serious, she has a memory like a steel trap."

Agent Harrison nodded as he listened to Ron. "Okay, that confirms why the fingerprints we lifted from the envelope and the note didn't belong to Jasmine." He handed a photograph to Ron who placed it on the table where Brick could see it as well. "That's Dr. Lynn Reznick."

Ron picked up the photo and stared at it. "No way, that woman looks like she's sixty years old."

"Sixty-two, actually," Harrison said. "This photo ran alongside her obituary in the Albany *Times Union*. She died ten years ago."

"What?" Ron set the photo aside and looked around the table. "That doesn't make any sense at all."

"It will." Harrison opened a folder and removed a file marked *Confidential*. "She was a psychiatrist whose identity was stolen by one of her patients."

"Oh man, this is crazy," Ron said. "Are you saying the therapist Jasmine was seeing was a fake?"

"Exactly." Agent Harrison handed Ron another photo. "Her name was Ellen Roberts. The fingerprints we got from the woman who jumped from the Bay Bridge identified her and were the only ones we lifted from the envelope and note. Court records gave us some insight into her troubled past and locating her next of kin. A sister in Saratoga Springs was the key to peeling back the layers and finding out who she was."

Ron shifted in his chair and rolled his eyes. "Bring it on."

Agent Harrison briefly referred to his notes. "Ellen Roberts grew up in Troy, New York. After graduating from high school, she was a student at SUNY Albany. In the second semester of her freshman year, she went off the rails and dropped out of school. She got arrested for shoplifting and drug possession. Both were misdemeanors and the judge gave her probation provided she went to rehab. She abided by that, and according to her sister, post-rehab she started seeing Dr. Reznick. Roberts stayed clean and sober for several years, even reenrolled at SUNY and started studying psychology."

"Well, that was convenient," Lieutenant Hughes commented.

Harrison agreed. "Apparently, she was doing well academically and was engaged to the guy she was living with. She was very excited when she found out she was pregnant with twins, but things unraveled when she had a miscarriage. After she and her fiancé broke up, she started seeing Reznick again. Two, sometimes three times a week. Although she seemed to be doing okay, her sister was concerned that she was becoming too dependent on her therapist."

"From what I understand, that's a fairly common phenomenon," Lieutenant Hughes said.

"It is," Agent Harrison confirmed. "Very strong bonds can develop, and according to information we were told by her sister, Roberts became unhinged when Reznick died."

"Of natural causes?" Brick asked.

"Yes, lung cancer. From diagnosis to her death was just a matter of weeks."

"I think I know where this is going," Lieutenant Hughes said.

Brick wasn't sure what she was thinking, but he was forming his own opinion. To him, it sounded as though Roberts was incapable of dealing with the kind of stressors that can trigger aberrant behavior. It was just a matter of when and to what degree she would act out.

Agent Harrison took a moment as he again referred to the report compiled by the agents in New York. "Roberts stayed with her sister for several weeks following Reznick's death. When she finally made a decision to visit a longtime family friend in North Carolina, her sister thought it was a good idea. To her, it seemed as though Roberts was moving forward from the miscarriage and the death of her therapist. Her sister received a few texts and was led to believe things were going well. Roberts sounded upbeat. There was no reason for concern until Roberts didn't return when she had planned to and didn't respond to texts or voicemail messages. The sister contacted the friend Roberts was visiting and was told she hadn't been in contact with her for over a year."

"Was she ever in North Carolina?" Ron asked.

"We don't know. Her sister did what she could as far as filing missing person reports, but there were never reasons to suspect foul play. Roberts was an adult. If she chose to disappear, she was entitled. Admittedly, there's some gaps in the timeline, but we were able to determine she spent some time in Richmond, Virginia. How she supported herself during that time remains to be seen. When she relocated to Maryland, she had reinvented herself as Dr. Lynn Reznick."

"Man, how can that happen?" Ron's frustration was evident as he continued. "I mean she came recommended by Jasmine's OB-GYN."

"Unfortunately, she's not the first impostor to slip through the cracks. As long as you have an internet connection and a printer, it's easy to fake credentials."

"Still, a couple of psych classes and she passes herself off as . . . a female Dr. Phil. Really?"

"Keep in mind, Ron, she had hundreds of sessions with the real Dr. Reznick. That was her training ground." Harrison shuffled through a couple of pages. "She was hired as a counselor at Patuxent Institution and according to tax records, purchased the bungalow in Jessup. Three years later, she opened her own practice in D.C. We found several positive reviews on Yelp."

Ron shook his head. "But I don't understand. How do you go from respected therapist to kidnapper to shooting a cop to killing yourself?"

Agent Harrison nodded. "Obviously, we'll never hear from Roberts, herself, and that's unfortunate. But one of our behavioral analysts weighed in. It's her opinion that Roberts may have had unresolved issues from the miscarriage. When Jasmine sought her counseling, she saw a woman struggling with motherhood. The very thing she desperately wanted for herself. Here was a chance to make it happen. It's probably not a coincidence that her former fiancé, the father of the twins she lost, was African American."

"So, what you're describing is a crime of opportunity," Ron said.

"Exactly."

Ron cleared his throat. "She already stole one woman's identity . . ." He seemed to be thinking out loud before directing another question to Agent Harrison. "It's hard for me to even say these words, but I gotta ask, do you think she was planning to kill Jasmine?"

"Yes." Harrison answered without hesitating but paused as if giving Ron a minute to process his confirmation. "That was the conclusion reached by the behavioral analyst, as well."

Ron pointed at Brick. "And if it wasn't for my man stopping me from confronting her twice . . . she might have killed me, too." Ron shook his head. "Shot with my own gun, that would have really sucked."

CHAPTER FORTY-ONE

To Brick, the things Agent Harrison had revealed went a long way toward bringing the big picture into focus. He could accept the theory that Ellen Roberts saw in Jasmine the life she believed she should have had. Her determination to make it happen explained the motivation behind her actions. In her distorted perspective, she may have even thought she was rescuing the twins from a seemingly incompetent mother. Had Roberts not killed herself, Brick could hear an attorney arguing that her behavior was the basis for an insanity defense. Convincing a jury might not have been that difficult until they heard she faked being a psychologist, drugged Jasmine and presumably held her hostage along with the twins, and shot a police officer. Instead, it was unlikely even a dream team could have saved her ass.

While Agent Harrison consulted his notes, Ron slumped against the back of his chair. Brick suspected that the realization of how close he and Jasmine came to losing everything was taking its toll. He could relate, the euphoria of surviving a life-threatening situation is often short lived. When it wears off, the aftermath can be jarring and last a long time.

"Questions, anyone?" Agent Harrison asked as he looked around the table.

"Is your investigation concluded?" Ron asked.

"Not entirely. We're trying to locate as many of her past patients as we can. Guess I shouldn't refer to them as patients, more like fraud victims. They deserve to know they were seeing a therapist who was a fake. And from them, we may gain more insight into the mind of Ellen Roberts. I suspect the Behavioral Science Unit will be studying and writing about her for a long time." Agent Harrison handed a copy of his report to Lieutenant Hughes. "I will, of course, keep you informed of anything else we discover."

*   *   *

"Do either of you need a break?" Lieutenant Hughes asked after Agent Harrison left.

"I could use one and a cup of coffee." Ron left for a Starbucks run with a request for a caramel macchiato from the lieutenant.

"Brick, there's something I've been considering, and I wanted to run it by you before I mention it to Ron. Getting back to work now might be therapeutic for him and working with you on the Yang case would give him the flexibility he may need. What are your thoughts?"

"Sounds good to me."

A few minutes later, Ron returned with the drink Lieutenant Hughes requested and a cup he set down in front of Brick. "Green tea, didn't want you to feel left out."

"Thanks."

"Least I could do for saving my life."

Brick raised his cup in Ron's direction. "Twice."

"Yeah, twice." Ron sighed loudly as he sat down. "That was rough." He took a sip of coffee. "I want to know; I mean I have to know, but hearing how close Jasmine came . . . I can't stop thinking about what might have happened if we hadn't rolled up when we did." He picked up his cup but set it back down. Ron's dreads swayed as he shook his head. He exhaled loudly. "She could have made it look like Jasmine killed herself while she took off with the twins for parts unknown."

"Ron, try not to think of what could have happened. It sounds to me like you two were at the right place at the right time," Lieutenant Hughes said.

"Maybe, but I kind of think it was something else. More like divine intervention?"

"That's certainly possible," Lieutenant Hughes said.

Brick agreed but wondered why Ron, who was far more religious, seemed conflicted.

"The problem is, if I believe it was an act of God, I need to find it in my heart to forgive Ellen Roberts." Ron gazed down at his left hand, seemingly focused on his wedding ring. "I think I'm a good Christian. At least, I try to be, but I don't know if I can ever forgive her."

"Ron, I think forgiveness is a process," Lieutenant Hughes said. "It doesn't have to happen immediately, and it might help if you speak with your pastor."

"You mean if he ever comes back from Vegas?"

Lieutenant Hughes grabbed a napkin and covered her mouth. She appeared to swallow hard before lowering the napkin. "I just came way too close to a macchiato spit take." She set her cup aside. "I had forgotten about the pastor's . . . let's say pilgrimage to Sin City." Her comment seemed to provide the comic relief to lighten the atmosphere in the room. "Anyway, remember the Employee Assistance Program has counselors available 24/7."

"Good to know. I'll probably take advantage of that when I get back to work. Hopefully, that will happen soon."

"How about now, with flexible hours?" Lieutenant Hughes paused as if trying to read Ron's reaction. "I think it would be mutually beneficial for you and Brick to work together on the Yang cold case."

"Seriously?"

Lieutenant Hughes nodded.

Ron smiled broadly exposing the gap between his front teeth. He gave Brick a high five. "Only a fool would pass up a chance to work with this guy."

"All right then, that's settled." She picked up the cup from Starbucks and took a drink before turning in Brick's direction. "Any new developments?"

"After discussing the files I found with Grace Alexander, I realized the need to talk with the Chief Financial Officer. I've set up an appointment with him for tomorrow morning." Brick cleared his throat. "I'm not looking forward to it, but tomorrow afternoon, a meeting with Blancato."

A smile crossed the lieutenant's lips. "Just put on your big boy pants."

Coming from anyone else, Brick would have found the comment condescending, but given the rapport he and Hughes had established, he took it in stride and laughed at her advice.

Lieutenant Hughes glanced at her watch. "We're going to have to wrap this up. I need to go over to District Court for the swearing in of the new U.S. Marshal."

"Any scuttlebutt on him?" Brick asked.

"I'm hearing good things, but it goes without saying, he's a political appointee. Ask me in a couple of months what I think." Lieutenant Hughes pushed back her chair, got up, and stepped over to the locked filing cabinet behind her desk. She entered a code and opened the top drawer.

"I believe these belong to you." She handed Ron his badge and service revolver.

CHAPTER FORTY-TWO

The gray, dreary morning didn't dampen Brick's enthusiasm for the day ahead. Thanks to Lieutenant Hughes assigning Ron to the Yang case, he was looking forward to working with his former partner, reuniting as a team to do what they had done so successfully. Brick didn't want to get ahead of himself but solving this cold case may have potential for working on others gathering dust.

Dress to impress. Brick muttered the words under his breath as he scanned the contents of his packed, but well-organized, walk-in closet. He felt compelled to carefully choose the suit he would wear to today's meeting as he recalled comments Grace Alexander had made about Alphonso Baez and after seeing several photos of him in *Washingtonian* magazine. The eligible bachelor appeared to be a regular at see-and-be-seen events, ranging from casual charity fundraisers to black-tie galas at the Kennedy Center. Based on the status-conscious mentality so much a part of life within the Beltway, Brick had reason to believe his and Ron's credibility would be judged by Lincoln University's Chief Financial Officer based on the cut of their suits and the fabric of their ties.

After selecting a dark suit, Brick reached for a navy blue–and maroon-striped tie hanging on a rack arranged by color. It had been several months since he had worn a suit and he was relieved this one still fit as well as it did on the day he bought it at Brooks Brothers. Just as he finished adjusting his tie, his cell phone pinged with a text from Ron.

"On my way."

Brick slipped his wallet into his pants pocket, grabbed his cell phone and keys, and headed downstairs to wait. As soon as he saw the Crown Vic pull up in front of his condo building, he felt his heart beat a little faster. For an instant it felt like what used to be the start of a typical shift.

"Looking good, partner."

"Thanks. You, too." Brick closed the car door and adjusted his seat belt.

"Yeah, based on what you told me about Baez, I thought about the teachings of Dr. King. You know, the saying about not judging a man by the content of his character, but where he buys his suits. Pulled out my best threads, even took a shower . . . last week."

"I don't recall that quote, but it sounds like you're ready." Despite what Ron had been through lately, it seemed his sense of humor was intact and for that Brick was grateful.

Ron pulled away from the curb and headed south on Connecticut Avenue. At 9:30 a.m., rush hour should have been winding down, but as he crossed the Calvert Street Bridge, traffic was at a standstill.

"What's going . . . oh, man, a motorcade."

"No worries, we've got plenty of time. How are things on the home front?" Brick asked.

"Good. Jasmine's mother is spoiling me along with the twins." Ron smiled as he patted his midsection. "Last night she made a baked ham and mac and cheese. No wonder I've regained the weight I lost and probably added a few pounds."

"And Jasmine?"

"Saw her yesterday for a couple of hours. We had a long session with one of her therapists and it went well. Jasmine doesn't remember much about the days in Jessup, but she said some things that make sense. It seems Reznick, or I should say Roberts, convinced her that she and the twins were in immediate danger."

"From you?"

"Right. Jasmine thought they were going to a women's shelter near Baltimore where they would be safe. It would give her time to figure out what she needed to do. She remembers driving to BWI and parking in the long-term lot. Then Roberts drove her and the twins to Jessup. From that point on, Roberts was in charge and controlled everything. There was no TV, radio, cell phone, internet."

"Power play—no communication with the outside world and total dependence on Roberts."

"Exactly. Right away, Roberts started drugging Jasmine. She said she lost track of time, and everything became distorted. Even when she was awake, she said she felt like she was in a hazy, sleep-like state. Hard to believe, but she doesn't remember being removed from the house by the SWAT team."

The distant sound of sirens grew louder as three motorcycles and a pair of police cars sped past followed by a couple of SUVs and a limousine.

"That's it? Definitely not POTUS."

"Yeah, whoever that was, one box lower on the organizational chart and they'd be riding the Metro to wherever they're going." Ron signaled to turn as he approached Massachusetts Avenue and merged into the lane behind a shiny black town car. "Is it just me or are there a lot more cars with diplomat plates these days?"

"Does seem that way. Just keep your distance."

"Absolutely. The last thing I want to do is a ton of paperwork for a fender bender that turns into an international incident. Plus, I've had my fifteen minutes; happy to fly under the radar, as the saying goes. Anyway, getting back to Jasmine. I guess it's possible she'll start remembering more details, but according to her treatment team, it's unlikely. The therapist thinks the best strategy going forward is reassuring her that I'm not a threat and that her home is safe. It may mean having her mother live with us for a while and I'm down with that."

"I would be, too, just based on the mac and cheese." That brought a laugh from Ron. "Seriously, whatever it takes, that's what you need to do."

"I know, and Lieutenant Hughes has offered to talk to Jasmine about Holly if I thought it would help. I haven't decided, but I'm leaning toward having her do that at some point. What do you think?"

"In court, hearing the same thing from two witnesses is always better than one. Plus, I think you can trust the lieutenant to sensitively explain Holly's texting games. So far, based on my experience with her, I'm impressed. Think about how her predecessor would have handled your situation."

"Oh, Blancato? If he thought it would have in any way reflected badly on him, I would have been under the bus in a heartbeat."

Ron drove to the north end of Lincoln University's campus and pulled into a parking space between a Lexus and a Volvo SUV. He placed the department-issued, official police business placard in the windshield of the Crown Vic. "Ready?"

Brick nodded. "I've been thinking, I want you to take the lead. Introduce yourself and then just refer to me by name. He'll probably assume I'm a detective, too, but we need to be careful to not misrepresent my position."

"Okay, but what if he asks about your role?"

"Then I'll explain."

"Roger that."

As they walked through the faculty parking lot, Brick looked around. "Get the feeling we're at the auto show?"

"Looks that way. I just hope they don't tow our wheels because it's an eyesore." Before heading up the stairs of the stately, ivy-covered Business Administration Building, Ron stopped and took a deep breath. "Ahh, filling my lungs with the rarefied air."

Brick laughed while agreeing with Ron's observation. Like many places in the nation's capital, this campus served as a reminder of the wealth some enjoyed that others were denied. After signing in at the security desk, Brick and Ron were given visitor badges and told an escort would be with them shortly. A few minutes later, they were handed off to the Chief Financial Officer's secretary, an attractive woman who appeared to be in her mid-fifties. She was wearing a classic Hillary Clinton–style pantsuit and a floral print Burberry scarf.

"Good morning. Mr. Baez will be with you as soon as he finishes his conference call." Together they took the elevator to the fourth floor and entered the double glass doors at the end of the hallway. "Please have a seat." She pointed to a beige leather sofa. "May I get you a beverage—coffee, tea, spring water?"

Brick and Ron took a seat but declined the beverage offer. From his vantage, Brick glanced at the telephone on the secretary's desk. There were four lines, and it appeared none were in use. After about ten minutes, Brick approached the secretary.

"Excuse me, on second thought, I would like a cup of tea."

"Of course, black or green?"

"Green, please."

"Detective Hayes, something to drink?"

"Yes, thank you. Coffee with cream and sugar."

Baez's assistant left, which was exactly what Brick had hoped for. He stepped behind her desk and listened outside the door to Baez's office for the sound of either a one-sided conversation or voices on a speakerphone. He didn't hear anything and sat back down wondering if there really was a call, or if this was Baez's way of letting them know whose time was the most important. Fifteen minutes passed while Brick drank his tea and Ron finished his coffee. Finally, the door to Baez's office opened.

"Gentlemen, right this way." Standing in the doorway, Alphonso Baez pointed to a pair of upholstered chairs in front of a modern glass and chrome desk. Behind the desk, a wall of windows provided a sweeping view of Key Bridge and the high-rise buildings in the Rosslyn section of Arlington County. Baez settled into his executive-style leather chair and faced Brick and Ron.

"Okay, let's get started."

It wasn't lost on Brick that from the man known to work the room, there were no introductions, no handshakes, nor an apology for keeping them waiting. Apparently, Baez didn't feel the need to waste his charm on two guys from the police department.

"Certainly," Ron said. "We appreciate you meeting with us and don't want to take up more of your time than is absolutely necessary."

Brick was proud of his protégé's polite approach. It's how he would have handled it himself even though Baez hadn't earned being treated respectfully.

Ron leaned forward, closing the distance between himself and Baez. "As I mentioned when I spoke with your secretary, we're looking into the death of Henry Yang, a former Lincoln University student."

With a look of boredom, Baez nodded his head.

"Were you familiar with—"

"Detective, the death of a student is very unusual. I'm sure everyone associated with the University at the time knew about it."

"I understand," Ron said in a matching condescending tone. "But I was about to ask if you knew Henry."

"Perhaps you're not aware, Lincoln U. has over 5,000 full- and part-time students. As Chief Financial Officer, I have little to no interaction with them."

Brick noticed the emphasis Baez placed on his title as he dodged Ron's question for the second time.

"I was not aware of the size of the student body—that's impressive." Ron paused. "But you didn't answer my question. From what I've learned, Henry Yang was interning at the Financial Aid Office."

Baez shrugged. "In that case, I may have met him."

"But you're not sure?"

"If you consider passing someone in the hall, exchanging pleasantries as meeting that person, then I suppose I did."

Brick wasn't buying it. Unless there was something to be gained, exchanging pleasantries didn't sound like Baez's style.

"Are you aware of the type of assignments interns may be given?" Ron asked.

"Detective, I am not a micromanager. It is the responsibility of my very capable staff, in whom I have total confidence, to supervise interns assigned to their offices."

For a split second, Ron glanced at Brick. A very subtle nod was their way of passing the baton.

"Understood. Sounds like we got ahead of ourselves. Do you know who would have supervised Henry during his internship?"

"Not off the top of my head, of course." Baez had dialed down the attitude. "I'll have my secretary check our records. She'll contact you with what she finds."

"Thanks, that would be very helpful," Brick said as he stood. He glanced over at Ron who was now also standing. "We appreciate your time."

Baez nodded as he pushed back his chair and stepped around his desk. As he ushered Brick and Ron out of his office, he shook their hands at the door.

Neither Brick nor Ron spoke until they left the building and headed toward the parking lot.

"Mission accomplished, partner?" Ron asked.

"I think so. What he didn't say told us a hell of a lot more than what he did."

"Yeah, and I liked the attitude shift when he probably figured he was off the hook." Ron unlocked the driver's side of the cruiser. "I'm not holding my breath until we hear back from his secretary."

CHAPTER FORTY-THREE

WHEN IT BEGAN operations in 2002, the Department of Homeland Security was temporarily located on the grounds of a former naval facility in the Tenleytown section of Northwest D.C. Eleven years later, it was still located at the Nebraska Avenue complex of two-story beige brick buildings scattered across several acres. After checking in at the guard's station, Ron drove to the parking lot across from the building housing the Office of Partnership and Engagement. He removed the car keys from the ignition and turned in Brick's direction.

"Ready to do this?"

"Ready as I'll ever be."

"What do you suppose the Deputy Director of the Office of Partnership and Engagement does?" Ron asked.

"Knowing it's Blancato, other than drawing a paycheck, probably not much."

"That might be a good thing."

Brick didn't disagree given Blancato's missteps during his tenure in charge of the Homicide Squad. Together they showed ID, signed in, and passed through a metal detector that looked like it was back in service after being retired from airport duty. Their footsteps echoed as they made their way down a drab hallway. At a reception desk a clean-shaven young man wearing a navy-blue shirt with the DHS emblem announced their arrival.

"Deputy Blancato is expecting you. Second door on the left."

"Have a seat, guys. Good to see you."

To Brick's ears, his former boss almost sounded sincere. As Blancato sat down behind his oversized mahogany desk, Brick noticed Blancato had gained weight and was sporting a gold wedding band on his left hand. Maybe third time would be a charm. Brick looked around at what he would easily describe as an executive man cave. Photographs of Blancato shaking hands with politicians, as well as local athletes and celebrities, filled one wall. On the opposite wall, a large, flat-screen TV was mounted. A mini-fridge was probably hidden under his desk.

"Sounds as though my successor doesn't understand the difference between cold case and closed case." Blancato leaned back in his chair. "I remember the hit-and-run case in Rock Creek Park and there's nothing cold about it. The driver was the son of an ambassador." Blancato picked up a paper clip and proceeded to unbend it into a straight line. "Diplomatic immunity—the equivalent of a get-out-of-jail-free card." Blancato shrugged before reaching for another paper clip. "I had no choice but to cut him loose and close the case."

"Do you remember the name of the driver?" Brick asked.

Blancato shook his head. "No. I think the ambassador was from South America." Blancato leaned forward. "Look, I don't like diplomatic immunity any more than someone who gets screwed by it, but it's a necessary evil we live with, especially here in D.C."

It seemed to Brick that Blancato had said all that he intended to say. "Thanks for your time."

After leaving the building, Ron commented that he thought Blancato knew more than he was willing to share.

"What makes you think so?" Brick asked.

"The way he was mutilating those paper clips. Maybe it's just a habit, but it reminded me of Captain Queeg rolling the tiny balls between his fingers."

"Channeling Humphrey Bogart in *The Caine Mutiny*?"

"Maybe." Ron stopped in his tracks. "Got to say I'm impressed—you knew my movie reference."

"Well, don't get too excited. That was easy. It's not like I'm ready to take the *Jeopardy* contestant test."

"I don't know. . . maybe you should."

After returning to the Homicide Squad, Brick pulled up a chair as Ron logged into his computer. "Somewhere in South America. I guess we should be glad he narrowed it down that much." Ron's computer displayed the State Department website. He entered the search criteria to obtain a list of ambassadors from South America at the time of the hit-and-run. "Here we go." Ron printed two copies of the list and handed one to Brick.

Fourteen countries starting with Argentina showed the name of their ambassador and the date of their appointment to serve in Washington. Brick scanned the list as he mentally visualized the map of South America. "Holy crap. Check out Paraguay."

"Whoa, Eduardo Baez." Ron dropped the list onto his desk. "Confirms what Blancato said—the driver was the son of an ambassador. Damn, Alphonso Baez is going to continue getting away with killing Henry Yang. That sucks."

"Pull up the State Department website again." Brick and Ron switched seats so that he had access to the computer. He entered *diplomatic immunity* and clicked on the document listing regulations. As he scrolled through the table of contents, he found the specific criteria to qualify for immunity.

"Ron, listen to this—family members forming part of the house-hold of diplomatic agents enjoy the same immunity."

"Yeah, so?"

"Alphonso Baez lives independently and flaunts it. If we can prove he wasn't part of the household at the time of the hit-and-run, im-munity may not apply." While Ron searched Virginia DMV records, Brick located Arlington County tax assessment records that con-firmed Baez purchased his high-end, owner-occupied condo eigh-teen months before the hit-and-run.

"C'mon, Ron, we need to talk to the lieutenant."

* * *

Brick and Ron took seats at the conference table and waited for Lieutenant Hughes to join them. They didn't have to wait long.

"Okay, guys, let's see if you can salvage this day for me," Hughes said as she sat down and uncapped a bottle of Pepsi.

"Based on our meetings with Alphonso Baez and your predeces-sor, we think we're on to something. When we met with Baez, he wasn't sure he ever met Henry Yang, other than possibly exchanging pleasantries in the hallway."

"So right there you knew he was being evasive."

"Exactly. We concluded the meeting with him thinking he had the upper hand. Our meeting with Blancato was also productive. He confirmed the driver of the hit-and-run was the son of an ambassa-dor from South America. After tracking down the driver, diplo-matic immunity protected him from being arrested."

Lieutenant Hughes nodded. "So, case closed."

"Maybe not. Blancato couldn't remember the driver's name or the country he was from, but we checked State Department records. At the time of the hit-and-run, the D.C.-based ambassador from Paraguay was Eduardo Baez."

"Guess we know where that DNA is going to lead, but Blancato was correct in not charging him."

"Not necessarily." Brick went on to advise the lieutenant of their findings of Alphonso's independent lifestyle. "And it's interesting that the high-end condo was purchased around the same time the fake scholarships were funded."

"Motive and means." Lieutenant Hughes knitted her brow. "Sounds like Yang discovered the fraud and in reporting it, walked straight into the lion's den. Proving that is going to be problematic, but do you think we have enough to prove felony hit-and-run?"

"Yes," Brick and Ron answered in unison.

"That carries a possible sentence of fifteen years," Brick added. "Since the scholarships were federally funded, the FBI will have jurisdiction over that investigation. It's sadly ironic the agency Yang was working so hard to join may ultimately be responsible for bringing his killer to justice."

"Ironic, indeed," Lieutenant Hughes agreed. "As far as I'm concerned, you have probable cause to arrest Baez, but we need to proceed with caution given the international factor. Why don't you guys take a break while I run this past the U.S. Attorney. I'll let you know as soon as I hear anything."

CHAPTER FORTY-FOUR

THE DAY AFTER presenting their findings to Lieutenant Hughes, Brick and Ron returned to the campus of Lincoln U. with a magistrate-signed arrest warrant. No escort was necessary as they took the elevator to the fourth floor and headed to the double glass doors leading to Alphonso Baez's office.

"May I help you?" Baez's administrative assistant looked surprised but sounded annoyed.

"We're here to see Alphonso Baez," Ron said as they approached the door leading to his office. They ignored her protestations that they needed an appointment.

"What the . . ." Baez put down his phone as he stood up behind his desk.

"Alphonso Baez, I have an arrest warrant for the felony hit-and-run resulting in the death of Henry Yang." Ron handed a copy of the warrant to Baez.

"This isn't worth the paper it's printed on." Baez threw the warrant into his wastebasket. "Obviously, you don't know who I am."

"I think we do," Brick responded. "Your father is Eduardo Baez." From the corner of his eye, Brick noticed the handcuffs Ron was holding. "Ambassador to Paraguay."

"Then you should know even if what you've accused me of is true, I have diplomatic immunity."

"Not according to the State Department, the U.S. Attorney, and the magistrate who signed the arrest warrant. Guess you didn't read the fine print on exemptions."

Baez sat back in his chair. The color drained from his face as Ron advised him of his Miranda rights. "I need you to stand and place your hands behind your back," Ron instructed.

It appeared Baez was complying as he slowly pushed back his chair and started to get to his feet. But instead of placing his hands behind his back, he reached across his desk for a metal letter opener. Holding the silver-plated mini-sword-shaped object securely in his hand, he lunged at Brick.

Brick felt pain as the object pierced his cheek just below his right eye and flinched as he heard what sounded like a balloon pop. The adrenaline surge coursing through his body had distorted his perception and for a moment it felt as if he were caught in a freeze frame. He was jolted back to the present when he saw Baez staggering backward before collapsing onto the floor.

Less than ten minutes had elapsed since Brick and Ron had walked into Baez's office. There was no way to anticipate that things would escalate so quickly, but now they had to deal with the aftermath. While Brick called 911 reporting an officer-involved shooting and the need for an ambulance, Ron holstered his weapon and knelt next to Baez. The bullet had caught Baez in his right upper arm. A bloodstain spread down the sleeve of his gray suit jacket. His eyes fluttered, and Brick was relieved to see Baez was conscious, at least for now.

"What . . . what's going on?" Baez tried to sit up but didn't succeed. "Am I . . . bleeding?"

"Try to relax. There's help on the way. I'm going to loosen your tie." While Brick undid the knot, Ron held his index and middle fingers against Baez's neck, checking his pulse rate.

"Elevated, around one thirty. Let's get his jacket off."

As gently as possible, Brick and Ron managed to remove Baez's jacket as he now appeared to be drifting in and out of consciousness.

"Alphonso, stay with us. You're going to be okay." Given the amount of blood pooling beneath Baez's shoulder, Brick wasn't sure he was telling the truth, more like wishful thinking. He glanced over at Ron. Beads of sweat ran down his face and he looked as if he might pass out.

"That's a lot of blood." Ron mouthed the words, but Brick understood the unspoken message.

Brick nodded as he stood and removed his belt. He knelt and with Ron's help wrapped the belt around Baez's arm. The flow of blood seemed to be slowing.

To Brick's relief, minutes after applying the makeshift tourniquet, the paramedics arrived along with campus security and police officers from the Second District. While the paramedics took over, Brick backed away. For the first time, he noticed Baez's blood on his hands and clothes. He used his handkerchief to wipe the blood from his hands as best he could. He picked up Baez's jacket from where it was lying on the floor and as he handed it to one of the police officers, a key fob fell out of a pocket. Brick recognized the familiar logo of Mercedes-Benz. He took a picture of the fob before handing it to the officer holding Baez's jacket.

Just after Baez was wheeled out of the office, Lieutenant Hughes arrived. Brick recognized the two veteran detectives from Internal Affairs who accompanied her.

"Are you guys okay?" Without waiting for a response, she stepped closer to Brick and focused on the injury to his cheek. "You need to get that looked at, but you're lucky his aim was off. A black eye is temporary, an eye patch is permanent." She turned her attention to Ron and repeated her question. He managed a less-than-convincing nod.

*   *   *

It was just after three when Brick's debriefing interview concluded. As expected, he and Ron had been separated before leaving the Lincoln U. campus, driven to Indiana Avenue, and questioned individually at Police Headquarters. After being seen by a nurse at the health unit and given an ice pack to reduce the swelling, his injury was photographed. As stressful as it was for Brick to retell what happened and answer the same questions asked by different investigators, he figured it was worse for Ron. Finally, he was free to go.

"Brick, when you're ready, I'll drive you home." The detective from Internal Affairs closed his laptop computer. "Given the blood on your clothes, you'll scare the shit out of a cab driver or people on the Metro."

"Thanks, I'm ready now."

Except for some small talk about the Nationals' less-than-impressive season winding down and the Redskins' upcoming game against the Cowboys, the twenty-minute trip was silent, for which Brick was grateful. When they reached his building, he used the back stairwell and made it to his unit without running into any neighbors.

Brick grabbed a large trash bag from under the kitchen sink before heading to the bathroom. He stripped off his suit and stuffed the jacket and pants into the bag. Shirt, tie, socks, and underwear followed. The clothes could probably be cleaned, but Brick knew he'd never wear them again. And it wasn't worth freaking out a dry cleaner in order to donate the suit to Goodwill. He stepped into the shower. With the water as hot as he could stand it, he grabbed a bar of Dial soap and scrubbed. He rinsed off and repeated the process two more times.

*   *   *

Wearing a lightly starched blue and white checked shirt and jeans, Brick locked the door to his apartment and headed to Boland's Mill.

"Jaysus, you look terrible."

"Eamonn's right, Brick," Rory said as he joined in the conversation. "I mean it's not like you ever look like you stepped out of a tanning booth, but you're pale as a banshee. Are you sick and what's with the black eye?"

Without going into a lot of detail, Brick explained what had happened.

"And this guy, Baez—is he going to be okay?" Rory asked.

"I don't know. He lost a lot of blood."

"Aw feck, that's not good."

Eamonn picked up a bottle of Jameson and a couple of shot glasses. "Rory can handle the happy hour crowd; let's go to my office."

Brick appreciated the suggestion and followed Eamonn to the back of the restaurant where a corner of the storeroom provided a workspace. Elvis was curled up and sleeping on Eamonn's desk. She woke, stretched, and head-butted Brick's arm a couple of times before jumping down and getting a drink of water.

Meanwhile, Eamonn poured a shot of Jameson for Brick and one for himself. Brick drank it down in one gulp.

"What happens now?"

"Ron will be placed on administrative leave or desk duty while the incident is investigated. The findings will be turned over to the U.S. Attorney's Office. If they determine the shooting was justified, that's it—done."

"And if they find it wasn't?" Eamonn asked.

"It will be presented to the grand jury. If they think Ron wasn't justified, they'll indict." Brick took a deep breath. "Hopefully, it will be determined to be a good shoot and the grand jury won't even be involved. But until that happens, it's a ton of stress Ron doesn't need especially after all he's been through." Brick threw back a second shot of whiskey.

Eamonn poured himself another and raised the glass to his mouth. "They say we're never given more than we can bear."

"They? Who's *they*, Eamonn?"

With the back of his hand, Eamonn wiped his mouth. "Who the feck knows . . . eejits, I suspect."

CHAPTER FORTY-FIVE

A week later

BRICK RETURNED TO the table he was sharing with Grace Alexander carrying two Bento boxes. He handed her the grilled salmon.

"Looks good, thanks."

"Seems like a fitting post-yoga meal." Brick unwrapped a pair of wooden chopsticks and broke them apart. "Even though I passed on the chicken and fish and went for the Korean brisket."

"Protein is protein. I don't judge." Grace smiled as she unfolded a napkin and placed it in her lap. "For a first timer, you did great."

"You don't have to say that just because I paid for lunch." Brick laughed as he sprinkled soy sauce over a generous portion of rice. "It's a tough workout. Probably good I didn't know that holding still can be so painful."

"Gets easier the more you practice." Grace lifted the lid on her Bento box. "Think you'll try another class?"

"Depends on how bad I feel tomorrow." With his chopsticks, Brick picked up a piece of avocado maki. "Of course, I can't use the old *I'm too busy excuse* since the Yang case has been turned over to the Homicide Squad. Back to being unemployed."

"Welcome to the club." Grace raised her glass of iced tea in a toast.

Brick was surprised by her comment and the gesture. "I thought you were offered reinstatement."

Grace nodded. "I was but I turned it down. I don't want to work with colleagues who automatically believed Baez's accusation against me."

"Changes your perspective, doesn't it?"

"Absolutely. People . . . I'm still trying to figure out who is Alphonso Baez. When I think about him committing a hit-and-run and assaulting you, makes me grateful that all he did was accuse me of plagiarism."

"Seems that was his preemptive strike to ensure the Yang case wouldn't be investigated."

"And it almost worked."

Brick took a taste of the spicy beef and reached for his glass of water. "Yeah, were it not for Lieutenant Hughes, he would have succeeded."

"True, the lieutenant gave the go-ahead, but you did the work."

"And unfortunately, Ron is paying the price."

"How's he doing?"

"Better, since Baez is expected to make a full recovery. It's traumatic. Lots of cops work their whole career and never fire their weapon. For Ron, it was a couple of hours into his first day back on the job."

"It's so hard for me to wrap my head around Baez being capable of doing the things he did. He's been with the University for quite some time and never did I think we had a killer in our midst." Grace looked perplexed. "What did we overlook?"

"Maybe nothing. You obviously recognized Baez was—"

"An arrogant asshole."

It was what Brick was thinking, but he didn't expect Grace to say it. He almost choked on a mouthful of rice. "It's easier to conceal being a killer than an asshole. And let's not forget, Baez is innocent until proven guilty."

"Didn't you tell me your game is Texas hold 'em?"

"Yeah, I did. Why?"

"You better work on your poker face." Grace smiled as she broke open an edamame pod and popped the beans in her mouth.

Brick laughed. "Convincing a jury to convict Baez of felony hit-and-run shouldn't be difficult, even for a relatively new prosecutor. On the other hand, proving premeditated murder to cover up embezzling scholarships funds could be problematic. Circumstantial cases usually are."

"I hope he gets convicted on both and is put away for many years." Grace paused as she seemed to gather her thoughts. "It makes me sad for Henry and angry that Baez got away with it as long as he did. But even though it's circumstantial, wouldn't you say it's a strong case? There's the money trail from Yang's spreadsheets to Baez's bank accounts. People have been killed for a lot less. And you tracked down the Mercedes that once belonged to Baez."

"True, and body shop records from the car dealer are strong evidence the car was involved, but the defense will probably argue it doesn't prove Baez was driving. Anyway, it's going to be a challenge but given its high-profile potential, it will be assigned to experienced prosecutors. I'd bet the rent on that."

"At least Baez can't play the diplomatic immunity card." Grace took a sip of iced tea. "I still don't understand how he got away with using that at the time Henry died. Even though his father was an ambassador, immunity shouldn't have been extended to him, right?"

Brick nodded. "There are limitations. According to tax and condo records, Baez was the owner and occupant of the property in Arlington when Henry was killed."

"Oh yes, the condo overlooking the Iwo Jima Memorial where he always hosted an extravagant Fourth of July party. Sorry, I interrupted what you were saying."

"Legally, he was living independently and not entitled to immunity granted to the ambassador's household members and staff."

"Sounds to me like someone didn't do their job. Anyway, I guess I just have to be patient and hope Baez pays for what he did. Trust that karma will see that he gets what he deserves." Grace finished the last piece of salmon in her Bento box. "Somehow, this seems to have all the makings of an episode of *American Greed*."

Brick wasn't familiar with the show, but this wasn't the first time he had heard the Yang case referred to as potential TV material. Lieutenant Hughes had said the same thing when she and Brick discussed Blancato's role in deep-sixing the case. It was an ongoing aspect of the case that Brick hadn't revealed to Grace but was thinking about a lot. A separate investigation was being conducted by Internal Affairs to determine if greed may have been a motivating factor in Blancato's actions as well.

"I'm getting a refill of iced tea; need anything?" Grace asked.

"No, thanks."

Grace returned to the table and sat down. After taking a sip, she smiled at Brick. "Think I'm taking a page out of your playbook."

"Really, how so?"

"Time away from D.C. to think about what I want to be when I grow up. I'm leaving tomorrow for a yoga retreat in Costa Rica."

"A one-way ticket?"

Grace shook her head. "Round-trip. Ten days, not three months." She glanced at her watch. "Oh, it's later than I realized. I need to get home and finish packing." Grace stood and so did Brick. "Thanks for lunch. I would give you a hug but I'm a little sweaty."

"Just a little? So am I, which is about the same as if we both ate garlic."

"You're right." Grace smiled as she stepped closer to Brick and shared a quick embrace.

"Have a great trip. I'd like to hear about it when you get back."

"That can be arranged," Grace said. *"Namaste."*

"Namaste." Brick watched as Grace walked away.

Although he hadn't mentioned that he also needed to pack, when Brick got home he finished preparing for his upcoming trip back to Chicago. It had been over a month since his weekend with Nora had been cut short and he hoped to pick up where they left off.

CHAPTER FORTY-SIX

BRICK HEARD HIS cell phone ping as the Uber driver exited the parking lot at O'Hare and merged with the traffic on the Kennedy Expressway. He checked the text message from Nora.

Everything ok but diverted to Logan. Delayed about 2 hrs. See you soon!

Brick responded with a thumbs-up emoji and slipped the phone back into his pocket.

Always have to expect the unexpected when traveling. Pack your patience. Brick recalled Nora's exact words from when they last spoke. Just in case, she said she would leave a key to her apartment and an admit slip for him at the security desk in the building's lobby. Not exactly how he had envisioned the weekend starting but since he wasn't being relegated to the guest suite, he wasn't discouraged. As much as he enjoyed the event-packed weekend in September until it abruptly ended, he was glad they agreed this one would be low-key, more focused on getting to know each other.

Montrose Avenue, Irving Park Road, Addison Street. As they passed the exit signs, Brick recognized the names and knew exactly where he was. About thirty minutes after leaving the airport, the Uber driver pulled into the circular driveway in front of Nora's building.

* * *

After picking up the key, Brick took the elevator to the fourth floor. Inside Nora's apartment, he glanced around the living room and set his suitcase next to her sofa. With time to kill, he locked the door and headed back outside. Even though he was anxious to see Nora, he welcomed some time alone to take a walk by the lake.

Brick noticed several empty boat slips as he entered Belmont Harbor. He guessed the remaining boats would soon be docked elsewhere for the season, but on this August-in-October afternoon a few sailboats dotted the lake. A swarm of dragonflies darted in and out as he walked south toward Diversey Harbor before finding a shady spot. He sat down on the concrete ledge and watched the gentle waves lapping the edge of the walkway. Certainly not as dramatic as the ocean but the effect was similar, including the squawking of seagulls flying overhead.

Despite some bicyclists and a few joggers and dog walkers, Brick felt as if he had the lake to himself. The same sense of calm he had experienced when he was here weeks before and during his days in Ireland, he felt again. Was it possible that a place could affect him so profoundly? If that was the case, wasn't D.C. doing the same thing but in a negative way? Maybe it was time to move to a place that was a clean slate. A place where a street or a building didn't automatically remind him of a bloody homicide scene he investigated. But was Chicago the answer? If today's weather was typical, who wouldn't want to live here? But Nora had already warned him about the extreme temperatures and as Eamonn had once cautioned, you have to experience a place when the weather is the worst to really know what it's like to live there. Something to consider, especially with climate change wreaking havoc on the planet.

His thoughts switched to his recent discussion with Lieutenant Hughes. The possibility of reinstatement to work cold cases was tempting, but involvement with the Yang case had resulted in an aspect he hadn't expected. Did his nemesis and former boss, Anthony Blancato, overstep his authority by invoking diplomatic immunity and shelving the case? If so, why did he do it? If he had acted with malfeasance, he deserved to face the consequences. Unfortunately, Brick wouldn't be watching from the sidelines. He was sure he would be dragged into the investigation based on what he had uncovered. Things between them had been strained for years, but Brick thought that ended when he retired. Now it seemed it may be ongoing with the potential to get ugly like a contentious divorce.

Thinking about reinstatement morphed into another idea. Maybe it really was time for a new career. What that would be, he wasn't sure, but at forty-two, Brick felt as though his window of opportunity for a second act was closing. A ping from his cell phone shook Brick from his reverie for which he was grateful. The glare on the screen caused him to squint as he read the text message from Nora.

Just cleared customs at ORD. ETA-45 mins. Almost home!

Knowing there would be plenty of time to figure things out when the weekend was over, Brick pushed aside thoughts of his future. For now, Nora deserved his undivided attention, and that is what he intended to provide. Before leaving, he took one last look toward the Ferris wheel at Navy Pier thinking it might be a Saturday night date destination.

As he headed back toward Belmont Harbor, Brick's path was unexpectedly blocked. He smiled as he yielded the right of way and waited patiently for a parade of Canada geese to proudly pass by.

PUBLISHER'S NOTE

We hope that you enjoyed *Duplicity,* the second in Shawn Wilson's Brick Kavanagh Mystery Series.

The first in the series is *Relentless.* The two novels stand on their own and can be read in any order. Here's a brief summary of *Relentless*:

 Cherry blossom season, Washington, D.C.'s most beautiful time of the year, is marred when veteran homicide detective Brian (Brick) Kavanagh is assigned to investigate a body floating in Washington, D.C.'s Tidal Basin. At first, Brick has no way of knowing how personal this will become, but as he relentlessly pursues the truth—and when he prevails—he finds little satisfaction in being right. The case breaks his heart.

"In *Relentless,* Shawn Wilson has introduced a memorable hero, a plethora of supporting characters, and a story full of twists and turns to keep any amateur detective or criminal enthusiast on his or her toes. Brick is the kind of personality readers will look forward to seeing again and again." —*BookTrib*

We hope that you will enjoy reading *Relentless*, Shawn Wilson's debut novel introducing the Brick Kavanagh Mystery Series and that you will look forward to more to come.

For more information,
please visit the author's website
www.shawnwilsonauthor.com.